OTHER BOOKS BY DOROTHY CANNELL

The Thin Woman
Down the Garden Path
The Widows Club
Mum's the Word
Femmes Fatal
How to Murder Your Mother-in-Law
How to Murder the Man of Your Dreams

God Save The Queen!

Dorothy Cannell

Bantam Books
New York Toronto London Sydney Auckland

This edition contains the complete text
of the original hardcover edition.
NOT ONE WORD HAS BEEN OMITTED.

God Save the Queen!

A Bantam Crime Line Book

PUBLISHING HISTORY

Bantam hardcover edition published February 1997

Bantam paperback edition / April 1998

CRIME LINE and the portrayal of a boxed "cl" are trademarks
of Bantam Books, a division of Bantam Doubleday Dell
Publishing Group, Inc.

ISBN 0-553-57468-X

Published simultaneously in the United States and Canada

Bantam Books are published by Bantam Books, a division of Bantam
Doubleday Dell Publishing Group, Inc. Its trademark, consisting of the
words "Bantam Books" and the portrayal of a rooster, is Registered in
U.S. Patent and Trademark Office and in other countries. Marca
Registrada. Bantam Books, 1540 Broadway, New York, New York 10036.

PRINTED IN THE UNITED STATES OF AMERICA

OPM   10 9 8 7 6 5 4 3 2 1

To my son Warren,

who also hears the sirens sing.

ACKNOWLEDGMENTS

To Dr. John and Barbara White of Lincoln, for taking me to the house that became Gossinger Hall and, most of all, for their unfailing love and kindness.

GOD SAVE THE QUEEN!

ONE

When she was three years old, Flora Hutchins went to live at Gossinger Hall in the village of Nether Woodcock, Lincolnshire. Upon first seeing the gray stone house with its turrets sprouting up all over the place, Flora had decided it was bigger than the cottage hospital where her mother had died, so it had to be Buckingham Palace. And when her grandfather came down the steps to meet her, looking so distinguished in his pinstriped suit, she was surprised he wasn't wearing a crown because she was so certain he had to be the King of England.

It took the little girl a few days to learn the true state of affairs. Grandpa was not the King, but Sir Henry Gossinger's butler. But that didn't mean Flora turned into a downtrodden little thing kept hidden away behind the broom cupboard door. When she got bigger she liked helping the series of housekeepers, who came and went as regularly as the seasons, to make the beds, dust the furniture, and peel vegetables for dinner. Grandpa wouldn't let her help him make up the special recipe he used to clean Sir Henry's prized collection of eighteenth-century silver, but Flora loved sitting with him at such times because then he would tell her stories about Gossinger Hall.

"Start at the very beginning," she would beg.

"Very well," Grandpa would reply. "The original part of this house was built in the twelfth century by Thomas Short Shanks, a henpecked baron whose wife, Lady Normina, agreed to let him go off and fight in the Crusades on one minor concession. He had to build her a house that would turn her eleven sisters green with envy."

"Lady Normina doesn't sound a particularly nice person, does she, Grandpa?"

"That's not for the likes of us to say, Flora," he would reply firmly as his hands kept polishing away at a piece of silver. "The story goes that Lady Normina was tired of the way her less-than-loving kin looked down their knobby noses at her. All because her husband had provided fodder for every second-rate town crier in England, by being disqualified from a major jousting tournament—plus fined a purse of gold—for galloping into the arena before Queen Eleanor had time to drop her hanky."

"Poor Thomas." Flora's tender young heart was always touched at this juncture of the story.

"Sir Thomas to you and me," Grandpa would say reprovingly. "He may have been dead for close on a thousand years but that's no reason not to pay him due respect."

"I'm sorry."

"Then we will continue." This would be said with a smile. "Truth be told, Flora, Lady Normina's sisters weren't the only ones she wished to outdo. In those days, kitchens weren't part of the main house. And, bent on keeping up with the Ostaffs who lived two castles away, Lady Normina insisted her kitchen be within easy distance of the house in order that she might spy on the shiftless cook; but not so close that were a leg of mutton to catch on fire her dream house would go up in smoke with it."

"I think I would have been scared of Lady Normina." Flora always hoped this did not sound too much like a criticism.

"By all accounts she was a masterful woman." Grandpa had usually finished polishing two or three pieces of silver by this time. "She didn't mind that the other ladies in the vicinity called her nouveau riche and terribly standoffish! Lady Normina thought them all pathetic creatures and understandably jealous that the rushes on her floors always stayed so nice and fresh. Her Ladyship had made a vow to her patron saint, Flora, that she would put a dent in the armor of any knight who didn't remove his shoes before setting foot inside her abode. And anyone who wanted to spit had to go outside."

"Did Sir Henry tell you all this, Grandpa?"

"Quite a bit has been written down, my dear. The Gossingers have always been great ones for keeping journals. But don't keep interrupting me, Flora, or I'll never be finished before it's time for Sir Henry's tea." Grandpa often picked up a clean polishing cloth about now. "It isn't hard to believe that Lady Normina's pride and joy was the garderobe."

"What's that?"

"An indoor toilet, something most people—even very rich ones—didn't have in those days, and so called because it doubled as a storage room for clothing, on account of the felicitous chemical composition of the fumes doing a bang-up job of keeping out moths. The word *wardrobe,* Flora, comes down to us from the garderobe."

"That's interesting," Flora would say dutifully, trying not to wrinkle up her nose.

"The sisters were beside themselves—with happiness we must hope—at their dear Normina's good fortune."

"Is the garderobe still here, Grandpa?"

"Of course it is," he would reply as he glanced up at the clock. "But it's locked up now. Do get down off that stool, there's a good child, and fetch the chocolate cake from the pantry for Sir Henry's tea."

Flora understood from listening to Grandpa that Gossinger Hall had once been the last word in luxury, by the standards of its time. John of Gaunt was said to have visited there on several occasions with his mistress Katherine Swynford. And, in this latter part of the twentieth century, the Hall still made for an interesting place to view on the days it was open to the public. The price of admission was modest, only two pounds per adult and fifty pence for any juvenile who made a sincere attempt to look short and sufficiently bored to pass for under the age of twelve.

Making even better value for the money was the inclusion in the tour of a pair of headphones and a hand cassette, which provided an audio guide to points of historical and architectural interest. However, the sad truth is that whilst it wasn't a bad place to visit, especially on early closing day at the shops, very few people who appreciated the comforts provided by even the most modest semidetached house would have wanted to *live* at Gossinger Hall.

Little Flora, with the ghost of the twelfth-century Lady Normina looming larger than life over her shoulder, was very glad that Sir Henry, at nearly sixty, remained unmarried. She quite liked Mrs. Warren who worked in the tearoom-cum-gift-shop. She was fond of Mr. Tipp, whose job description was stable boy even though he was close to the same age as his master, Sir Henry. And she adored her grandfather, even though she sometimes thought crossly that he loved the Queen better than anyone else in the world.

Her childhood seemed to pass through her fingers like an enchanted daisy chain, all pastel colors and gentle fragrances. School in the village. Sir Henry giving her toffees and patting her on the head. Sunny afternoons spent rummaging for cast-off finery in attic trunks, so she could dress up and pretend to be one of Lady Normina's handmaidens. And Grandpa telling her other stories about earlier times at Gossinger.

There was the one about Queen Charlotte paying an afternoon visit that ended with a terrible stain upon the family honor, when it was discovered that the silver tea strainer Her Majesty had brought with her (no doubt assuming Lincolnshire to be a primitive place) was missing. The Gossinger heir at that time was a wild young man, up to his powdered wig in gambling debts, and it was naturally suspected that he had pocketed the tea strainer to sell at the first opportunity. As a result the Gossinger family was not received at court until the reign of George V, and even in present times the taint lingered, causing unkind people to whisper that the Gossingers were not one hundred percent true blue.

Flora spent countless hours hunting for the strainer, which was said to be shaped like a swan, in all the nooks and crannies she could discover. It would have been so wonderful to have gone running in to Grandpa with her hands behind her back and say "Guess what I've found? Sir Rowland didn't steal the tea strainer after all! It was here all the time!" It would have been Flora's small way of repaying her grandfather for making up to her all the love she had missed by her mother's untimely death. And for the fact she never seemed to have had a father.

Grandpa, she knew, would have been immensely

pleased to have the Gossinger honor thus restored. But that wasn't all. Holding the tea strainer in his hands would have been a magical moment for him. His great passion was the silver he polished for Sir Henry, which made it surprising, Flora always thought, that there was one story he would never tell her even though she was sure he knew all about it: how the superbly crafted silver collection he loved so much had come into the Gossinger family's possession in the first place.

Flora never did find that tea strainer. And suddenly, as if she had gone to bed one night a child and awakened the next morning a young woman, Flora was seventeen. And before she had time to turn around, a big change occurred at Gossinger Hall. Mabel Bowser appeared on the scene.

On the fateful day in question, Flora had been looking out the window of the sitting room she shared with her grandfather when she saw a woman in brown tweeds get off the sight-seeing coach and set foot inside the tearoom-cum-gift-shop that served as the public entrance to Gossinger. *Why, she looks just like the reincarnation of Lady Normina,* Flora thought, and a strange little pang of fear quivered up her spine.

Miss Mabel Bowser certainly had the ironclad look of a woman who would send her man off to the Crusades without first packing him a lunch. And no one, including Flora, could ever have suspected that her heart was beating fast under her forty-five-year-old bosom as she opened her handbag. It was a chilly day in October, and Mrs. Warren took her entry fee money by dint of inching the tips of her fingernails out of the sleeve of her cardigan. Or, to be accurate, cardigans. Mrs. Warren was bundled up in at least three, and did not appear to be joking when she declared the radiators that lined the walls were neither use nor ornament. Unless, that is, you happened to be a "bally" dancer and wished to practice your arabesque.

Undaunted, Mabel Bowser embraced the chill of centuries bearing down on her from the towering stone walls of the great hall. Meanwhile, two women school-teachers from her sight-seeing coach were less than enthusiastic. They groused that their headphones would have to do double duty as earmuffs. Mabel was able to hear their petty complaints because she had declined Mrs. Warren's offer of a personal electronic guide. She hadn't wanted any encumbrance to bring her down to earth. Being a woman of substantial build, she walked on air somewhat at her own risk. Besides, the device would have stamped her as a visitor, and Mabel Bowser wanted to pretend for one glorious hour that she dwelt in the musty splendor that was Gossinger Hall.

From her childhood days in the flat above her parents' secondhand shop, Mabel had yearned to be part of Britain's upper crust. With this commendable goal in mind she had taken to wearing dowdy tweeds, lisle stockings, and pudding-basin hats. She had applied herself to elocution lessons with a dedication that would have pleased Henry Higgins no end and gave her sister Edna, who still lived in Bethnal Green, a sad little pang. But what does a woman whose idea of personal fulfillment is an evening spent at the dog races know about bettering oneself? Shortsighted Edna would not have bet a fiver that on that visit to Gossinger her sister's schoolgirl dreams of moving up a class would be amply rewarded. But fate has been known to pull a few strings. For outside the garderobe, which was locked and had a "Keep Out" sign posted on the door, Mabel Bowser collided with Sir Henry Gossinger himself.

With a somewhat awkward bow, the baronet introduced himself. Sir Henry wasn't a man designed by nature to bend at the middle. And being a true aristocrat, he spoke to her in a voice that sounded as though he had a mouthful of hot plum tart.

"Frightfully sorry, m'dear. Shouldn't be let out on m'own without a Seeing Eye dog."

What address! What *savoir-faire!* Mabel couldn't make head nor tail of what Sir Henry was saying, but she knew instantly that he was everything she had ever wanted in a man. Stout, balding, and three inches shorter than herself.

"It was my fault," she assured him. "I wasn't looking where I was going." A simple apology, but one elevated to operatic proportions by the throb of passion in her voice.

Sir Henry said something she couldn't follow, to which she responded with a series of heartfelt nods. Within moments Mabel discovered that if she watched his lips closely she could understand his every other word. It was miraculous! Like going to France and realizing you didn't need the phrase book to get off the ferry.

Smiling kindly at her, Sir Henry explained that the garderobe was kept locked because a shift in Gossinger's foundation had enlarged the (Sir Henry got extra-mumbly here) seating area to the point of making it dangerous. A toilet by any other name is not the same. Mabel Bowser was captivated by Sir Henry's chitchat on the subject of his twelfth-century loo.

Perspiration bathed her face in dewy luminosity. For all she was a sizable woman, she felt herself grow fragile. Was she dreaming, or had Sir Henry just offered to personally escort her around his historic abode? She didn't go so far as to imagine he had fallen in love with her at first sight, but she did wonder if the baronet recognized in her a person of his own kind. Mabel Bowser trembled in her brogue shoes when Sir Henry put his hand on her elbow to guide her across the great hall.

Less than half an hour later, Sir Henry showed her Gossinger's remarkably fine collection of eighteenth-century silver, which was displayed in glass cases in the former buttery. He assured her that Hutchins, the butler, was responsible for the silver's cleaning and of course she would not be expected to so much as dust this room were she to accept his offer and make Gossinger her home.

Admittedly, it wasn't a lengthy courtship. But times have changed since Lady Normina was betrothed before she was fully out of the womb (she was a breech birth) to Thomas Short Shanks in 1172. Emotion may have wrought Sir Henry more than usually indistinct, but Mabel Bowser had no trouble making it crystal clear that she would marry him without waiting to get her best frock back from the cleaners.

The wedding took place several weeks later at St. Mary's Stow. It was a tastefully small affair with only Sir Henry's nephew Vivian and Miss Sophie Doffit, a third cousin who strongly resembled the Queen Mother, in attendance. It didn't do, of course, to count Hutchins, his seventeen-year-old granddaughter Flora, and Mrs. Johnson, the current housekeeper, seated respectfully at the back of the church. Mr. Tipp, the elderly stable lad, didn't come because someone had to stay behind in case burglars stopped by and took the huff at the lack of hospitality. And Edna couldn't come up from Bethnal Green to witness her sister's triumphal walk down the aisle, because she was in hospital having an operation for piles, as she insisted on calling them. But that was all for the best. Edna would have had trouble saying the minimum and trying to look educated.

With nothing to cast a blight except a fleeting regret that she had not married Sir Henry when she was of an age to provide him with a son and heir, the fledgling Lady Gossinger had every anticipation of living happily ever after. In the ensuing years she grew ever more tweedy. No one would stamp her as nouveau riche, thank you very much! Lady Gossinger's concept of life as lived by the gentry was based on certain novels written in the 1930's and 1940's—in particular, those by Dame Agatha Christie.

To the former Mabel Bowser, the Golden Age meant a time when breakfast was laid out in a grand parade of silver-domed dishes on a twelve-foot sideboard. Gentlemen went fox hunting, or busied themselves doing nothing in their libraries, while their wives concentrated on their herbaceous borders. And the discovery of a corpse on the premises was not permitted to delay mealtimes by more than one hour, even though the cook's favorite carving knife was stuck up to its handle in the victim's back.

It goes without saying that Lady Gossinger, née Bowser, never seriously expected anyone to be murdered under her nose. Her married life moved contentedly forward until came that ill-fated day five years later when Sir Henry dropped his bombshell and the rose-colored scales fell from her eyes. Afterward, Mabel was to remember with bitter clarity how very chipper she had been feeling only an hour before her brave new world was blown utterly to smithereens. And she would reflect with a pinched and sour smile, very much like the one worn by Lady Normina on her marble tombstone, that she would never have guessed in a thousand years that a girl as seemingly unimportant as Flora Hutchins would have to be dealt with, one way or the other.

TWO

It was a Saturday afternoon toward the end of March. Young Vivian, as Lady Gossinger still called her nephew, even though he was now twenty-nine years old, had come up for the weekend. Although not handsome, he was certainly more than presentable with his thick brown hair, hazel eyes, and aristocratic features. There were four of them gathered in the tower sitting room. This was not an excessively cheerful apartment, being reminiscent of the one in which Anne Boleyn had spent her final days wondering how she would wear her hair for her last public appearance.

Sir Henry and her Ladyship were seated side by side on heavy carved chairs with the look of the judgment seat about them. Across from them, on a settee with oak arms and wafer-thin tapestry cushions, Vivian and Miss Sophie Doffit sat improving their posture. Sir Henry's cousin was as much a daily fixture as the bird's nest in the niche above the window, having (by dint of forgetting to repack her suitcase) extended her week-long visit at the time of the wedding into permanent residence.

Lady Gossinger moved to cross her legs, remembered that doing so was common, and handed out smiles like toffees from a paper bag. If the atmosphere seemed the least bit strained it was only because two of the little family gathering were chilled to the marrow. The stone fireplace was empty, except for the bare bones of a rusted grate. And, despite recent work on the radiators, central heating at Gossinger still came down to closing the windows and wearing woolen underwear.

"I appreciate your having me underfoot." Vivian addressed his aunt and uncle whilst wishing that they might all adjourn to the chapel, which he had always thought the coziest room at Gossinger. Failing that, he could only hope that Hutchins would soon arrive with a couple of hot water bottles along with afternoon tea.

"Stuff and nonsense. You're never a scrap of bother!" Lady Gossinger's voice vibrated with a heartiness that threatened to put further cracks in Gossinger's ancient foundations.

"How kind of you to say so, Mabel!" Miss Doffit rubbed her hands together to get the circulation going. "Sometimes I start to worry, as old people will, that I may have outstayed my welcome by a few weeks."

"Not at all, Sophie. We have enjoyed your visit." Her Ladyship was able to speak with sincerity, because she firmly believed that life among the better families required having a poor relation hovering gratefully in the shadows. And then there was that resemblance to the Queen Mother, which made riding in the backseat of a taxi with Cousin Sophie a bit of a thrill, even as she warned the old lady that waving out the window in that particular way might be a treasonable offense. Lady Gossinger drew a forbearing breath.

"Never mind, Sophie! Although, if you'd only listened a little harder before interrupting me, dear," she laughed to soften the rebuke, "you would have realized I was talking to young Vivian. I was saying that *he* isn't a scrap of bother. We're quite awfully fond of him, isn't that right, old bean?" Lady Gossinger raised her voice an octave or two as she turned to her husband and gave him a bracing pat on the knee.

"Oh, absolutely, Mabel!" Sir Henry chomped down on his words and slowly regurgitated them, in the manner of a man whose thoughts were elsewhere. "Couldn't be more fond of the young cub if he were m'late younger brother Tom's boy."

"Vivian *is* Tom's son, dear," Lady Mabel said with wifely patience.

"Oh, yes, quite, quite! Old family name, Vivian . . ." Sir Henry lapsed into reverie. A whoosh of icy wind came down the chimney, while rain began to beat at the narrow lattice windows in the stop-and-start manner of an untalented child practicing scales at the piano.

In truth, Lady Gossinger had developed a deep affection for her acquired nephew. It was born the instant Vivian had made it plain he had no wish to take up residence in the ancestral home when he came into the title upon his uncle's death. He would, he had given his word as a gentleman, be happy for his aunt to continue living at Gossinger for the many, he hoped, years allotted to her.

"We only wish you'd come up to see us more often, young Vivian." Her Ladyship gave him one of her cultivated smiles. "Positively topping having you here. But mustn't push our good fortune. We know how it is with busy young men-about-town, don't we, Henry?"

"Oh, absolutely. Not always an old fuddy-duddy.

Remember being young m'self once upon a time. Seemed the thing to do, I suppose." The baronet's faded eyes strayed to the longcase clock, which had neither ticked nor tocked in living memory, but still appeared, perhaps by some imperceptible change of facial expression, to be able to communicate the time to its master. "What's it you've been doing with yourself recently, m'boy? Serving queen and country?"

"In a manner of speaking, Uncle Henry." Vivian Gossinger tucked his feet under the faded strip of Persian carpet for warmth.

"Has someone been keeping secrets?" Lady Gossinger chided him with a raised finger that almost got blown off her hand by the force of the wind now taking rude peeks up Cousin Sophie's skirts. "That won't do, will it, dear? Your Uncle Henry and I have your very best interests at heart. And there's absolutely nothing you can't tell us that you wouldn't tell your own mummy and daddy if they were still alive."

"In that case, if you're one-hundred-percent sure you want to hear this, Aunt Mabel!" Avoiding looking at the brass rubbing of Lady Normina on the wall that always gave him the willies, Vivian Gossinger announced: "To put it in a nutshell, Aunt, I've recently taken up employment selling men's toiletries door-to-door."

"You have done what, dear?" Lady Gossinger plunged back in her chair and immediately sprang forward again, after getting the Tudor Rose imprinted on her spine. She was shocked by what she had just heard. Deeply so. But part of her enjoyed being shocked. It was the proper response from someone with her responsibilities to the Family. Unless—was it possible young Vivian had been pulling her leg? Yes, that had to be it! Chuckling to show she hadn't taken the bait, her Ladyship wagged her finger at her naughty nephew.

"Shame on you for telling such whoppers! Going

around from house to house with your little sample
case, indeed! We should stand him in the corner for
trying to frighten us, isn't that right, Henry?"

"Sorry, m'dear! Must have fuzz in my ears, or the
old brain's gone on the blink. Missed what you were
saying, but sure you're right as always." Sir Henry
passed a hand over his bald pate. He appeared considerably more interested in the sound of the rain, now playing a Beethoven concerto on the windowpanes, than in
his nephew's earthshaking pronouncement.

"I'm not joking, Aunt Mabel."

"But surely, Vivian!"

"I'm currently a Macho Man representative. But if
it's any consolation, Aunt, I'm not frightfully good at it.
I'm always getting lost. And I don't like being set upon
by toy poodles with capped teeth and false nails."

"Is someone talking to me?" Cousin Sophie immediately realized her mistake and said that it must have
been her tummy asking for a scone with butter.

Lady Gossinger ignored her. "Vivian, for the sake of
the family, listen to Auntie! There must be something
else you could do to supplement your allowance. Something that would be more suited to your position in life.
How about becoming an M.P., dear? You wouldn't
have to take a lot of nasty exams, and think what you'd
save on meals by going to all those roast chicken din-
ners."

"I'm sorry to upset you, Aunt Mabel." Vivian looked
remorseful. "But I think I should stick it out with Macho Man Products a bit longer. Character-building and
all that. It really is a pretty decent outfit. And they do a
frightfully good body cream and an oatmeal-and-
avocado face mask, if Uncle Henry should be interested."

Sir Henry made a noise deep in his throat and did an
excellent job of appearing lost in thought, but Lady
Gossinger could not hide her distress. Face masks and

body creams! Was she learning something about her nephew that she would rather not have known? Was she about to discover that he kept Persian cats and liked to do his own flower arranging? Of course, this sort of thing cropped up in the best families; they (whoever *they* were) said that Richard the Lion Heart . . . So perhaps—Lady Gossinger took a reviving breath—the well-bred thing to do was to be broad-minded. But that didn't mean, surely, that she had to encourage young Vivian.

"I'm afraid," she bit down on her lip, "that your Uncle Henry's going to blame himself."

"Because of the job?"

"That's right, dear. Anything else is entirely your own business." Lady Gossinger basked for a moment in the glow being shed by her halo. "Henry blames himself for everything. Comprehensive schools, the Common Market, take-out curries, you name it. And, strictly between you and me, young Vivian," Lady Gossinger glanced at her husband, who sat oblivious two feet away, "I worry, as any devoted wife would, that he spends far too much time in the Penitent's Room off the chapel. But funnily enough, dear, that gives me an idea."

"It does?"

"The perfect solution, Vivian. I know you're not all that churchy, but you could come and live at Gossinger for a while and do some voluntary work at Lincoln Cathedral. Wouldn't that be jolly? We're only about sixteen miles away. That's minutes in the car." Her Ladyship was bubbling over with enthusiasm. "I think it would be particularly nice, dear, if you helped out in the information booth. You could tell people where to find the famous Imp and how at one time the cathedral's copy of the Magna Carta used to be kept in an old biscuit tin, and then there's that funny little legend about the Swineherd of Stow. Americans in particular love that sort of thing."

While Lady Gossinger was taking a well-earned breath and Vivian was wondering how he could tactfully explain that he would rather live in a bus shelter than at Gossinger, Cousin Sophie decided that having counted to three hundred and thirty-one she might reasonably reenter the conversation. Sitting up very straight, with her hand on the standard lamp beside her as if holding a scepter, she came out strongly in support of her Ladyship.

"Mabel is right, as always, Vivian. Voluntary work is one thing, but the other kind—where one receives remuneration—is never a suitable occupation for people of our sort. One of my brothers went to work for the Bank of England. And it killed our daddy. Have you," Cousin Sophie's cushiony soft face grew troubled, "ever worked in a bank, Vivian?"

"No, Cousin Sophie."

Miss Doffit gathered Vivian's hands between her own and squeezed, revealing surprising strength for an old lady, so that his eyes watered. "I suppose I'm old-fashioned, but I can't help thinking it a very vulgar occupation—delving into people's money problems. I don't know that I can think of anything more discreditable, except perhaps working in one of those second-hand shops that thrive on the spoils of people fallen on adversity." Cousin Sophie resolutely blinked away a tear. "Oh dear, here I go again, rattling on as if my opinion is of the least importance. Have I been making a nuisance of myself again?"

"You could never do that." Vivian Gossinger was moved to respond by centuries of good breeding and his aunt's silence, which had not helped the chill in the room. "You're a national treasure, Cousin Sophie."

"And you are so like your dear father, may our Father in heaven rest his soul!" Miss Doffit smiled mistily.

"You know I sleep in his old room. And I must admit I have grown very fond of it and the way the wind whistles so cheerfully through the windows. Would you believe it, Vivian, sometimes I forget for weeks on end your daddy once telling me that particular bedroom is haunted by that ill-bred young woman who put a wicked curse on Gossinger Hall in the eighteenth century."

Miss Doffit eyed Sir Henry, saw he looked cross, and hung her head as if wishing it would drop into a conveniently placed executioner's bucket. "May I," she gathered herself together, "make myself useful by going to see what is keeping Hutchins from bringing in our tea?"

"It is unlike him to be unpunctual." Lady Gossinger fussed with the strand of pearls around her neck. She hadn't caught more than a stray sentence here and there of Cousin Sophie's ramblings since the part about the depravity of secondhand shops. What would the old lady think if she knew about the one in Bethnal Green? Hard as her Ladyship had worked at obliterating her past, Mabel Bowser's legacy lingered. And at that moment, although she was even more fond of her husband than she was of young Vivian, Lady Gossinger could have strangled the man.

In a burst of insensitivity a few weeks previously, Sir Henry had purchased the late Mr. and Mrs. Bowser's former shop, and the flat above, as a present for his wife's fiftieth birthday. On presenting her with the deed, Sir Henry explained that he had prayed upon the matter and had become convinced she would want this piece of property for sentimental reasons. Also, it would make a nice little nest egg. Sir Henry had said this looking at peace with himself and the world. And to think of the wonderful present she had hidden away for his birthday coming up shortly! Lady Gossinger had only contemplated hitting him for an instant before she remembered that doing so would have put her back on a par with the likes of Edna. Truth be told, it wasn't a bad investment. The building had been let for the last ten years to the same tenant. Even so, for weeks after her birthday Lady Gossinger had walked around with her arms close to her sides, for fear that if she raised them an inch a telltale whiff of Bethnal Green would escape. Now she stopped fiddling with her pearls and drew in her elbows.

"A bit odd, Hutchins being late. Never met such a stickler for time. And here it is ten minutes past four," Sir Henry said, looking at the clock, whose hands were locked in prayer as they had been ever since the pendulum had stopped, according to family legend, one midnight long ago. The baronet cleared his throat. "It's about Hutchins that I've been wanting to have a word with you all. But felt it could wait. Didn't want to spoil anyone's tea. Thought you'd all take the news better on full tummies."

"Is Hutchins ill?" Vivian Gossinger forgot about good posture and leaned forward, elbows on his knees, the epitome of well-bred concern for a family servant.

"He's not dying?" Lady Gossinger sounded quite put out, feeling—quite rightly—that Hutchins should have notified his employers of his intention. "Well, I must say he's been doing a very good job of looking well."

"No, no! He's not got an appointment with the Grim Reaper. Nothing like that!" Sir Henry shifted further back in his throne chair, which was not made for seating comfort, as the expression on his face bore witness. He started to speak, being anxious to get on with what he had to say, but being a gentleman, allowed a lady to go first.

"Hutchins isn't especially old, Vivian," said Cousin Sophie, who took great pride in being eighty-four, and staunchly resented people in their seventies putting themselves forward as elderly.

"But come to think of it, he must be close to retirement age," said Vivian. "Even so, Uncle Henry, I always assumed Hutchins would never leave Gossinger until he was carried out in his coffin. Particularly as he has his granddaughter here."

"Ah, yes! Little Flora!" Sir Henry spoke quite fondly. "Of course, she's grown up now and works about the house or in the gift shop. But when Hutchins first brought her here after her mother died, she was only about four or five. Really quite a playful little thing. Quite like having a puppy about the place. I remember she used to like going up into the trunk room and playing dressing-up games."

"Hutchins seems quite devoted to her," Cousin Sophie broke in, once more forgetting that fate had allotted her a permanent place in the shadows. "Human nature being what it is, people always make lots of fuss when a man, and one who is not," she conceded, "particularly young, takes on the upbringing of a child. But think of that woman who last week had quadruplets, or whatever they're called, at age sixty-four!"

"Cousin Sophie," Vivian Gossinger's lips had thawed out sufficiently to allow a smile, "you've been at it again, reading the tabloids."

"No, no, it was a proper newspaper! And I'm sure I heard the same story on the wireless, about this retired schoolteacher from Bridlington, who married a much younger man and decided she wanted to give him a child. Some people would say a pipe rack would have made a more suitable gift, but I thought it quite brave of Mrs. Smith." Cousin Sophie nodded sagely. "Her story made me think about you, Mabel."

"Me?" Lady Gossinger did not sound pleased. "I am *not* years older than Henry!"

"No, no, of course not." The old lady backed into

her corner of the sofa. "It was because you always seem
so young, not much more than a girl really, that I began
to think how lovely it would be if you and Henry were
to have a baby. A boy, of course. And I could make
myself useful looking after it." Sentimental sigh. "You
wouldn't mind, would you, Vivian?"

"Mind your looking after it?"

"No, dear! Mind being supplanted as Henry's heir."

Giving Cousin Sophie a cross look, Lady Gossinger
said: "In the course of leaping from one subject to another we have lost track of the fact, Henry," she turned
to her husband, "that you were about to tell us something or other about Hutchins. Sorry about that, old
bean! But out with it now. You have my undivided
attention."

THREE

Flora hadn't forgotten that her grandfather had asked her to take afternoon tea up to the tower room. But she had lost track of time. This was partly because a button had popped off her white blouse while she was serving a customer in the gift shop, and she'd had to go and sew it back on. At which time she had noticed that her hair was slipping out of its knot and she also had a run in her tights. However, the main reason she failed to look at her watch was that this was Grandpa's birthday and she was obsessed with making sure that their little sitting room looked as festive as possible.

It was always a cozy apartment, with lots of books on the shelves and Grandpa's chair drawn snugly up to the fireplace, but today Flora wanted everything perfect. She had filled a blue and white china jug with winter pansies and put it on the drop-leaf table. The iced chocolate cake she had made early that morning looked very tasty on its silver doily and she had strung balloons from the backs of the two dining chairs. Grandpa would pretend to be surprised and they would have a merry supper, but Flora could not rid herself of one disappointment, that the birthday present she so longed to give him was not to be.

A couple of weeks previously she had screwed up her courage and written to Her Majesty, telling her about Grandpa and the marvelous silver polish he made up in accordance with an old family recipe. Flora had explained that the silver polish was sold at the Gossinger Hall gift shop and that people made special trips, often driving many miles to buy it. Would it be asking too much (she had underlined these words) to hope that Her Majesty might consider granting one of her Royal Warrants for this excellent product?

After rereading the letter several times to make sure she hadn't made any spelling mistakes or grammatical errors, Flora had taken it down to the postbox, her heart thudding all the way. That night when she went to bed she had lain awake a long time picturing Grandpa's look of stunned delight when her dream for him came true. Even though she knew it was foolish, Flora had begun hoping for a reply by the end of the week. Perhaps it would be written by a lady-in-waiting requesting that a bottle of the silver polish be sent to Buckingham Palace. To be tried out on the royal silver collection. But now more than a fortnight had passed, and Flora was beginning to think that she might never receive a response. Perhaps Her Majesty, if she ever saw the letter, had decided that Miss Flora Hutchins was either a complete crackpot or the cheekiest person alive.

Mrs. Bellows, who was the housekeeper at Gossinger Hall for a few years when Flora was a child, had enjoyed making up stories to entertain the little girl on rainy afternoons. Of course they weren't as good as

Grandpa's stories, but she had told some awfully jolly ones about Her Majesty and life at Buckingham Palace. And those stories had remained with Flora long after Mrs. Bellows found that Gossinger Hall didn't agree with her lumbago and went to work somewhere else. They had portrayed Her Majesty Elizabeth II as a woman with a tender heart who wanted to be a real Mum to each and every one of her subjects. And years afterward, particularly when she was feeling down, Flora would weave her own versions of Mrs. Bellows's Queen stories.

"I think I've been completely taken in," Flora said out loud as she adjusted a candle on the chocolate birthday cake, "but I've no one to blame but myself. Only a real twit would expect the Queen to care two hoots about homemade silver polish. Thank goodness Grandpa doesn't know what I did: I see now that he would be completely mortified by my impudence. Unlike Mrs. Bellows, he views Her Majesty as a sacred personage who has never eaten baked beans in her royal life and is to be revered from the appropriate distance. It was just that I wanted this to be Grandpa's best birthday ever, because I think he sometimes worries about growing older. He wonders what will become of Sir Henry and Gossinger Hall when he reaches an age at which he is no longer able to take care of them. And," Flora sighed, "Grandpa knows he's the only person I have to love me. In some ways he still thinks of me as a little girl. But maybe that is changing."

She moved over to the mirror above the bookcase and stood tidying her hair back into its knot. She had baby-fine dark hair that wasn't ideal for constraining with rubber bands and pins, but her grandfather had always urged her not to cut it short. Perhaps, thought Flora, that's because my mother had lovely long hair and he needs to see something in me that reminds him of her. All of which made it most surprising that

Grandpa had said, quite out of the blue, at breakfast that morning: "Flora, why don't you think about doing something different to your hair? Something a little more modern."

"Well, that proves it," Flora informed her reflection, "his birthday is getting to him. He's taken to wondering if he should give me a shoosh out of the nest. Most girls would have taken off long ago, I suppose. But I could never leave Grandpa, and," she bit her lip, "I have to admit, there's another reason I like being at Gossinger, even though her Ladyship is a pain in the neck. It's because of Vivian." A blush crept up her cheeks and she imagined what her grandfather would say if she confessed to thinking about a member of the family by his first name. "But I can't help it." Flora turned away from the mirror and pressed her hands against her face. "I'm like one of those pathetic girls in fairy stories who fall in love with the handsome prince. Although, come to think of it, Cinderella wasn't so pathetic, she got to marry him. And anyway, I didn't develop a mad pash for Vivian at first sight. I must have been five years old the first time I saw him. And he scared me senseless until I was at least seven because I always seemed to be in his way when he was rushing up the stairs. It wasn't until he played marbles with me one afternoon that I decided he was the nicest person alive, next to Grandpa. And I must have been at least sixteen before I reached the point where just hearing that he was coming to Gossinger for the weekend was enough to make the world spin out of control."

It was then that Flora glanced at the mantel clock and discovered it was ten minutes past four and she was already well and truly late in taking tea up to the tower room. Rummaging through a drawer, she grabbed up a clean apron and dashed along to the kitchen, where Mrs. Much, the current housekeeper, was tapping her foot and looking at her watch.

"So sorry." Flora grabbed up the nearest tray and headed out into the hall. Five minutes later, after carrying up two more trays and depositing them on the oak trolley stationed for the purpose on the landing, she pushed open the heavily studded door and entered the room, looking, as Lady Gossinger had so often thought with deep satisfaction, exactly like a maid in a Christie novel.

"I'm ever so sorry to be late!" Luckily Flora's heavy breathing was lost in the rattle of wheels over the stone floor. A teaspoon went flying over the edge of the trolley and Vivian leaped to his feet in a futile attempt to catch the silver missile.

"I don't understand why you're here at all, Florie." Lady Gossinger had adapted the girl's name in this way, believing it better suited to her lowly station in life. "Now, don't stand there, child, looking as if you're waiting to have your adenoids removed. Where is your grandfather?"

"He's all right, is he?" Sir Henry inquired. "Not feeling under the weather, I hope? Isn't like Hutchins not to bring up the tea himself. I've known him to crawl up those steps when he was half dead with pneumonia."

"It's my fault." Flora kept her eyes on her hands as they moved among the cups and saucers. "Grandfather asked me particularly to fill in for him because he wanted to keep an eye on things below. There's a tour going on, a whole classful of schoolboys, and Grandfather was afraid the teacher wouldn't be able to keep them from getting rowdy and out of hand."

"Quite right, we wouldn't want that." Sir Henry accepted a linen serviette and arranged it over his knees.

"Grandfather will be upset with me." Flora handed Miss Doffit a cup and saucer. "I forgot to watch the clock, and I'm really sorry for keeping you all waiting for your tea."

"Cheer up! No harm done." Vivian, having run the teaspoon to earth between Cousin Sophie's feet, helped out further by handing round a plate of scones.

"Do sit down, there's a dear," Lady Gossinger instructed her nephew. "Florie mustn't be rewarded for failing in her duties." She looked sternly at the girl. "I do hope we are not going to see more of this irresponsible behavior."

"No, your Ladyship." Flora looked suitably chastened. And Lady Gossinger sat back well satisfied; she had thought for a moment that she had glimpsed young Vivian winking at the girl, but immediately realized the impossibility of such a thing. It must have been a twitch. And even had young Vivian's good manners and staid demeanor hidden a lascivious nature, Lady Gossinger certainly didn't believe Florie capable of bringing out the beast in any man.

She was a plain girl, pale and rather thin, with her dark hair pulled suitably back into a bun. And whilst not appearing exactly dim-witted, Lady Gossinger thought charitably, she didn't exactly sparkle with intelligence. But to give Florie her due, she wasn't carrying on with the butcher's boy and had never been caught wearing her Ladyship's clothes or taking a nip of the sherry kept for visits from the vicar. And it had to be admitted that, in addition to making herself useful helping out the series of housekeepers who came and went, she had done a good job assisting in the gift shop. Mrs. Warren—who rarely found much to be happy about—said that the take at the end of the day had tripled since Florie had started doing some of the buying, as well as selling bottles of Hutchins's silver polish.

"Is there anything else your Ladyship will be needing?" Flora finished filling up the teapot from the hot water jug, then waited with hands gripping the handle of the trolley for any further instructions.

"No, that will be all for now, Florie. Unless," Lady

Gossinger turned to her husband, "you would like her to run down and fetch more scones?"

"Sorry!" Vivian rose from his chair. "I seem to have eaten three. How would it be if I went down to the kitchen for more? Not right for Flora to have to pay for my sins, is it?"

Lady Gossinger looked ready to debate this point, but Sir Henry said he didn't want any more scones. Smiling somewhat absently, he got up and paced the room. "Run along, Flora," he said, "and don't you come back to collect the tea things. Can't have you getting the wind knocked out, not when your grandfather's going to want you in his corner. Send Tipp, that's the idea. Decent enough chap, Tipp. Likes to make himself useful."

"Yes, Sir Henry." Flora made a hurried exit and failed to shut the heavy door behind her.

"My goodness, old bean! What is it about Hutchins? You were going to tell us, and now you make that strange remark to Florie about her being a support to her grandfather." Lady Gossinger set down her teacup on the nesting table beside her chair and looked with fond concern at her husband's back as he stood peering out the leaded panes. Something about his posture told her that he would have been tempted to leap, had he been a little thinner and the windows a good deal wider. Young Vivian and Cousin Sophie were very much aware of the charged atmosphere. Both sat absolutely still. *My dear, sensitive Henry,* thought Lady Gossinger. *He's agonizing because Hutchins has been with him for donkey's years and he's been noticing things . . . things I have missed, that indicate that the man is slipping. This business of Flora being sent up with the tea, it's not at all the way things are done at Gossinger Hall.*

"It's all right, Henry," her Ladyship said aloud and moved as lightly as her brogues would carry her over to the window. "I understand what you're trying to tell me, dear, and believe me, it doesn't make you a bad person. Quite the reverse. I think you are being incredibly courageous to act upon your convictions in this way."

"You do, m'dear?" Sir Henry looked flabbergasted. "Don't know how you found out. But couldn't be happier you're taking it this way. Been worried you might have trouble accepting the situation."

"I know you think I'm too sensitive for my own good," Lady Gossinger patted her hair and tried not to dislodge her halo, "and believe me, I do feel enormously sorry for Hutchins, but if the time has come to put him out to pasture, dear . . ." Her eyes met her husband's, and the shock she saw in them caused her to feel a small flutter of unease. "That is what you wanted to tell me, isn't it, Henry?"

"I'm afraid not, Mabel." The baronet took one last longing look at the window before squaring his shoulders. "To make a long story short, I've decided to change my will and leave Gossinger Hall to Hutchins."

"You've done what, you bloody varmint?" Lady Gossinger's bellow would have done a barrow boy proud. It sent echoes vibrating all the way to Bethnal Green, where Edna was giving one of her customers a wash and set and wondering how her grandson Boris was behaving himself on his school visit to Lincolnshire.

FOUR

Mr. Leonard Ferncliffe was a man of science. He had taught the subject to eleven-year-old boys in expensive school uniforms for more than a decade, and now made a discovery which he believed to be of monumental importance to the world at large and to himself in particular: He did not like children. In particular, he did not like children of the male persuasion. To put it even more bluntly, he detested them with every fiber of his being, which consisted in part of a Burberry raincoat, beige twill trousers, and the lightweight wool socks that his mother washed for him by hand and dried in a nylon bag.

If life had gone according to plan, Mr. Ferncliffe would not have found himself in the position of leading the school outing that ended up at Gossinger Hall after a rampage through the city of Lincoln. Eric Stodder,

the history master at New Church Preparatory School
For Boys, had made all the preparations for what had
become for him an annual pilgrimage, when with two
days to go he came down with chicken pox. Whereupon
the headmaster called Mr. Ferncliffe into his office and
told him he was Stodder's lucky replacement. At first it
hadn't sounded a particularly hellish assignment. Stodder rang up from his sickbed to say that he had chosen
Lincoln because it was loaded with history and there
was a very decent tie shop in the Bailgate.

So far, so good, Mr. Ferncliffe had been thinking at
the precise moment when Tom Collier, a usually coop-
erative boy, was sick all over his seat companion on the
coach while they were still in the thick of London traffic. From then on, the day skidded downhill at a break-
neck pace. Edward Whitbread had loftily imparted the
information that his father called Lincoln the poor
man's York. The castle was a joke. Lucy Tower wasn't
worth the climb. And let's face it, Edward said, if
you've seen one cathedral, you've seen them all.

Understandably, Mr. Ferncliffe took his revenge by
replying the same might be said of sweet shops. So,
although he'd been informed by Mr. Stodder that there
were some very good ones on Steep Hill, they wouldn't
waste time paying any of them a visit. Equally understandably, the boys, having decided they now had nothing to lose, turned into rampaging monsters. Making it
most unlikely that any one of them would, at any future
date, be presented with the keys to the city of Lincoln.

Now, as Mr. Ferncliffe stood in Gossinger's Great
Hall with twenty-two sullen schoolboys either tossing
their headphones and cassettes in the air or leaning with
ostentatious boredom against the radiators, he was torn
between a longing to go home to his mother in Earl's
Court and a desire to do something really desperate—
such as flee to the pub down the road and order a glass
of Babycham.

Mr. Ferncliffe was not particularly struck with Gossinger Hall. He had spotted two daddy longlegs investigating cracks in the walls and was convinced there were incubators filled with them all over the place. But after making a heroic attempt not to check his trouser cuffs for spiders, he ordered the boys around him in a circle and began quizzing them on what they had learned during the tour. Regrettably, there was more than an hour to kill before the coach driver would come to the rescue.

"We wanted to see inside the garderobe," said Scott Lowell.

"I expect you did, so you could have put up a sign that read 'John of Gaunt Sat Here.'" Mr. Ferncliffe gamely reminded himself that he had only thirty years to endure until retirement.

"And we haven't seen even one ghost!" Barry Taylor-Hobbs sounded thoroughly disgusted. "Edward Whitbread's father grew up near here and he says there's supposed to be a curse on this place."

"And I'm sure Mr. Whitbread is correct, as always," Mr. Ferncliffe said. "Let us move to the center of the room, boys, so we can look at the fireplace and try to imagine what life must have been like when it was responsible for heating all of Gossinger Hall."

"It looks like an old barbecue pit." Tom Collier had not returned to his usual stolidly cheerful self since being sick on the coach.

"If we threw our blazers up in the air," Lionel Robbins suggested helpfully, "we could knock down some of those tatty old pennants; then we could burn them to see if the smoke really does go up through the hole in the roof."

"It wouldn't. The shutters are closed." Mr. Ferncliffe had to raise his voice to be heard above the ensuing war cries that would have made the Scots and the Picts think twice about crossing the border. It was shocking how quickly the boys degenerated into the sort of little hoodlums their ingenuous parents thought belonged to people who watched television soap operas for a living. "I'm sure," Mr. Ferncliffe continued manfully, "that you have all benefited enormously from learning that the word *curfew* derives from our ancestors' habit of covering the fire at night, for safety reasons, when everyone went to bed."

The only person who showed any sign of listening to Mr. Ferncliffe doing his stuff was the dark-haired waif of a girl in the old-fashioned maid's outfit who had appeared as suddenly and silently as a ghost at his elbow. Now a school blazer went whizzing past her head, knocking her smile slightly askew, as she informed him that the tea and gift shop would be closing in thirty minutes.

"There's some mocha walnut cake left, sir," she added.

"Is there?" Mr. Ferncliffe's heart lifted.

"It's very good cake. My grandfather makes it and we've had visitors say it's the best they've ever tasted."

"Homemade?" Mr. Ferncliffe's bruised spirit warmed to this simple Lincolnshire lass. He pictured himself pouring his heart out to her over a cup of milky coffee. The boys' pounding footsteps and raucous laughter subsided into sporadic echoes, reminiscent of thunder retreating behind a distant hill. This girl, being a plain-faced little creature, would be touchingly grateful that he, in his Burberry raincoat and well-polished shoes, treated her like a person capable of insight and sensitivity. She had freckles, he now noticed, unusual in someone with dark hair. Mr. Ferncliffe was particularly susceptible to freckles.

She would fall head over heels in love with him, he decided, while passing him the sugar. And afterward—poor thing—she would reflect with a bittersweet smile that her half hour with a handsome stranger had

spoiled her for any other man who might come her
way. Mr. Ferncliffe tended to indulge in these romantic
fantasies. His mother was unlikely to find out about
them and make difficulties, as she had done on the
occasion he had turned a lunch date with a young lady
into a commitment of sorts by ordering a bottle of
French wine.

On this occasion, however, Mr. Ferncliffe took the
fantasy a step further than usual. He pictured the Lincolnshire lass twining her fingers through his hair and
gazing mistily into his eyes as she vowed to murder as
many of the boys as would make him happy. This of
course would put him under an obligation to her, which
would require that he bid her *adieu* with particular gen-
tleness.

"I'm sorry." He shook his head to bring her face
back into focus. "I didn't catch what you were saying?"

"I was suggesting respectfully, sir," she stood on tip-
toe and cupped her hands around her mouth, "that if
you were to stuff the young gentlemen with cake and
chocolate biscuits you might get a moment's peace and
quiet and my grandfather won't read you the riot act if
he catches you."

"Your grand— Do you mean Sir Henry Gossinger?"
Mr. Ferncliffe was knocked off-balance when one of
the boys collided with him at full tilt before collapsing
in a heap with his classmates on the floor. Had he been
taking mental liberties with a young woman from one
of Britain's better families?

"Sir Henry?" The girl looked down at her uniform,
clearly wondering if Mr. Ferncliffe had mistaken it for
fancy dress. "No, sir, my grandfather is Hutchins the
butler. He usually keeps a close eye on the tours. And it
is a wonder he hasn't been in to have a word with you
about making these lads behave themselves." She hesitated, her fingers working busily to replace a strand of

hair into the bun at the nape of her neck. "You haven't seen him, have you, sir?"

"I don't think so." If Mr. Ferncliffe sounded vague, it was because his mind was fully occupied in feeling taken down a peg. This nondescript young woman didn't find him irresistible. In fact, he was sure she wasn't the least bit impressed with him or his Burberry raincoat. Quite possibly she despised him as the worst sort of weakling. A man who let schoolboys trample him into the ground.

"Grandfather has gray hair," she said.

"Does he?" Mr. Ferncliffe applied his scientific mind to this piece of information and came up blank.

"He parts it close to the middle."

"Really?"

"He's of medium height and . . ."

"Is he lost?" Mr. Ferncliffe knew the moment the words popped out of his mouth that he had hit the nail on the head and he felt his spirits lift: Here was the damsel in distress his heart was always seeking. What did it matter that she failed to see him as a knight in shining armor? He would prove to her that chivalry was his middle name. Actually, his middle name was Herbert, but that was a disclosure that could be made much later, over a glass of red wine. If he were to help her, he must first ask one vital question.

"And your name is?"

"Flora." She evinced appropriate maidenly surprise. "And Grandpa isn't lost. It's just that I can't find him in any of the usual places. Most times when there's a tour going on, he stays close to the old buttery where the silver collection is kept, but . . ."

"I'll help you look for him." Mr. Ferncliffe put his hand in his raincoat pocket and produced, instead of a sword suitable for slaying dragons, a notepad and pencil. "Let me just take down a few details and then, if we don't find your grandfather in a very short time, I can spare you the distress of phoning up the police."

"But it isn't that serious." Flora backed away from him, narrowly missing stumbling over a couple of boys on the floor, who along with the rest of the group had opted to be quiet as they listened in on the unfolding drama. "I'm sorry, sir, that I said anything to make you think I was worried. Grandpa is probably in the kitchen right now having a cup of tea with the housekeeper."

"But what if he isn't?" Mr. Ferncliffe's voice rang out with unusual fervor. "What if the poor old chap has wandered away from the building and is even now heading down the road, a pitiful prey to oncoming traffic?"

Flora pressed her fingers to her temples, drew a deep breath, and mustered a smile. "Grandpa is in full possession of his faculties. He's as sensible as you are, sir." A derisive snicker from one of the boys filled in a tiny pause. "Thank you for your kindness but, honestly, you've got enough on your plate looking after twenty boys without worrying about me or Grandpa."

"Twenty-two." Mr. Ferncliffe put the notebook and pencil back in his pocket and tried not to look as rejected as he felt, when Flora Hutchins disappeared through an archway to his left. He told himself that he was better off without her, that she couldn't even count, and that his mother would have hated her. Then his eyes totted up the number of boys present in the grand hall and he discovered Flora was right. There were twenty of them. So where were the other two?

Mr. Ferncliffe was about to pose this question to the remaining little horrors when Edward Whitbread came sauntering forth from the direction of the tea shop.

"Awfully good cream cakes," he announced, as if this explained everything.

"How dare you wander off on your own?" Mr. Ferncliffe, unable to prevent his voice from sounding pathetically shrill, dug a hand into his raincoat pocket and got stabbed by the pencil.

"I wasn't on my own, sir," responded Edward with the arrogance he had learned at his father's knee. "I was with Boris Smith. He said he was going to look at the rude screen in the chapel. Thought it would be full of carvings of saints with their clothes off. Disgusting, some people's minds." Edward sighed heavily. "Anyway, sir, I thought that for the good of the school I should go along to keep an eye on him. After all, he's not like the rest of us, is he?"

Mr. Ferncliffe gnawed on the inside of his cheek. It was true Boris Smith was not cut from the same cloth as his fellow classmates. Each year New Church Preparatory School For Boys offered a free place to an undeserving youngster from a less than affluent background. Boris was one of the recipients of this largesse, and Mr. Ferncliffe had pondered, on more than one occasion, the wisdom of the school's board of governors. Such as the time Boris's science experiment turned out to be a demonstration in blowing up the chemistry lab. But Mr. Ferncliffe knew Edward Whitbread to be an instigator. He found it impossible to believe he had tailed after the other boy to keep him out of trouble.

"So where is Boris now?" he asked frostily. "Stuffing himself with cream cakes in the tea shop?"

"I don't think so, sir." Edward smirked at a couple of his pals who were only too eager to egg him on. "I gave up on Boris after he started in on some cock-and-bull story about his Aunt Mabel being Lady Gossinger. As my father says, it really doesn't do to try to help these people. If you'll believe it, Mr. Ferncliffe, Boris said he was going to sneak into the family's private quarters and surprise the old girl." Edward looked sickeningly virtuous. "I wasn't prepared to be a party to that, sir; so I went to the tea shop expecting that you would be along soon with the rest of the chaps. And the woman at the counter, a good sort for that kind of person, insisted I have something to eat to keep my strength up for the coach journey home."

Mr. Ferncliffe ground his teeth. Duty demanded that he go in search of Boris, but he wouldn't have been the least disappointed to discover that the other missing party, the butler named Hutchins, was a particularly maladjusted vampire who had bitten the boy on the neck before escorting him on a tour of the dungeons. Ill-wishing not being an exact science, it is rarely one-hundred-percent successful, even in places with the shadowy history of Gossinger Hall. And it would not have lightened Mr. Ferncliffe's emotional load to know that Boris Smith was blithely unaware that he was in deep trouble.

This was typical of young Boris, who tended to live entirely in the present. He had promised his grand-mother Edna to behave himself on the school trip. And at the time he had meant every word. He had agreed that although her bleached blond hair might be deceiv-ing, she was getting too old for any more shocks to her nervous system. He had also promised that he would not go telling any of the kids in his class that his Great-Aunt Mabel was her Ladyship of Gossinger Hall. Gran had explained that if the board of governors got hold of that piece of information they might order her to cough up the school fees for the last four terms. And then where would they be? Out on the street with a mattress and a saucepan, that's where. Boris had assured Gran, before heading off to join his classmates, that he under-stood completely.

But, typically, he had forgotten his promises. He modestly refrained from taking credit for getting into mischief with Edward Whitbread, because his had only been a supporting role, requiring little more than a promise that he would keep his mouth shut about their visit to the medieval toilet and subsequent high jinks.

And afterward, in the spirit of camaraderie, Boris had told Edward about Great-Auntie Mabel. The other boy had crossed his heart and promised not to blab and Boris almost trusted him; but suddenly it seemed to him that, given the chance that this afternoon's activities would catch up with him, he might as well go whole hog against Gran's wishes and beard the old bat, otherwise known as Lady Gossinger, in her lair. Perhaps he could squeeze five pounds out of her.

Boris had been about to open the door marked "Private" when it swung open with a groan that startled him into sitting smartly down on his bottom and scooting under a table covered with pamphlets to avoid getting barked in the shins. Before he could get up, two men came out and started talking, and he decided to stay where he was rather than be ordered to scram and in all likelihood lose his opportunity to sweeten up Great-Aunt Mabel.

"Must say I feel the most frightful cad," said the elderly man with the bald head and the stoutish build of one who rarely, if ever, refuses custard with his pudding. "Hate to see a woman cry."

"Afraid it came as a bit of a blow to her, Uncle Henry," responded the younger man, who looked to Boris like a real toff.

"I suppose you think I should have told her in private, eh, Vivian? No need really for you or Sophie to be there. Knew that, of course. But I'm a coward by nature." The elderly man looked deeply sorrowful. "Always have been, always will be, I suppose. That's why I married Mabel in the first place, if you want the whole truth of it."

"There's no need to bare your soul to me. Some things best left unsaid, Uncle Henry."

Boris realized these two starchy-mouthed geezers were talking about Gran's one and only sister, his Great-Aunt Mabel.

"Hang it all, Vivian," the older man said, "got to talk to someone. Made a damn silly mistake the day I met Mabel. Thought she'd come after the job as housekeeper. Been advertising for one all week in the paper. Never occurred to me she was part of a tour group. She looked the part, do you see? Like a housekeeper, I mean. And she wasn't wearing the headphones, so you can understand, can't you, m'boy, how I got the wrong end of the stick?"

"I don't get what you're saying, Uncle Henry."

"Know it sounds damn odd, m'boy, but when I asked her if she'd be happy at Gossinger, she thought I was popping the question. So what was there for a chap to do?"

"You could have told her she'd misunderstood."

"There is that." Sir Henry looked dolefully down at the floor. "But there is also, when all is said and done, the matter of atonement. Of recent years I've become something of a religious man. No point in letting the chapel go to waste, if you understand what I'm saying, m'boy."

"Not precisely." Boris could see that the young man named Vivian was striving not to look disappointingly thick.

"Never was much good at explaining m'self." Sir Henry squared his shoulders and looked his nephew in the eye. "But to try and put it in a nutshell, I rather got the idea when Mabel was so stuck on marrying me that I was being handed a penance that might in its small way make some reparation for the sins of the past. Not my past, if you get what I'm saying, Vivian. Dull sort of fellow. Never been sufficiently interesting to get up to any great wickedness."

"Then whose past, Uncle Henry?"

"Enough said, m'boy."

"It's not that business about the family silver?"

"Mustn't even discuss it, Vivian; walls have ears,

don't you see, gave m'father my solemn oath when the poor chap was coughing out his lungs on his deathbed. That's when he told me the story. Just as your father told you before he passed on. That's how it works, family tradition and all that." This was a lengthy speech for Sir Henry and he wasn't done yet. "I hope you understand, m'boy, that in making the decision to leave Gossinger Hall to Hutchins, I feel I've done m'damnedest to move our family one step closer to laying the past to rest."

"I'm sure you've done what you think is best, Uncle Henry," responded Vivian, "but to be perfectly frank I don't suppose that is a whole lot of consolation to Aunt Mabel at this moment."

"You could be right." Sir Henry stood there, looking very much like a stuffed owl to Boris, who was still hiding out under the table. "But when all's said and done it's not as though Hutchins would turn Mabel out of the house after my day. I haven't yet spoken to him about m'plans, but I haven't a doubt in the world he'd invite her to make Gossinger her home for as long as she liked."

"And she could be a second mother to Flora?" Vivian raised an eyebrow. "I may be wrong, Uncle, but I rather got the impression from Aunt Mabel's outburst upstairs that she would sooner be dead than stay on under those conditions."

"You think she put it that strongly, do you?" Sir Henry looked crestfallen until he remembered something. "But it's not as though she won't have options, m'boy. I plan to leave her a tidy sum, enough money to keep her in reasonable comfort. And she has the flat in Bethnal Green, you know. She's got a sister there, and after I'm gone I would think she'd want to get back to her roots. Nothing like your own people, is there? Fact of life." Sir Henry breathed an audible sigh of relief. "Give Mabel time, she'll come round."

"If you say so, Uncle Henry."

"She's a good woman, wouldn't want you to think I'm not damned fond of her after all these years."

Pull the other one, it's got bells on, thought Boris. He shrank back closer to the wall as Sir Henry looked around him in an absentminded sort of way and said that he thought he would go and look for Hutchins and have a chat with him about the situation. Whereupon Vivian Gossinger said that he would toddle down to the pub for a pint. And after bleating on a bit more like a pair of sheep, the two of them strolled off along the corridor, leaving Boris to get to his feet and ponder.

The boy found it impossible not to feel a twinge of sympathy for Great-Aunt Mabel, even though she'd never done anything halfway nice for Gran. But there was no denying that he saw the possibilities in the situation. Right now Auntie was bound to be feeling all alone in the world, betrayed by her husband, abandoned by the stupid nephew, so how could she fail to view a visit from Boris as a little ray of sunshine sent like a gift from God to lighten her darkest hour?

Boris opened the door marked "Private" and went up narrow twisting stairs that were partially lit by a window that was the shape and approximate size of an arrow. It was like climbing out of a well, he thought, and he'd probably smell like a frog for at least a week. Boris felt a flicker of affection for the council flat where he lived with Gran. It mostly smelled like toasted cheese or fish-and-chips.

By the time he reached the top of the stairs and found himself on a narrow landing, facing a door, he was convinced Great-Aunt Mabel would burst into tears of joy when she saw him. His only fear was that she would also smother him with sloppy kisses or, even worse, want to hold him on her lap. But, he reasoned philosophically as he lifted his hand to tap on the door, if he ended up with ten pounds in his pocket it wouldn't be so bad.

Boris knocked a second time. Not getting any answer, he turned the heavy iron handle with both hands and pushed open the door. There were two ladies in the funny round room. One was lying on a sofa and the other one, who looked a lot like the Queen Mother, was bending over her, talking in a singing sort of voice.

"It's Cousin Sophie, Mabel . . ."

She hadn't noticed Boris and he thought it only polite to interrupt. "Hello," he said, his voice coming out louder than he meant it to, "I've come to visit you in your hour of need, Great-Aunt Mabel. I am your sister Edna's only grandson, Boris, and this moment my heart is overflowing with—"

He never did get to say with what, because his Great-Aunt Mabel sat bolt upright on the sofa and emitted a piercing scream before sending a pillow sailing toward his head.

"Get out, you little monster," she yelled, "before I have you taken outside and hung, drawn and quartered!"

"But, Auntie, I love you . . ."

A second pillow hit him squarely in the chest and, taking the hint, Boris headed out the door, where he came upon a very thin elderly man wheeling an empty tea trolley toward him.

"Afternoon, young master," said Mr. Tipp.

Rarely, in all his eleven years, had Boris felt more embarrassed. But he managed to display a loftiness worthy of the New Church School uniform.

"Someone should lock her Ladyship up in the garderobe," he said, before turning and running full tilt back down the stairs. Luckily, or so he thought at the time, he didn't collide with Mr. Ferncliffe who one minute before had abandoned his search for his missing pupil, and gone to drown his sorrows in a cup of tea.

FIVE

"Dear Mabel." Cousin Sophie's crooning voice came at Lady Gossinger through a thick fog. "I think you have been quite astonishingly brave. Lie back on the sofa, dear, and give your poor head a rest, while I pour you a nice cup of lukewarm tea."

"Is he gone?" Her Ladyship cracked open an eye before remembering that her life was over.

"You mean that horrid little boy, dear?"

"Edna's grandson? He was really here? Lord help me, I hoped he was just a nightmare. But I was actually talking about Henry. Flown the coop, has he? Or is the old bean cowering behind that half-open door, waiting for me to call out that I appreciate no end his letting me in on his plans to change his will and leave Gossinger Hall to Hutchins?" The wronged wife held up her hand in a futile attempt to stop the tower room spin-

ning at a crazily lopsided angle that threatened to top-
ple her off the sofa into an undignified heap.

"Henry became very flustered, as well he ought, Mabel." Cousin Sophie tried not to sound as if she were
thoroughly enjoying the situation, but her hands trembled with excitement as she filled a cup from the silver
teapot. "He said something about women liking to be
alone at times such as this and hurried from the room
as if all the devils in hell were after him when you
started to go into convulsions. As any reasonable person
would have done under the circumstances," Cousin Sophie hastened to say. "Such a shock, and right after
eating cheese scones. It's a wonder you are still with us,
Mabel."

"And I suppose young Vivian was only a couple of
steps behind his uncle, and neither one of them had the
consideration to close the door behind them." Lady
Gossinger blinked back a tear.

"It was the boy—Boris, I think that was his name—
he left the door ajar. Good manners are rarely to be
found in young people today." Cousin Sophie hesitated,
then added in an obvious attempt at fanning the flames:
"Flora did the same thing, if you remember, after she
brought in the tea."

"And to think that stupid little nobody will be
queening it here at Gossinger after Henry kicks the
bucket. If that isn't enough to make you spit! As my
sister Edna would say." Her Ladyship's face turned an
almost fluorescent purple. "Having a bit more class, I
think I'll settle for killing myself."

"But surely that would be a little premature! Bear in
mind, dear, that Henry hasn't changed his will yet. And
in this uncertain world anything could happen. For instance, though one hesitates to mention it, Henry might
pass away before he sees his solicitor. Admittedly it's a
remote possibility, but life can play some very funny
tricks at times." Sophie shook her head philosophically.

"Henry's as healthy as a horse."

"But he *is* laboring under a great deal of pressure." Cousin Sophie tiptoed over to the sofa with the cup of stone-cold tea, most of which had slopped over into the saucer. "Drink this down, Mabel, and remember you are not alone. I am in your corner."

On this encouraging note the old lady went over to the door and, at the moment of closing it, saw Vivian Gossinger on the stairs. The young man was standing at such an angle that she could not be sure whether he was coming or going, but as far as she was concerned it made no difference.

"Go away!" Flushed with power, she mouthed the words at him. "Your Aunt Mabel doesn't want to see you. She has the greatest distaste for men at this moment."

"Whatever are you mumbling about?" demanded Lady Gossinger.

"Nothing, dear. Just thinking about how best to help you." Cousin Sophie tried to smooth out her face, but traces of triumph still showed around the edges of her mouth when she turned back into the room. Her eyes fixed for a moment on the oak cupboard by the fireplace where the bottle of sherry was kept in readiness for a visit from the vicar. A tiresome man, the vicar, with a nose like an old boot. But in all likelihood he would say that God had presented her with the opportunity for which Sophie had pined during her five-year visit to Gossinger Hall. At last she was needed. Sorely needed. And if she played her hand correctly, Mabel's gratitude might cause an old lady to feel secure at last that she would not abruptly find herself out on the street with a shopping cart and a sudden desire to join the Salvation Army.

Pictures filled Sophie's head. Happy pictures, beginning with breakfast in bed and ending with having her pillows fluffed by hands eager to smooth out any and every crease that might mar a perfect night's sleep for Mabel's guardian angel. Unfortunately, these hopeful images were shattered when Lady Gossinger dropped her Royal Derby teacup and saucer with a fearsome clatter and burst into noisy sobs.

"Oh, go away, Sophie, do!" Her Ladyship's flailing hand found a damask serviette and she blew her nose three times—very hard. "Get out, I say. I honestly can't bear to look at you."

"But why, Mabel?" The old lady felt a bubble burst deep inside her, and tears welled in her eyes. "What have I done? What in heaven's name have I said?"

"You were there! A witness to all my lower-class instincts running amuck! You heard me screaming at Henry like a bloody fishwife. And if that wasn't enough, you had a ringside view of the bloody encore when Boris showed up. So now if it's all the same with you, I'd like to try and pull myself together before I crawl back into the gutter where I belong."

"Better an honest fishwife," Cousin Sophie dabbed at her tears with an arthritic knuckle before bending down with great dignity to pick up the broken pieces of china, "than a mealymouthed coward."

"*What* did you call me?" A gasp went down the wrong way and her Ladyship started to cough.

"You heard me." Cousin Sophie straightened and walked over to the wastepaper basket by the fireplace. "And I'm surprised at you, Mabel, for talking about giving up without even attempting to fight for your rights as Henry's wife. Somehow, although I've never set eyes on her, I'm certain your sister Edna would have more backbone."

Lady Gossinger was stung to the quick. "But what in heaven's name can I do?"

"May I suggest, Mabel," Cousin Sophie had brightened considerably at the success of her less than subtle ploy, "that you exercise your womanly wiles."

"What—throw myself into Henry's arms and start blubbering all over his waistcoat?" Her Ladyship vented her contempt in a hollow laugh. "Those sort of dramatics might work if I were blond and beautiful with a face that looked as though God made it yesterday morning. For your information, Sophie, I look like a clown when I cry. Thanks all the same, but I think I'll hold on to what little dignity I have left."

"I couldn't agree with you more, dear. That was going to be my suggestion, Mabel: that you compose yourself before seeing Henry again. At which time you tell him you're sorry you went off the deep end because you now wholeheartedly agree with his decision. In fact," Cousin Sophie sat down in one of the judgment-seat chairs across from Lady Gossinger, "you think he's an absolute saint for acting upon his conscience, and never have you loved him more dearly, or been prouder to be his wife, than at this moment in time."

"And what will that do?"

"Henry will realize he married a treasure."

"And?" Lady Gossinger raised a derisive eyebrow.

"With luck, he'll start wondering if he isn't behaving like an absolute cad. Especially, dear Mabel, if you suit action to words and *turn up the heat.*"

"You're talking about the *radiators?*"

"No, dear." Cousin Sophie glanced toward the door as if fearing someone might have his ear to the keyhole. "I'm talking, if you will excuse the vulgarity, about *sex.* Men are such babies when it comes to all that nonsense. Or so I understand from listening to some of the television chat shows. And I do not think it would hurt, and might well do the world of good, if you were to make a concerted effort, perhaps two or three times a week, until Henry got the point."

"Which is?" Her Ladyship had not felt this uncomfortable on her wedding night.

"That he should leave Gossinger Hall to you, or at

least to Vivian—which would amount to the same thing, because that young man has made it plain he would never want to live here. You know what I am suggesting: see-through nighties, bedroom eyes and all that sort of thing. Of course that may well seem an insurmountable task, especially for someone who is through the change of life. . . ."

"I am nothing of the sort!"

"No, of course not." Cousin Sophie struggled to rally from this monumental blunder. "What was I thinking? It is just that . . . you are so very . . . mature for your age."

"I'm sure you are trying to be helpful," said Lady Gossinger without much sincerity, "but if it's all the same with you, I'd like to be by myself so I can really enjoy being miserable."

"The wisest course of action, Mabel." The old lady forced a quivering smile. "But do think about my suggestion. Men are so susceptible to a little cheese-cake . . . I think that is the term used by the married women of my acquaintance. Meanwhile, dear, I will try to make myself useful by going to see why Tipp has not been up to remove the tea things. Perhaps he overheard your upset with that awful boy and thought it best not to come in until you had recovered."

"Forget about Tipp! The last thing I need at this moment is that old geezer buggering about when I'm trying to pick up the pieces of my life!" Lady Gossinger knew she sounded common as muck, and she didn't much care. "For all I friggin' well know, Henry has left Tipp a manor house in Cornwall!"

"You mustn't worry about that, dear." Cousin Sophie spoke in a depleted voice. "There isn't any family property left besides Gossinger. Unless you count the Dower House."

"Oh, go away!" Her Ladyship was about to pick up another cushion and hurl it full force, when the door opened and closed, leaving her alone in the room. Blessed silence. At last she could enjoy her misery to the full. She stood at the window, a sturdy woman in sensible tweeds with tears plopping off the end of her nose.

From the window, she could see the Dower House which Cousin Sophie had mentioned, separated from Gossinger Hall by the road and a market garden. A handsome Tudor dwelling, it had been built on the site of Lady Normina's twelfth-century dream kitchen. But the Dower House wouldn't provide a refuge for a dispossessed widow, because it was leased to the family who operated the garden and there was as little likelihood of getting them out as—Lady Gossinger gulped down a sob—as there was of Hutchins conveniently dropping dead before Henry signed his new will.

What it comes down to, old girl, the former Mabel Bowser thought, *is the age-old question: Are you a woman or a mouse?* She could feel her spine stiffening. She was beginning to sound like Lady Gossinger again. No more sniveling. The time had come for action.

She went over to the cupboard by the fireplace and removed a small object from behind the bottle of sherry. Tempted to shore herself up with a glass of liquid courage, she decided the last thing she needed was to picture the vicar lecturing her on the wages of sin. Best to do the dirty deed, if it was at all possible, today.

On this uplifting note, Lady Gossinger left the tower room. She went down the shadowy stairs and entered the Great Hall without meeting a soul; but there was something present—a stirring beneath the silence that made her wonder for the first time if the old tales about Gossinger's being haunted might perhaps be true. Or was it only her silly conscience that made her feel the tiniest bit uneasy? Oh, ballocks to that, decided her Ladyship as she headed down the narrow passage toward the tearoom and came face-to-face with the very person she was seeking.

"Ah, there you are!" she boomed in a voice now fully restored to its earthquake dimensions. "I have a little job for you to do. Won't take but a moment, and afterward you can sit down to a nice cup of tea and a cream bun."

At that precise moment, Mrs. Much the housekeeper was making tea in a pot whose insides she had steeped in bleach overnight. Setting the kettle back on the ancient cooker, she patted her permed hair and gave her apron strings a resolute tug, while giving the kitchen a scathing glance. This room wasn't any more cheerful than the rest of Gossinger, having been built at the turn of the century with an emphasis on reminding the household staff that fallen arches went with the job.

"If I don't get away from this dreadful house I'll end up throwing myself off the roof, and then there'll be another ghost come to haunt Sir Henry and her Ladyship," Mrs. Much said aloud. "And only three months ago I was thinking I'd landed the job of my life."

Mrs. Much was speaking to Mr. Tipp, who sat at the scrubbed wood table studying the small piece of paper he held in his skeletal hands. At sixty-five, Mr. Tipp was far from a robust-looking man. Indeed, one feared the least breeze might turn him into a set of wind chimes.

"It's not to be wondered at." He folded the piece of paper into a postage-size square, and managed to sound as if he were listening to the housekeeper's lamentations for the first time.

"Let me put it this way, Mr. Tipp." She set a chocolate biscuit in his saucer and settled her comfortably large person into the chair across from him. "There's some people that have ambitions to be doctors or bank managers or the like, but when I was a little girl, all I dreamed about was growing up into a woman who cleaned other people's houses. There's nothing thrills me like scrubbing and polishing, unless it's taking down an armload of curtains and putting them in the wash."

For a moment Mrs. Much's face took on a glow reminiscent of a full moon in an unclouded sky. "Think on it," she clasped her serviceable hands, "the boundless joy of scrubbing out a bath until it's white as driven snow! No one, and that's the gospel truth, Mr. Tipp, will ever know the happiness I get from bringing back the shine on a piece of lino so's it looks better than new."

"I take your meaning, Mrs. Much."

"But the working conditions has to be right, if you understand me, Mr. Tipp. It's not sufficient that I get to live at Gossinger Hall and make decent wages. I can't find professional fulfillment when I'm told off for taking down the tapestries for a wash."

"I doubt no one could make themselves any clearer." Mr. Tipp took a sip of tea, which tasted of bleach, but told himself manfully that it was an acquired taste and he would get to like it. He would have liked to ask for another chocolate biscuit but did not wish to appear greedy.

"Mr. Hutchins carried on about those tapestries like I was a cold-blooded murderer." Mrs. Much's face darkened. "It quite ruined my afternoon, until I told myself, who needs this job, when all is said and done. I've no idea where he's disappeared to all this time, but good riddance is what I say. Let him report me to Sir Henry and her Ladyship. And let them give me the push. It's no skin off my nose. I've a cousin as thinks I could get on where she works, but I won't say any more about that," Mrs. Much crossed her fingers, "in case I jinx myself. What I don't understand is why you stay on here, year after year, Mr. Tipp. It's not like they've ever made a proper position for you now that there's no horses in the stables."

"Haven't been for thirty years, not since old Major had to be put down, but it doesn't bother me none being the odd-job man. When I see something that needs doing I write it down, and sometimes I come up with quite a list." Mr. Tipp picked up the folded piece of paper he'd been fiddling with before he started drinking his tea. He looked at it with an expression of pleased pride before tucking it in his jacket pocket. "I'm the last of a long line of Tipps that have worked at Gossinger Hall since no one quite remembers when. Which is more than can be said for Mr. Hutchins. Not that I mean any disrespect, I'm just saying that's one difference between us, along with him being Sir Henry's right-hand man."

Mr. Tipp looked decidedly anxious, and Mrs. Much hastened to put his mind at ease.

"Trust me not to breathe a word. My late husband would tell you I'm loyal to a fault. Such a lovely man, snuffed out like a light in his prime when he fell asleep in the bath and drowned." She dabbed at her eyes in respectful memory of the deceased. "It's a shame, that's what I call it, Mr. Tipp, you being the junior here, at your time of life. My pride wouldn't stand for it—" Realizing this was hardly tactful, she added quickly, "but I suppose it would be hard for you to find another job so close to retirement. Where will you go when that time comes? Do you have any family," Mrs. Much got up to pour him another cup of tea, "any relatives at all who would offer you a home?"

"Not that I knows about."

"You poor man." She handed him the sugar bowl by way of a consolation prize.

"Sir Henry will see me all right."

"I wouldn't bank on her Ladyship," Mrs. Much said darkly.

"She's not the easiest to please," Mr. Tipp conceded, "but she does love Gossinger Hall something fierce."

"Well, good luck to her!" Mrs. Much resettled herself at the table. "Don't take offense, because it's clear you have your loyalties, but I can't pour my heart and soul into a place where there's not one fitted carpet or a color television in sight and the plumbing dates back to the Dark Ages. I couldn't believe what I was seeing when on my very first day Mr. Hutchins took me up one of those stone staircases and showed me that horrible pit toilet. I've never seen such a disgusting place in my life. And I couldn't have been more thankful that it's kept locked and I wasn't to be put in charge of one of the keys and told to go in there and clean once a week."

Mr. Tipp tried to look sympathetic, but as a man who had dreamed of mucking out the stables as his father and grandfather had done before him, he found himself somewhat at a loss for a response. So he wisely said nothing.

"I'll be glad to get out of this place." Mrs. Much got to her feet again and with a heartfelt sigh removed Mr. Tipp's teacup from his hands. "Flora's a nice enough girl, but I wouldn't say she's company. Not much spark to her, but I'm not one to pull people to pieces. Maybe she's not strong. She's pale enough to be a ghost, which isn't to be wondered at after growing up in this tomb of a house! Sometimes if I wake up in the middle of the night," Mrs. Much gave a trembly laugh, intended to indicate she wasn't a coward by nature, "I hear noises deep down inside the walls that sound like screams."

"There's a lot of stories told about strange doings at Gossinger Hall over the centuries." Mr. Tipp lowered his voice. "You'll have heard tell about the Queen's tea strainer that went missing. But did you know there's some as say one of the maidservants was blamed, and punished, for taking it? Seems to me, considering there's been one or other of us working here down through the years, that she was a Tipp like people say." This confession was made with a curious hint of pride. "And it could be that it's her screams you hear of a dark night, and her who put a curse on Gossinger Hall."

"There's a curse on the windows all right." Mrs. Much was looking out the one above the kitchen sink. "All those horrid little panes with so much lead on them it looks like cross-stitch. Give me a nice picture window and double-glazing any day. Mrs. Frome, the lady I worked for before coming here, had the loveliest big windows. It was that sort of house, if you can picture it, Mr. Tipp. Only five years old, with fitted cupboards everywhere you looked and all the pictures bought to match the curtains. They purchased every bit of furniture brand-new when they moved in, Mr. Frome insisted on it. And, as I told him when Mrs. Frome was taken away in the ambulance never to come home again, he could take comfort in knowing he'd nothing to regret. Don't go reproaching yourself that you didn't buy one of those self-cleaning cookers, I said when Mr. Frome cried on my shoulder like a baby. Those sort of gimmicky things take all the fun out of housework. And it was true. I'd loved every minute of scrubbing the racks so you'd never think a Yorkshire pudding had come out of that oven."

"That's a sad little story." Mr. Tipp looked up at the clock as he spoke.

"It was an overdose that took her." Mrs. Much teared up. "Accidental, of course, because what woman with a fridge that makes ice cubes and a Laura Ashley bedroom would want to make away with herself? And I took it especially hard, because before Mrs. Frome I was with Mrs. Ashford who passed away, without a word of warning, minutes after finishing a bowl of mushroom soup." Deciding that was enough reminiscing, Mrs. Much turned away from the sink. "Is something wrong, Mr. Tipp?"

"I wonder if I should go back upstairs to collect the tea things," he replied vaguely, getting to his feet, then sitting back down again. "Flora came along to the kitchen a while back, when you were busy elsewhere, and told me Sir Henry had asked for me to tend to that task, but when I went up to the tower room her Ladyship threw a cushion."

"That woman's off her head."

"She didn't throw it at me," Mr. Tipp hastened to explain. "There was a boy there, a boy in school uniform, with spiky hair and freckles, at the top of the stairs."

"Perhaps he'd escaped from the tour group?" Mrs. Much suggested, as if talking about a lion at the zoo. "But however that may be, Mr. Tipp, it's now almost six o'clock and it worries me you'll be in hot water if Mr. Hutchins suddenly pops up and finds out you haven't cleared away those tea things and brought them down here. Now, that wouldn't matter if you was planning to hand in your notice along with me, but you've just been saying that's not the case. So why don't you put your skates on and explain to her Ladyship—if she's still in the tower room—that you didn't like to disturb her when she was all upset?"

"She was more than upset, she was . . ." Mr. Tipp scratched his head as he searched for the right word, "she was . . . distraught."

"Over this schoolboy?"

"He said . . ."

"Yes?"

"That he was her sister's grandson." Mr. Tipp looked ashamed of himself for gossiping about his betters. He certainly knew that if Hutchins had been present he would have branded him a traitor to his class.

"And why should that get her Ladyship wound up like a grandfather clock?"

"Perhaps he's a bad lot."

"Come to hit her over the head, because she'd forgot his birthday?" Mrs. Much sounded as though she might be warming to the lad.

"And there was more. I couldn't help overhearing . . ."

"Of course you couldn't."

". . . Lady Gossinger was talking to Miss Doffit about Sir Henry . . . something about him changing his will." Mr. Tipp hovered like a shadow at the kitchen door.

"Well, I never!" Mrs. Much was all ears to hear more, but (wouldn't you know?) at that very moment Flora came into the kitchen by way of the outside door, wearing a damp mackintosh and a strained look on her face. Strands of hair had escaped from its coil to hang limply against her neck. And it seemed to Mrs. Much that the girl had brought some of the gathering darkness of late afternoon into the room with her.

"Here, let me help you off with that coat," the housekeeper said, "and Mr. Tipp, why don't you leave going up to the tower room for another few minutes and put the kettle on so Flora can have a cup of tea? It's plain to see something has upset her real bad."

"No, I'm just being silly." The girl evaded the hands that were trying to undo her mackintosh buttons and sat down at the kitchen table. "I've been out looking for Grandpa, thinking he might have . . . had to go out on an errand, but of course he has to be here in the house."

"Well, I can't say as I've seen him since early afternoon," Mrs. Much said. "But I've been busy around the place myself and figured he'd be polishing the silver; although I can't say for certain this is his day for it." Sensing Flora needed cheering up she went on, "I must say Mr. Hutchins does a lovely job of keeping all those christening cups and whatnots sparkly. That polish he makes up is a miracle. I for one have never used anything that removes tarnish the way it does, along with giving a shine that's not to be beat." Mrs. Much hoped she did not sound as if she felt compelled to give the devil his due: It was clear it would take more than the cup of tea Mr. Tipp carried to the table to bring the girl out of the dumps.

"I am being silly," Flora repeated. "It's not likely, is it, that a flying saucer landed on the lawn and an army of little green men made off with Grandpa for outer space." But her laughter was hollow.

"Could be they wanted that recipe for silver polish!"

It was unlike Mr. Tipp to attempt a joke, and Flora found herself smiling. Suddenly she was quite sure her grandfather would turn up any minute now and make nonsense of her concerns that he wasn't overseeing the tour group. And as if to prove her right, the door to the corridor opened. But it wasn't her grandfather who entered the room. It was Vivian Gossinger, with his tie askew and his usually well-groomed hair flopping over his forehead.

"Miss Hutchins," he spoke gently, "you'd better come at once. There's been the most dreadful accident in the garderobe. Your grandfather has fallen in and—"

"Is he badly hurt?" She came slowly to her feet.

"I'm so sorry, Flora. He was dead when he was brought out." Vivian took hold of her hand. "God bless him, we won't see Hutchins's like again at Gossinger."

Six

It rained on the day of Mr. Hutchins's funeral, and that was a twist of the knife because Flora had always loved rainy days. Grandpa used to say that Lincolnshire rain was the softest in all England. When she was a little girl and it started to rain she would picture God wearing a pair of Wellington boots as he walked around his estates in the sky carrying a giant watering can.

Sometimes, if Flora screwed up her eyes just right, she could see God's face in what most people would think was just another woolly cloud. She would smile at the idea of the Deity taking time out of his busy workday to peer down at the earthly garden he had planted so long ago, to make sure he didn't miss sprinkling the tiniest continent or flower. And she would remind him that her name was Flora.

Even when she was all grown up she still loved the

way the world looked when it was smudgy and out of focus, as in a picture she had drawn herself and then rubbed out because she hadn't got it quite right. And the best-ever part of rainy days was knowing that afterward when the sun came out the world would be put back exactly as it always was, only better because it would be all polished up, in just the same sort of way that Grandpa polished the silver every Tuesday and Thursday.

But it was different on the day of the funeral, because Flora knew that when the rain went away and the sun came back out nothing would be the way it was before the accident. It was as though all the bits and pieces of her life had got put away in the wrong drawers. And all the drawers had locks on them and she didn't have any idea where to start looking for the keys. The key to the garderobe had been found on the floor by Grandpa's feet when he was discovered. Along with a piece of paper on which he had written the words: GOD SAVE THE QUEEN!

When the time came to leave for the church service, Flora put on her courage along with the black coat and the hat that looked like a fruitcake which Lady Gossinger had insisted on lending her for the occasion. As she was getting into the car she overheard Miss Doffit telling Sir Henry she was glad it was raining, because funerals weren't supposed to be pleasant little outings with a picnic hamper from Fortnum & Mason stowed in the backseat of the car, along with a plaid traveling rug to be spread out on the cemetery grass. Flora did not hear Sir Henry's response, because Vivian, who had opened the car door for her, now closed it very quickly.

The service, which was held at St. Sebastian's—a rather vulgar-looking late-Victorian church with flashy stained-glass windows, located midway between Nether Woodcock and Maidenbury—included all Mr. Hutchins's favorite hymns. There were no flowers, by request.

And Flora noticed when the coffin was brought down the aisle that it was a little dusty on top, but she tried not to think how this would have vexed her grandfather. It was important to focus on uplifting thoughts.

In addition to the Gossinger family and its employees, there were a goodly number of people lining the pews; but not so many that it looked as though free raffle tickets had been handed out at the door. The rector, Mr. Aldwin, was a roly-poly figure with a twinkle in his eye that even the solemnity of the occasion could not quite banish.

"Isn't he a lovely man?" piped up a voice from the back of the church. "Such a nice change from the old rector. Mr. Roberts used to stand in the pulpit like he was stuck in the dock at the Old Bailey, falsely accused of cold-blooded murder."

Then Sir Henry, there was no mistaking his mumbling voice, said, "You look like you're about to faint, Mabel, m'dear. Awfully stuffy in here. Don't suppose they ever open those confounded windows."

One of the differences between Mr. Aldwin and his predecessor was that where Mr. Roberts had been partial to the occasional glass of sherry, Mr. Aldwin liked a pint of Guinness when the occasion arose. Despite only being on the job a couple of weeks, the rector spoke with boundless affection and admiration of the Dearly Departed, concluding with the assertion that Mr. Hutchins had ever been a good and faithful servant of the Almighty.

"He was that and all." A woman's voice floated up from behind Flora. "Devoted, that was Mr. Hutchins. Worked for the almighty Gossingers most of his life and ends up in the toilet. Doesn't seem right, that's what I say!"

Fortunately, at that moment the organist struck up the final hymn and Mr. Aldwin, now looking positively jolly, plunged into the first verse of "Shall We Gather

At the River," while beating time on the rim of his
pulpit. And soon almost everyone was joining in with
equal gusto, causing Mrs. Much, who sat in the second
pew, to whisper into Flora's ear that it sounded like a
sing-along down at the pub.

"And I'm not sure your Grandpa was that sort, dear.
You know, the kind to be doing a knees-up at The
Golden Fleece."

Neither did you like him very much, thought Flora. It
was a comfort to have Sir Henry step forward to take
her hand, as if she were still a little girl with stubby
pigtails, and lead her from the church.

"Must say you're holding up frightfully well,
m'dear," he said as they stepped out into the rain that
bounced off his bald head. "But shouldn't be afraid to
break down, you know. I'm not ashamed to say I've
shed a few tears m'self. Even caught her Ladyship having a bit of a sniffle this morning."

"It was pitiful to see her so upset. Only a good
woman would take the loss of a servant, even one of
Hutchins's sort, so much to heart." Miss Sophie Doffit
spoke up from right behind them, then added softly,
"Surely no one could possibly think Mabel wasn't genuinely shocked by what happened."

The old lady was wearing a pale pink hat with
downy feathers adorning one side, and a matching
edge-to-edge coat quite unsuited to the weather. Her
resemblance to the Queen Mother was more startling
than usual. Several children who had been brought
along, and told to behave themselves or be very sorry
afterward, began jumping up and down and pointing
excitedly at Miss Doffit.

This rude display stopped abruptly, however, when
the naughty little things noticed a woman standing at
the edge of the path who looked like a witch. Her cloak
was a mustard-and-black plaid and she had extraordi-
narily long purple fingernails. At that moment she was

staring at one little boy in particular in a lip-smacking sort of way. He let out a terrified squeal when she beckoned to him with one of her claws and offered him a piece of barley sugar.

The parents immediately rounded up their offspring and marched them away, while Flora stood looking into space, unaware that the witch woman had taken a couple of steps toward her before apparently changing her mind and retreating. By this time Lady Gossinger had emerged from the church on her nephew Vivian's arm. It was impossible, with the rain now pelting down, for Flora to get a clear view of her face.

The drive to the cemetery and the walk down the mossy path to the graveside was also mercifully blurred by the steady rain. To the accompaniment of depressed-looking trees rustling in the chilly breeze, the rector imparted to the standard verses, including the one about "ashes to ashes," a heartiness that again bordered on the jovial.

In a voice that carried on the wind, Miss Sophie Doffit declared the new rector was a vast improvement on Reverend Roberts, who had frightened her into deciding to forgo laying up treasures on earth, in order to have a hope of being admitted to the outskirts of heaven. Where, from the sound of it, she added, the vast majority of people lived in council houses in less than salubrious neighborhoods. Someone coughed. And Vivian held a black umbrella over Flora's head.

The mourners, who included the witch woman with her mustard-and-black cloak flapping like a live thing, closed into a dark, silent huddle when the coffin was lowered into the grave. Flora found herself worrying that old Miss Doffit would move a little too close and fall in headfirst, thereby putting her knickers on view to all and sundry.

They would be pale pink, Flora decided, trimmed with handmade lace and little ribbons. It was easier for her to think about something like that than to dwell on the fact that the one person in the world whom she loved was gone forever. Suddenly she realized that they hadn't sung *all* Grandpa's favorite hymns in the church.

Much to her own surprise, Flora opened her mouth and began singing "God Save the Queen" in the reedy off-key voice that had caused the music teacher at the village school to call her aside one day and suggest (in the kindest possible way) that in future she should just open and close her mouth like a fish.

A boy, the one who hadn't been particularly brave when the witch offered him a sweet, giggled.

Flora didn't hear, nor did she notice when first Vivian and then several other straggling voices joined hers, until everyone was singing. She tossed a handful of moist earth onto the coffin and turned to walk quickly —almost at a run—away from everyone including the Gossingers, toward the waiting car.

Sir Henry had made the arrangements for her driver. He was married to Mrs. Warren who worked in the gift-shop-cum-tearoom at Gossinger, and would herself be traveling back to the house with Mrs. Much and Mr. Tipp. Flora wasn't eager for chitchat, but it seemed unfriendly to sit in state in the back of the car. So she climbed in front with Mr. Warren and gave him a smile that was clouded by the brim of her hat.

"You sit quiet, little lass," he told her, "I'll have you home in next to no time." The words, so kindly spoken, sent a chill through her, because the emptiness waiting for her back at Gossinger Hall was so enormous she was afraid she would get lost in it and never find her way out.

Mr. Warren said he knew a shortcut back to Gossinger Hall. He was a man in his late forties with a scholarly face and a receding hairline. Nothing worried him, his wife had been heard to say on many occasions with exasperation. Perhaps he was having an off day, but he didn't strike Flora as a particularly good driver. He hummed hymn tunes as they bounced on and off a few curbs, pruning a few hedges along the way, and almost clipping a bus stop. Flora tried not to clutch the edge of her seat.

After motoring haphazardly along winding country lanes, they wound up in Maidenbury, a middle-size town in the opposite direction from Gossinger. Mr. Warren said—without appearing too embarrassed by the detour—that he was sure he could find another shortcut.

"There's no rush," Flora assured him, and thanked God for seat belts as they skidded to a stop at a crossroad, narrowly missing a man cloaked in rain and carrying a bulging briefcase. She was about to roll down her window and inquire if he were all right when, to her amazement, the man opened the car door and climbed, without so much as a by-your-leave, into the backseat.

"Keep looking straight ahead," he said in a pleasantly modulated voice. "I've just been to the local bank and made a rather large withdrawal."

"That's very interesting, mate," replied an unruffled Mr. Warren as Flora brought a hand up to her throat, "but I'm not driving a bus."

"Public transport just isn't in the cards today." The stranger settled himself comfortably. "Not after the grueling time I had conducting my banking transaction, with a gun in one hand and a note saying how much in the other. To make matters worse, the young woman teller wasn't particularly polite. I'm thinking of writing out a complaint on one of those little evaluation forms. Of course," the man conceded, "she could just have been having an off day."

"We all have them," agreed Mr. Warren, as he attempted to pass a bus and narrowly avoided a collision with an oncoming lorry.

"Ah, well," said the man in the back, "I'm sure you nice people will understand I feel like pampering myself. Which means, if it's not too much of an imposition, that I'd like to lean back in this very comfortable seat while you keep this car moving. Anywhere will do. I'm not concerned so long as it is in the opposite direction from Maidenbury. And speedily, if you please, because as you might surmise I am in something of a hurry."

"You just robbed a bank? And you can't afford a taxi?" Mr. Warren let loose a laugh, clearly intended at shoring up Flora's spirits; but she noticed that he put his foot down on the accelerator as instructed.

"Sorry, I don't have any small change. Nothing under fifty-pound notes." The man in the back chuckled softly to demonstrate that he too had a sense of humor. He tapped out a merry little tune on the briefcase as they shot forward into the mist.

"But you do have the gun?" Flora suddenly had the oddest feeling that her grandfather, not Mr. Warren, sat next to her. She could hear him saying as clear as day: *"Now you know what's expected of you, Flora. At all times, in all situations, we represent the Family."* And she felt her spine stiffen as she said, "Because if you don't have a gun, Mr. Bank Robber, it would be rather silly for me and Mr. Warren to sit here like a pair of lemons. Wouldn't it?"

"By Jove, I like your spirit," said the man.

"Let's just assume he has a gun, lass," chimed in Mr. Warren.

"You're right," Flora conceded, "because it seems to me he'd have to be the biggest dimwit alive to hitch a ride without a means of protecting himself. For all he knows we could be a couple of homicidal maniacs going on our wicked way after digging graves all afternoon." She raised her hands, grimy palms up.

"I've a feeling his sort doesn't scare easy," Mr. Warren whispered as he swerved around a lorry and sent a cyclist pedaling into a shop doorway.

"You're wrong," said the bank robber in a weakened voice as they bounced over a couple of potholes. "Your driving has the potential to scare me to death. Forget what I said about speed, old chap. We don't want some busybody of a policeman hightailing after us."

"You don't have to worry about that," Mr. Warren replied equably; "we turn here," he gave the steering wheel a mighty spin, "onto a country road that hardly sees any traffic at this time of day."

"I don't want to be a pain in the rear, if you will pardon the pun," said the man in the backseat, "but I do have a tendency to car sickness. It helps if I try not to think about it, so how about telling me a bit about yourselves?"

"You'd find us ever so boring," Flora assured him.

"Not at all. I'm a people person. One has to be, in my line of work. I offered my gun to the woman standing next to me at the bank, explaining that it would get her to the front of the queue in a hurry, and she repaid my kindness by going into hysterics. But let's get back to you two."

"We're on our way back from a funeral," Mr. Warren told him.

"Not someone near and dear, I hope?"

"My grandfather."

"Left all alone in the world, she is," put in Mr. Warren. "Her mother died when she was tiny and her father," he cleared his throat, "was also taken away from her at an early age."

"Poor little orphan! Please accept my condolences." The man sounded so completely sympathetic that it was easy to forget he was a bank robber.

"Grandpa took a fall."

"Wasn't pushed, was he?" Interest added a slight cockney edge to the man's voice, where before it had been upper-crust. And the thought flashed through Flora's mind that he had many voices and probably almost as many faces.

"Of course he wasn't pushed," she retorted as the car slammed to a stop and immediately lurched forward again. "It was an accident. Grandpa must have turned dizzy and—"

"Sorry to interrupt your sad story, my dear. But the truth is I'm beginning to feel somewhat dizzy myself. One regrets looking a gift horse in the mouth, but our friend's driving doesn't appear to agree with me. So, if it wouldn't be too much bother, I'd appreciate being put down at the next corner."

"If you say so, mate." Mr. Warren managed to sound disappointed as he drew to a bumpy stop. "I don't suppose," he added as the rear door opened, "you're the sort that takes from the rich and gives to the poor."

"Afraid not!"

"Just thought I'd ask, but if that's not in the cards," Mr. Warren reached down the side of his seat and pulled out a sheet of paper, "perhaps you'd fill out this evaluation form—shouldn't take but a minute—and put in a good word for me with the boss."

"I'd be delighted," said the man with what sounded like genuine enthusiasm. "Many thanks for the lift." So saying, he climbed from the car and was instantly swallowed up by the mist.

"Interesting people you meet on this job," was all Mr. Warren said as he shifted gears and took off in what Flora hoped was the general direction of Gossinger Hall. She felt a little shaken, but she wasn't by any stretch of the imagination close to hysterics. Hadn't Grandpa instilled in her from an early age that people from their walk of life did not make scenes, even when no one important was looking?

"Imperturbability," he used to say, *"is the first require-*

ment of a good servant. We are not easily distressed, Flora, and rarely impressed."

As the car bumped on down the road, Flora closed her eyes and pulled up mental snapshots of her happy childhood, when the world beyond the village existed only in the magical universe of make-believe and she had believed Grandpa would live to be as old as Noah in the Bible. She was sorry when Mr. Warren placidly announced that here they were, back safe and sound at Gossinger. Knowing that when she went inside all the happy memories would be blacked out by the dark shadow of the garderobe, Flora went into the kitchen reluctantly. Mrs. Warren, looking almost like a stranger in her best hat and coat, was there with Mrs. Much and Mr. Tipp.

Sally Warren was a woman who thrived on trouble of all sorts, big and little. And fifteen minutes of enthusiastic retelling of her favorite deathbed stories had ensured that quite a festive atmosphere prevailed. Admittedly, there weren't any balloons or crepe-paper streamers, but little sandwiches, butter-cream fancies, and gingerbread were set out on the table, along with the big earthenware teapot and milk jug.

I can't do this, thought Flora. *I can't sit down to a party tea, with people who want to celebrate the fact that the name that Death pulled out of the hat this time wasn't theirs. Grandpa is in that dark hole in the cemetery with nobody to talk to him but the wind. And he never did like people who moaned. . . .* It was with a feeling of almost giddy relief that Flora realized there was something she had to do, right away. She had to phone the police station and tell them about the bank robber. It would be criminal to keep quiet and help let the man escape just because he had been a bright spot of sorts in an otherwise horrible day. Grandpa had spoken quite a bit about people who broke the law and how they ruined the lives of ordinary people like himself and Flora.

SEVEN

Twenty minutes later, Vivian stood in his impeccably well-bred way, at the tower sitting room window, with a cup of tea in his hand and a lock of hair falling fetchingly over his forehead. He was chilled to the bone, despite having remembered to pack woolen underwear for this visit, and he spoke partly in the hope that exercising his vocal cords would help warm him up.

"A police car just drew up outside," he said.

"You're making that up, young Vivian." Lady Gossinger brought a hand to her throat and her eyes bulged even as she turned toward her husband and attempted a lighthearted laugh. "It really is awfully naughty of him to tease us, don't you think so, old bean? What do you say, shall we make him stand in the corner?"

"Let me take a look, m'dear." Sir Henry moved with noticeably lagging steps to join his nephew at the window. "It would appear, my dear," he said at length, "yes, I think I can say quite definitely that it would appear to be a police car."

Lady Gossinger made a gurgling noise that she hoped would be taken to be the wind.

"Even if it is a police car," contributed Miss Sophie Doffit in her most soothing voice, "it does not mean that there is a policeman inside."

"That's true," Vivian Gossinger said gently, "but given the law of averages, I'd say it's a pretty safe bet."

"Then," Cousin Sophie plucked at the sleeves of her pink cardigan and came up with an answer, "they've undoubtedly come about the television license. With all you have to do, my dears," she encompassed Sir Henry and Lady Gossinger in her smile, "I don't suppose you remembered to pay it, did you?"

"That must be it." Her Ladyship seemed desperate to grasp at straws. "My sister Edna will have such a laugh when she hears about this. Time I was taken down a peg, that'll be her thinking. But it's not as though we're going to be in serious trouble, is it, Henry?"

"Of course not, m'dear." He crossed the room to stand beside her, but not close enough to be touching. "Sensible chaps, the police, won't hear *them* carrying on as though a murder has been committed."

A heavy silence settled, like dust covers, over the room and at least one of the occupants had trouble breathing. Then Vivian said that he would go downstairs and see if he could find out what was going on, and Cousin Sophie gamely offered to accompany him, in the hope perhaps of buttering up the police with an offer of cheese scones.

"Well, now m'dear . . ." Sir Henry took a seat across from his lady when they were alone but was unable to think of anything else to say.

"Another cup of tea?" she suggested and, receiving a

negative shake of his bald head, sat studying her brogue
shoes. They still bore traces of mud from the graveside.
Terror lodged like a chicken bone in her throat. *Does
Henry have an awful picture inside his head of me luring
Hutchins into the garderobe on some diabolic pretext and
shoving him headfirst into the antiquated W.C.?* Lady
Gossinger had not been present when the dead butler
had been found, but Vivian had described in unflinch-
ing detail how the man had been wedged in up to his
ankles. And Henry, desperately trying not to break
down, had added that Hutchins had been spared plung-
ing three stories to his death by the caving in of the
ancient stonework.

*Why would the police be here if not because they suspect
foul play?* Her Ladyship's mind darted this way and
that, like a laboratory rat desperately seeking a way out
of its cage before a giant hand came down on the scruff
of its neck. Should she confront the issue head-on and
ask Henry if he suspected that by telling her he was
about to change his will and leave Gossinger Hall to
Hutchins he had led her down the primrose path to
murder?

"We need to talk about Mrs. Much," she heard herself say instead.

"What's that, m'dear?"

"She's given notice; says she's found a better position."

"Ah!" said Sir Henry.

"Wouldn't you say it's jolly suspicious, her bunking
off at a time like this?"

"How's that?"

"I didn't like to say anything and worry you,
Henry," Lady Gossinger drew a rallying breath, "but
I've come to wonder if the woman is one-hundred-
percent honest. One of the briar rose teacups is missing
and—" She was about to add that this being the case,
one could only wonder what other dishonesty lay

within the scope of Mrs. Much's villainy, but Sir Henry
interrupted her.

"Oh, that!" He looked decidedly awkward. "Broke a
cup m'self the other day. Forgot to mention it, sorry
about that, m'dear."

"Well, it wasn't the only thing that's gone for a
walk." Lady Gossinger took a restorative sip of tea. "I
can't find that shoehorn—the nice long one with the
horse's-head top that my sister Edna sent us for a wedding present. Now, why ever are you looking like that,
Henry?"

"Got it in my bedroom, Mabel; been using it to practice m'golfing. Should have said something, but thought
you would worry I'd send a ball through the window."

"You have every right to keep your little secrets."
Her Ladyship had no trouble sounding noble. The conversation—whilst not going the way she had planned—
was not a dead loss. "Perhaps you have trouble believing I mean that, dear," she managed to squeeze a tear
out the corner of her eye, "especially after the dreadful
way I carried on when you told me you were planning
to leave Gossinger Hall to Hutchins. But as God is my
witness, Henry, I regretted my outburst the moment it
was out of my mouth, and I've been tormented ever
since by the thought that the man's death may have
been a judgment on me for being so dreadfully un-
Christian."

"Wouldn't think so." Sir Henry chewed the words
over thoughtfully. "All of us known to fly off the handle at times. If anything, I blame m'self for the way I
handled the matter."

"How awfully dear of you, Henry!" Tears that were
real this time moistened Lady Gossinger's eyes. "I've
been worried you might think that perhaps it wasn't an
accident after all and that I . . . well, you know, had a
hand in what happened to him."

"Rubbish, m'dear. Thought never crossed my mind."

"I suppose the thing to do," her Ladyship sniffed without worrying whether doing so might be considered common, and continued, "is to fix on what we are going to do about poor little Florie."

"Been doing some thinking about that m'self," Sir Henry said.

"What I would like to suggest, old bean," his wife said with a watery smile, "is that we send her up to Bethnal Green."

"To live with your sister Edna?"

"Of course not, dear, I wouldn't do that to my worst enemy." Her Ladyship was so carried away by her own magnanimousness that she almost let slip that no one should be subjected to Edna's dreadful grandson. And that wouldn't have done at all. Lady Gossinger had not told her husband about the boy trying to force his way into this room on the day Hutchins died. For reasons lodged in the dark corners of her soul she preferred to keep that bit of information under her garter belt. "No, what I have in mind for poor little Florie," she continued, "is to let her have the flat above my parents' old shop for a while."

"Thought it was already occupied."

"Not anymore. The tenants were obviously fly-by-nights: After ten years at a ridiculously cheap rent, they've moved on to greener pastures." Lady Gossinger tensed, thinking she heard plodding footsteps on the stairs. Did they herald the arrival of the police? A heart-thudding moment passed in which she waited for a fist to thump on the door. But nothing happened. "I received a letter of intent to vacate a few days ago, Henry," she said, still sounding a bit rattled even to herself, until she realized that she was hearing the approach of the tea trolley. Mrs. Much tapped and entered the room.

"All done, are we?" she inquired with a smile, sounding, thought a disgusted Lady Gossinger, like a ward maid talking to a patient sitting on the bedpan. Really, it was a pity the woman had given in her notice, or she would have had to be sacked on the spot. As for Mrs. Much's fancy new job, her Ladyship didn't believe a word of it.

"No, we are not finished with our tea yet," she replied in a voice that was the fruit of all those long-ago elocution lessons, and would have had Edna in stitches. "Run along, do, Mrs. Much, and come back in half an hour."

"Hate to put her to all that trouble, Mabel; all those stairs, you know." Sir Henry, having visited his private chapel that day, in addition to attending the funeral service, was in a particularly Christian mood.

"Oh, don't you mind about that," Mrs. Much assured him with cheerful familiarity. "I'll be glad to get back to the kitchen. Things were getting interesting when I left. And there's nothing I like more than a little mental stimulation, unless it's scrubbing the right sort of house from top to bottom on my hands and knees." Mrs. Much gave a happy thought to getting away from this house where she was sure more than one poor lass had been put on the rack for burning the breakfast toast.

"Go on," said Lady Gossinger in a voice as chilly as the dregs in the teapot.

"I'm sure you'll get the whole story from Mr. Vivian. Such a nice young man. He came down to the kitchen just minutes after the policeman arrived to talk to Flora and Mr. Warren about what happened. Constable somebody-or-other, and he sounded confident as ever you could wish that they'll be making an arrest very shortly."

Her Ladyship made a choking sound.

"Fred Warren?" Sir Henry asked. "I can understand this copper chap having a word with Flora, but why the dickens is he talking to Warren?"

"Because it was him what drove the getaway car,"
Mrs. Much explained reasonably.

"The what?" Sir Henry looked only a couple of de-
grees less dumbfounded than his wife.

"For the bank robber."

Lady Gossinger stood up and immediately sat down
again. When she could find her voice, she crisply ordered Mrs. Much to start at the beginning. And somehow she managed to look deeply shocked when the
woman revealed what she'd learned of Flora's ride back
from the funeral with Mr. Warren and the man in the
backseat. But inside, her Ladyship was singing—in a
rather deep baritone—a paean to joy and reprieve. How
silly she'd been to think the police would suspect foul
play in Mr. Hutchins's death! The very idea was non-
sensical. But if the bank robber had walked into the
tower sitting room at that moment, her Ladyship would
have been tempted to kiss him full on his wicked lips.

Instead, she succumbed to her pent-up passion by
bestowing a peck on her husband's cheek when Mrs.
Much left the room with the loaded tea trolley.

"And Sophie thought the police were here about the
television license." Sir Henry let out a lengthy sigh.
"Couldn't have been that, of course. Don't have a television. Poor little Flora."

"Yes, terrible experience for her, after all she's been
through," agreed Lady Gossinger. "But life goes on and
she'll find herself on the mend when she goes to Bethnal Green."

"Are you sure that's for the best, m'dear?"

"Don't you, Henry?"

"Well, I had thought we'd need her here. May take
a while to replace Mrs. Much, and with Hutchins
gone . . . you do see the difficulty, m'dear."

"We still have Tipp," said her Ladyship.

"Not suggesting he fill Hutchins's shoes, are you?"
came the unusually testy reply. "Wouldn't do, Mabel.

Never said as much before, but never really cared for Tipp. Listens at doors, you know. And peeks around corners. One day the fellow's going to hear or see more than's good for him. Kept him on because his family's worked here since time began . . ." Sir Henry stopped. He looked pointedly toward the door, which nobody ever seemed to remember to close properly on their way out. Nobody, that is, except Hutchins, who had also never committed the solecism of tapping before entering a room.

"I wouldn't doubt that's Tipp out there now," Sir Henry continued in what he believed to be a whisper.

"Far more likely to be Mrs. Much," Lady Gossinger countered. "She's probably rearranging the tea trolley before she unloads it to carry the tea things downstairs."

"Won't argue that with you, m'dear." Sir Henry rubbed his knees, which were a little sore from the time spent kneeling in prayer that day. "And forget what I said about Tipp. I've possibly never been fair to him. Not the poor fellow's fault one of his forebears, a maid here in the house, was suspected of stealing Queen Charlotte's silver tea strainer."

Sir Henry noticed that his wife's eyes had strayed toward the oak cupboard where the sherry was kept. He took the hint. Deciding he could also benefit from some liquid reinforcement, he poured a glass for each of them. "There you are, m'dear." He handed her a glass. "Now what was I saying? Ah, yes! Talking about Tipp. When all's said and done, he's no worse than Cousin Sophie when it comes to listening at keyholes and hiding behind corners. Remember the night m'father was dying—"

"All most interesting, Henry," Lady Gossinger downed most of her cream sherry in a single swallow, "but let us get back to talking about poor Florie. I still say that she needs to start a new life. Seems to me, Henry, we owe her that small kindness." Her Ladyship's halo tilted somewhat tipsily over her left eye as she spoke these words, but she did not miss the fact that her husband was looking at her with a mingling of admiration and affection.

"You're right, m'dear, as always." Sir Henry lifted his glass to her in salute. "We'll let little Flora have the flat free for a year and a day. Reminds me of my ancestor, the roguish Sir Rowland. The one responsible for acquiring the silver collection and possibly for the disappearance of the tea strainer. Which would let Tipp's ancestress off the hook. Sir Rowland was in the habit, so I understand, of granting free rent of one of his cottages for that length of time to any maidservant who took his particular fancy. Sounds good. But it's also said he expected to be paid in other ways. But let's hope that was before he married and put his nose to the grindstone. But enough of that, m'dear. Back to the present. As you say, sending little Flora up to Bethnal Green will give the poor child a chance to forget and . . ."

"And what, Henry?"

"No need to upset yourself, Mabel." Sir Henry glanced at his wife, raised the sherry glass to his lips, and took a desperate swallow. "Nothing cut-and-dried, you understand, but this idea of yours will allow me time in which to decide whether I'd be doing the right thing."

"About what, old bean?" Lady Gossinger had to raise her voice in order to make it heard over the sudden thumping of her heart.

"Leaving Gossinger Hall to little Flora." Sir Henry said the words very fast with his eyes shut. "Seems to me, after kneeling in prayer the better part of the day, to be a possible solution, now that my faithful Hutchins isn't around to be the beneficiary."

"Someone had better start praying," muttered Lady Gossinger as she picked up the sherry bottle in what could only be described as a menacing manner.

EIGHT

Mrs. Much stood outside the tower sitting room and silently offered Mr. Tipp her handkerchief, then wondered if she had done the right thing, because it was so heavily starched she was afraid he might use it to slit his wrists. Her heart, which after her husband's death she had never given completely except to fitted carpets and colored toilet seats, ached for this elderly man who had so little meat on his bones that a vulture would have turned up its beak at the prospect of having him for elevenses.

Poor man! And him doing his bit, coming up to help take down the tea things! But this was neither the time nor the place to stand having a discussion with Mr. Tipp on the really nasty things Sir Henry had said about him, before launching into that statement about leaving Gossinger Hall to Flora Hutchins. Mrs. Much, whilst naturally surprised by that piece of news, wasn't particularly interested in any will that didn't have her name in it. She set off down the stairs carrying a tray loaded with crockery while her maligned coworker followed behind with a bunch of cutlery in his hands, wearing the expression of one about to pay another visit to the cemetery.

Only a few more days in this monstrosity of a house, Mrs. Much reminded herself as she crossed the flagstones toward the kitchen, then she would be starting in on her new job. Of course, it wouldn't be like working for the late sainted Mrs. Frome, but then beggars can't be choosers. And in all fairness it wasn't to be expected that anyone, including Her Majesty the Queen, would be capable of upholding Mrs. Frome's high standards.

"Where did you say you'll be working next?" Mr. Tipp tried hard to look interested.

"I don't think I did say." Mrs. Much pushed open the kitchen door with her elbow without causing the heavily laden tray to do one wobble. "It's not that I'm a secretive woman by nature, but after this last experience I've decided you never know what you'll find when you get to a new place, so I'm only cautiously optimistic about going to work at Buckingham Palace."

Mr. Tipp's dropped jaw said all Mrs. Much needed to hear.

"It's another of these old places," she conceded, "but I hear from my cousin who works there—the one what put in a good word for me—that it's been kept up lovely. I'm to start out as a chambermaid in the real sense of the word; I'll be working in the bathrooms. . . . You don't suppose, Mr. Tipp, that there's a garderobe at Buckingham Palace, do you?"

"I wouldn't think so; there's not many places in England as can compete with the wonders of Gossinger Hall."

"You've eased my mind. Set yourself down, Mr.

Tipp, and I'll make us a nice cup of tea," Mrs. Much offered kindly. There was no one but them in the kitchen. But someone had thoughtfully put away the remains of the funeral feast and done the washing up.

"Looks like that policeman took them all into custody," said Mr. Tipp—referring to Mr. and Mrs. Warren, Flora, Mr. Vivian Gossinger, and Miss Sophie Doffit.

"Oh, surely not, the police car wasn't big enough." Mrs. Much took the cutlery away from him before he could do himself an injury, as was a risk given his depressed state of mind, and wondered whether it would be wise to make some physical overture. She had held Mr. Frome's hand after his wife died and the poor man had ended up sobbing in her arms like a two-year-old and saying he was afraid to sleep alone. She couldn't picture Prince Philip sobbing in her arms, but one never knew.

"I was just making a joke." Mr. Tipp sat hunched at the kitchen table. "About the police, I mean."

"Well, I think it's nothing short of marvelous," said Mrs. Much, "that you're up to seeing the funny side of anything after getting an earful of Sir Henry holding forth. A real man, that's what you are, my friend, and don't never let anyone tell you different."

"That's kind of you to say." Mr. Tipp proved himself a worthy recipient of the handsome compliment bestowed upon him by taking a manful sip of tea heavily flavored with bleach from another pot cleaning. "Between you and me," he continued through pursed lips, "it did knock me back some, hearing Sir Henry talk about leaving Gossinger Hall to Flora."

"And I can't say as I blame you." Mrs. Much sat down across from him with her own cup of tea. "But what I really had mind to, Mr. Tipp, was the spiteful things he said about you." She debated whether to repeat them—word for word, by way of refreshing his memory—but decided to eat a piece of gingerbread instead.

"Oh, I didn't take none of that to heart," replied Mr. Tipp. "It's always said listeners never hear nothing good about themselves, and if I hadn't come up to the tower to help you down with the tea things I'd not have heard Sir Henry talking about me. So I brought it on myself, there's no saying different."

"You were just being kind." Mrs. Much was moved to hand him a fat piece of gingerbread.

Mr. Tipp kept his head down as he sat twisting his fingers that were already whittled down to the bone. "Sir Henry's always treated me fair and kind. Never no reason for me to complain. He's missing Hutchins, that's what has him saying things he don't mean. And it could be that he's . . . what you could call worried."

"Because of losing Hutchins and then me giving in my notice?" Mrs. Much inched her chair closer to the table. "Well, I can see that's upsetting. Not to be the big-I-am, and strictly between you and me, Mr. Tipp, but I won't be easy to replace. There's not many as would climb up on ladders and take down all those dirty old paintings where you can't see the faces, because they look like they've been dipped in the fish-and-chip pan, and then give them a good scrubbing with steel wool."

"You're one in a million, no question." Mr. Tipp took another sip of tea, which may have been the cause of his strained expression. "I'm certain sure Sir Henry and her Ladyship won't know how to manage without you. And it's not like they don't have troubles enough already. Sometimes, mostly of an evening, I get to wondering if Sir Henry's worried that it wasn't any accident what happened to Hutchins."

"Why, whatever makes you say that?" In leaning eagerly forward Mrs. Much stuck an elbow in her piece of gingerbread and had to get up and wash off her arm.

Having made an uncharacteristically sketchy job of doing so she returned to the table and plied Mr. Tipp with more tea.

"Well, if you do remember the day of the accident—"

"Who could forget it!"

"What I'm meaning to say . . ." Lowering his voice, Mr. Tipp looked anxiously around the room as if afraid someone might be hiding in the pantry with an ear to the door. "Do you remember me telling you that afternoon as how I heard Lady Gossinger and Miss Doffit talking about Sir Henry changing his will?"

"It's coming back to me." Mrs. Much nodded her head.

"Perhaps I oughtn't be repeating any of this." Mr. Tipp's lips twitched and he stared down at his slice of gingerbread as if afraid it would leap up and bite him.

"I think you need to get anything that's bothering you off your chest," came the encouraging advice. "Trust me, you poor little man, I'll never breathe a word to a living soul."

"It was like this," Mr. Tipp slid down low in his chair, "her Ladyship was mortal upset because Sir Henry had just broken the news as how he was about to change his will and leave Gossinger Hall to Hutchins."

"Well, I never!"

"So you do see . . ."

"Yes, of course I do!" Mrs. Much almost added that she wasn't a pea-brain, but bit her lip in time. "You think that wicked woman upstairs, with her put-on voice and jumped-up airs, murdered Mr. Hutchins before Sir Henry had time to see his solicitor and sign on the dotted line."

"I'm not saying her Ladyship did anything . . . anything at all." Mr. Tipp looked more like a rattling bag of bones than ever as he shifted in his seat. "I'm only thinking that Sir Henry could be wondering and getting himself all worried. The doctor didn't raise a question, did he? Said there'd have to be an inquest—that's my understanding; but from the sound of it, no one seems to be expecting a fishy sort of verdict."

"I supposed most people was thinking along the same lines as myself," said Mrs. Much, "that Mr. Hutchins had gone up to check on the garderobe, as he was always doing to make sure it wasn't getting in a worse state of repair—though why it mattered don't ask me. And then he came over faint, as who wouldn't in such a nasty unhygienic place, and perhaps bent down to clear his head, only it didn't do any good and he pitched headfirst into that hellhole of a toilet."

"It could have happened that way." Mr. Tipp tried valiantly to sound as if he believed it. "It's not like Hutchins was locked in, was it? Now I do say as how that would have been suspicious. But the door was open, how wide I don't rightly know, but enough to make Mr. Vivian Gossinger notice, because it was always a strict rule about the garderobe being kept locked. Only Hutchins and Sir Henry had keys to it, leastways as far as I know."

"Let's have another cup of tea while we chew this over," suggested Mrs. Much.

"I'll make it—" Mr. Tipp started to rise.

"No, you stay put." This was said with great firmness. "I'll not have you straining yourself lifting that great heavy kettle that by my guess has been around since the Iron Age."

"I'm stronger than what I looks."

"The wiry sort often are," Mrs. Much agreed, fearing she had hurt the poor little man's feelings. "I wouldn't be surprised to hear you'd done some boxing in your time."

"No," Mr. Tipp shook his head, "my ma and pa wouldn't have allowed none of that, being as they was Chapel people."

"Oh, yes, my uncle was one of those. They're always very keen on sin," said Mrs. Much knowledgeably as she returned to the table with the fresh pot of tea and began doing the honors. "But even someone more middle-of-the-road like myself, Mr. Tipp, thinks murdering someone over a will isn't the way to earn your crown in heaven. Now you know," she handed over his cup and saucer, "I've never much taken to Lady Gossinger; but to give the devil her due that's a sight different from thinking she'd finish off Mr. Hutchins."

"Could be it wasn't her." Mr. Tipp stared into his cup as if hoping a floating tea leaf or two would provide some answers.

"Talk about turning the tables," Mrs. Much sat down, looking thoroughly confused, "haven't you been telling me her Ladyship's the one with the motive? And you don't have to read detective stories to know there's always got to be one of those. But hold on a minute," she exclaimed, apparently picking through the bones of a new idea. "Seems to me there is one other person what mightn't have been jumping for joy on account of Sir Henry deciding to leave the ancestral home outside the Family. And that's Mr. Vivian Gossinger."

"Wouldn't never have been him." Mr. Tipp answered with unusual conviction. "Mr. Vivian's never been overly fond of Gossinger."

"Then he's got more sense than you'd ever guess from looking at him front or back." Mrs. Much spooned sugar into her tea and stirred the pattern off the inside of her cup. "But that's not the same as saying he'd be merry as a kitten with two tails and a dead mouse if his uncle upped and told him the house was being left to Hutchins. Don't ask me why anyone would want to live here; there's never been any accounting for bad taste. And who knows what Mr. Vivian—such a soppy name for a man—Gossinger is like when he thinks nobody's watching. From what Mrs.

Warren tells me, there's bad blood in the family from way back."

"Sally Warren thinks there's bad blood in her own husband on account of him forgetting more times than not to put those plastic liners in the dustbins," said Mr. Tipp stoutly.

"Well," Mrs. Much glanced at the clock on the wall and decided she didn't need to get back to work for another half hour, "if you don't think it was Mr. Vivian Gossinger who did the dirty deed, who else could it have been, except her Ladyship? There's no one else as stood to lose by that will. Unless," Mrs. Much sipped her tea as she considered the matter, "Miss Doffit got the wind up her petticoats, thinking as how she could be out her bread and board if Mr. Hutchins took over. Between you and me, Mr. Tipp, I've a soft spot for the old lady, but there's no denying she's nuttier than a squirrel's pantry. And awfully spry for someone closing on ninety years of age."

Mr. Tipp shook his head. He did not see Miss Sophie Doffit as a likely suspect. "I've been mulling it over in my head," he said, "and I got to thinking that if it do be the case that Mr. Hutchins was murdered it could be that the will happened to come in handy for someone who wanted him out of the way for different reasons."

"I think I see what you mean," said Mrs. Much. "If the police was to cotton on that what happened wasn't any accident, they'd be bound to latch onto Lady Gossinger being the person with the number one motive. And if she managed to wiggle out of the net, there was always her nephew and that poor dotty old lady. Doesn't bear thinking about, does it? Not if it was someone else up to no good. Now, don't get me wrong, I'm not convinced by a long shot Mr. Hutchins didn't just fall in that toilet all on his own doing." Mrs. Much gave another glance at the clock. "But I must hand it to you, Mr. Tipp, there's a lot more to you than meets the

eye. Seems to me you ought to set yourself up as the
likes of one of those private detectives."

"That's kind of you to say." Mr. Tipp's scraggly face
creased into a smile. "Course, if I was ever to do anything like that, it could only be as a sideline, a sort of a
hobby so to speak, seeing as how I wouldn't never want
to leave Gossinger."

"And here was me thinking I could be your girl
Friday." Mrs. Much turned pale in the middle of a
chuckle. "The trouble is, Mr. Tipp, that even if someone did overhear Sir Henry talking about changing his
will . . . or what I suppose is more likely, somebody
blabbed, that doesn't leave a whole lot of other suspects.
Just you and me, when it comes right down to it."

"There's Sally Warren."

"So there is," Mrs. Much stood up and began gathering together the tea things, "and if we're playing detective and looking for a reason for *her* to want Mr.
Hutchins out of the way it could be that he'd found out
she'd been helping herself to money out of the tea shop
till and was going to tell Sir Henry. Perhaps," she tried
unsuccessfully to sound charitable, "the poor soul found
herself in a financial bind on account of her husband
losing his old job at the market garden across the way,
because the owner's son had come to work for him and
Mr. Warren had to start driving a taxi."

"I wasn't accusing Sally," said Mr. Tipp.

"Then who?"

"We have to do this fair."

"All right." Mrs. Much stood doing a balancing act
with the crockery. "You give me a couple of seconds to
get this lot in the sink and I'll play Mr. Sherlock
Holmes and tell you why you could be the one, and
then—turnabout being fair play—you have a go at
coming up with a reason for me doing away with Mr.
Hutchins." Turning off the taps, she added a dollop of
washing-up liquid. "There," she said, arms up to the

elbows in soapy water, "now I can concentrate, Mr. Tipp. Although why I'd be standing here with my back to you if I really thought you was a murderer I don't know."

"But if I did do it?"

"Well, that would have to be because you'd always wanted to step into Hutchins's shoes."

"I never did."

"But that's what you would say." Mrs. Much up-ended the teapot on the draining rack. "And if we're making this up, I'm going to suppose you've always hated being at Mr. Hutchins's beck and call, especially when you've said your family has worked at Gossinger for hundreds of years. Oh, how," she warmed to the scenario, "it must have rankled, never having a proper position here after a lifetime of service!"

Mr. Tipp opened his mouth a crack.

Mrs. Much, however, was in full flood. "Yes, I know as how you're going to say you're still officially in charge of the stables, but I'd think all that does is rub salt in the wound when there's nothing out there on four legs, unless you count a couple of broken-down old tables. And then to find out Sir Henry had gone and left this place to Mr. Hutchins!" She rinsed off the milk jug. "Well, it's not to be wondered at, my friend, if you went a bit barmy and made sure the only thing he'd be inheriting would be a place in the cemetery."

"You've stitched me up tight as a glove. To tell you the truth," Mr. Tipp twisted his hands together, "Mr. Hutchins was never quite my cup of tea."

"Much too bossy by half," agreed Mrs. Much in the sanguine voice of one who knew herself to be free of this fatal flaw.

"What I minded, though I never did let on, was how Mr. Hutchins would never let me help out polishing the silver." Mr. Tipp continued to ruminate. "It got me to wondering if he was afraid I'd make off with a piece, because of that maidservant way back in my family as was thought by some to have pinched the Queen's silver tea strainer."

"I don't suppose it was that." Mrs. Much felt called upon to soothe the poor little man's wounded feelings before he burst into tears and she ended up having to give the table another wipe. "Possessive, that's the word for the way Mr. Hutchins carried on about that silver. Anyone would think it had been in *his* family for two hundred years. Although, I've always thought that when you've had something for five or six years it's time to get rid of it and have a change. As Mrs. Frome, God rest her soul, often said to me, if I can't afford new I'd rather do without."

Mr. Tipp, who by this time could have quoted verbatim the many acute sayings of Mrs. Frome, merely nodded his head.

"And now it's time," Mrs. Much gave the sink a final buff with the drying-up cloth and checked to make sure she could see her face in the taps, "for you to fill me in, Mr. Tipp, on why you think *I* should be added to the list of suspects."

"That's a bit of a puzzler right off the top."

"Now, don't be afraid to hurt my feelings." Mrs. Much sat down at the table and turned on a beaming smile. "If I can dish it out I can take my own medicine."

"It's not that I really think——"

"Of course not."

"But if," Mr. Tipp addressed a spot slightly to the north of her head, "I was a proper detective it could cross my mind that you was more than a little worried on account of Mr. Hutchins acting so cross on account of you washing those tapestries and so on that he might have seen you got a bad reference and that could have dashed your hopes of going to work at Buckingham Palace."

"Well, I never!" Mrs. Much tried to sound admiring. "Mr. Tipp, you've certainly got an imagination."

"Left to himself, Sir Henry's a bit of an old softie."

"Well, her Ladyship isn't."

"But it's Sir Henry as always writes the references. I've thought on that sometimes," Mr. Tipp was back to looking Mrs. Much in the eye, "and I wonder if it could be because she's a touch nervous about her spelling, same as I am."

"Well, I doubt anyone could accuse her of going to Oxford or Cambridge. Except on a day trip, that is." Mrs. Much had begun to recover from having been put —figuratively speaking—in the dock. But there was no denying that Mr. Tipp had set her to thinking along some rather dark lines. "It seems like we've covered everyone what could possibly have wanted Mr. Hutchins out of the way. There wasn't anybody else in the house that day save for young Flora, and you couldn't possibly think she would . . . not her very own grandfather what brought her up from when she was a kiddie. Unless . . ." Mrs. Much looked around the antiquated kitchen and realized anew how desperately anxious she was to escape Gossinger Hall. "Unless," she continued, "young Flora saw herself being chained to this house so long as her grandfather lived and took what she thought was the only way out."

Mr. Tipp did not appear to be listening hard to what she was saying. "There was other people here the day Mr. Hutchins died," he said slowly. "There was that tour of schoolboys and their teacher from some swanky London school."

"So there was."

"And if you remember, Mrs. Much, one of those schoolboys was Lady Gossinger's nephew. His name was Horace. Or it could have been Boris."

"That's all very interesting, Mr. Tipp, but why in the world would he murder Hutchins?"

"I'm not thinking he did; but I do mind that when I met up with him outside the tower sitting room he said something that didn't strike me as strange at the time, Mrs. Much, but when I thought on it later, it fair gave me the shivers. That boy said as how someone should lock Lady Gossinger up in the garderobe."

"Gracious!"

"Suppose," Mr. Tipp's face seemed to flesh out in his evident enthusiasm for his theory, "Boris, or whatever his name was, got Mr. Hutchins to show him the garderobe and then locked him in for a joke. It's the sort of thing schoolboys do; leastways they did in the stories I read in *The Schoolboy's Annual* when I was but a lad myself. And like as not he meant to go and let Mr. Hutchins out, but either he forgot or he couldn't get away from his teacher again."

"Oh, if that isn't the nastiest suggestion you've put forward yet," said Mrs. Much, "a kiddie of his tender years responsible for the death of a fellow human being!"

"Yes, but not with—what's the word?—*intent.* When he went to let him out, Hutchins was dead from his heart giving out or whatever." Mr. Tipp shook his head. "Leastways, that's the way I see it."

"I suppose it's nicer to think we're dealing with someone that pulled a silly stunt instead of a cold-blooded killer who worked it all out beforehand." Somewhat unsteadily, Mrs. Much got to her feet and went over to the pantry, where she kept an extra cardigan hanging on the back of the door. "It's bad enough when you read about murders in the papers, like that woman what disappeared from the launderette in Grimsby the other week, or that old man as was last seen not too far from here. But you don't never expect it on your own doorstep, so to speak. Now, like as not you've let your imagination run away with you, Mr. Tipp, and brought me along for the ride, but it seems to me we might do right to phone the police. That was ever such a nice young man who came to talk to Flora and Mr. Warren about the bank robber."

"He did do a thorough job of asking questions, didn't he?" Mr. Tipp took a look at the clock and he, too, got to his feet. "I suppose they soon get the knack of it—asking probing questions I mean, so as to get people telling them things they never meant to let slip."

"Yes, very clever when you come to think of it," Mrs. Much responded in hollow tones. Her mind had settled like a damp rag on her former employer Mrs. Frome, who had been so kind as to remember her devoted housekeeper in her will, made within a few months of succumbing to an overdose. And before Mrs. Frome there had been nice, kind Mrs. Ashford, who had also left Mrs. Much a tidy little remembrance before falling afoul of the mushroom soup.

What, heaven help her, would be the outcome if the police started poking into the deaths of those two ladies? Wasn't it almost a foregone conclusion that they would leap to the decision that they were dealing with an old hand at murder? Mrs. Much took a couple of slow, steadying breaths. It wasn't like Sir Henry would have gone and left her anything in his will? Unless—an icy hand clutched at her heart—Sir Henry was the sort who believed it only right and proper to leave a little something to his housekeeper, even if she hadn't worked for him more than a few months.

Afraid of betraying the fact that she wasn't one-hundred-percent calm and collected, she walked over to the window. Where she could just make out the figures of Flora and Mr. Vivian Gossinger standing in apparent conversation in the garden. For the first time Mrs. Much pondered the question of why Sir Henry had decided to bequeath Gossinger Hall to his butler, but as quickly as it came the thought was wiped out of her head. She suddenly felt horribly defenseless with her back to the room. She wasn't afraid of Mr. Tipp. No, what scared her was feeling that someone . . . or something . . . was hovering beyond the kitchen door, soaking up her fear, having already taken in every word of her and Mr. Tipp's conversation.

Turning back to face him, she said in what she hoped was a casual way, "Perhaps we shouldn't go to the police at this stage of the game, Mr. Tipp. It's not like we've anything really to go on, when it comes right down to it."

"And I don't think Sir Henry would be best pleased at us interfering, as he'd be bound to see it. So what do you think, Mrs. Much, of the two of us keeping our eyes and ears open?"

"But I won't be here," she replied. "I'll be at Buckingham Palace trying to talk the Queen into fitted carpets."

"So you will. Meaning it's all up to me, isn't it?"

Mr. Tipp sounded heroically excited at the prospect of embroiling himself in another period of treachery and intrigue in the shadowy history of Gossinger Hall. But there was not time for Mrs. Much to try to talk him out of playing Sherlock Holmes, because the door bounced open and Miss Sophie Doffit entered the kitchen to announce that Lady Gossinger had made herself ill following the funeral. The old lady did not add that her Ladyship had achieved this result by drinking the entire contents of a bottle of sherry. She demanded a pot of extremely strong coffee and bore it away with what Mrs. Much, in her nervy state, sized up as a strangely triumphant smile.

NINE

For Flora, the days after the funeral got all jumbled together like scarves thrown higgledy-piggledy in the drawers of a dressing table. There were only a few distinct moments: Being in the garden with Mr. Vivian Gossinger, and telling him it was difficult to believe that Grandpa was dead and feeling safe for the first time in days when he put an arm around her. Sir Henry asking if she'd like to get away for a while and live in Bethnal Green in a flat that had once belonged to her Ladyship's parents.

And now Flora sat in the middle of a long carriage on an early morning train to King's Cross. There were two men seated opposite her, separated from her by the laminated table. She saw that the one next to the aisle wore a clerical collar, but otherwise she hardly noticed them. Her two suitcases were in the overhead rack and her face was pressed to the cool of the window. Flora had only been to London once before when she was a small child; come to think of it, she had never been anywhere much.

Her whole world had been Gossinger from when she was three years old and Grandpa had explained that he wasn't the King of England, but only Sir Henry's butler, and that no crowns went with *that* job. To the *chuff-a-chuff-chug* noises of the train, the memories returned in soft shining colors behind her closed lids: Watching while Grandpa went about his work. Telling him that she loved him more than gingerbread or playing dressing-up in the trunk room, and even more than rainy days.

Flora remembered the time when she had begged him to promise he would never die and leave her, the way her mother had done, or at least not until she was nine hundred and ninety years old. On that occasion she had hugged him passionately, and promised him that when he was too old to be a butler anymore they would go and live in a little house by the sea at Cleethorpes and then it would be her turn to read him bedtime stories.

Shifting her position slightly, Flora sensed rather than saw that one . . . or perhaps both . . . of the men opposite were watching her, but she didn't wonder what was attracting their attention. Unlike the train, which was rushing past another station, her mind had traveled back again to the time when her world was real and safe. She had sometimes missed her mother, but had never felt too bad about not having a father. When she was still very young she had concluded that God had temporarily run out of these items at the time she was about to be born in the same way that the cake shop might be out of Bakewell tarts on a particularly busy day. What Flora got instead was Grandpa.

And she had never stopped feeling lucky. He was

sometimes a little stern and not much given to hugs or kisses, and a few times, such as when he sent her to bed early because she had said that Sir Henry had big ears, she had decided Grandpa loved everyone at Gossinger more than her, and the Queen more than anyone in the whole world. But even at that moment she had known in the kernel of her heart that Grandpa would have burnt at the stake, without a wince, if anything or anyone had threatened harm to his little girl.

Flora stared out the window at fields and trees and scatterings of houses speeding past as if fleeing an invading army. She felt terribly small and lost, in much the same way that a nun might have done at the time of the Reformation after being booted out of the convent by Henry VIII's henchmen without so much as a spare set of undies and being told not to loiter. *I expect I look just as odd and out of touch with the world,* thought Flora, *as if I was wearing a rough woolen habit and one of those meek faces that comes from praying all day and half the night in a cell the size of a pantry.*

Her glance passed over the heads of the two men sitting opposite her and focused on the women in the carriage, particularly the ones of about her own age. They all looked so . . . Flora floundered for the word, so . . . *alive.* Some were smartly dressed. Others looked as though they hadn't had a bath or washed their hair in recent memory. But none of them looked as though they were going up to London for the first time in their lives. Studying a red-haired girl dressed like an Edwardian tramp with a silver stud in her nose and her eyelashes weighed down with mascara, Flora fingered the knot at the nape of her neck and felt a twinge of envy. She remembered the time when she bought a lipstick—Persuasion Pink was the color—and how Grandpa could not have looked any more disappointed if she'd told him she'd earned the money to buy it standing on street corners talking to strange men in fast cars. Grandpa hadn't forbidden Flora to paint her face like a circus clown. He'd merely reminded her, without raising his voice, that what she wore and how she comported herself must always reflect for better or worse on Gossinger Hall. Flora had come close to saying something defiant on that occasion, but she had noticed that when her grandfather turned away his shoulders were a little stooped and his hair was closer to white than gray. It was the housekeeper at the time, a Mrs. Jolliffe, who'd spoken up in Flora's defense.

"No harm in a bit of lipstick, Mr. Hutchins. Even the prettiest girls" (her tone made it plain Flora could not count herself in this fortunate category) "don't like to go around with their faces bare as a baby's bum. And Flora's at that age. Wanting to make the most of herself. Don't tell me you haven't seen the way she colors up when Mr. Vivian Gossinger comes for a stay and so much as tells her good morning?"

"I never!" Flora had cried, being mightily tempted to hurl the hateful lipstick at Mrs. Jolliffe's smiling face.

"Indeed not!" This time, Mr. Hutchins broke with precedent and raised his voice in addressing the housekeeper. "I take extreme offense at the suggestion that I have not brought up my granddaughter never to behave with any degree of familiarity toward members of the Family."

"You can't stop a girl from thinking, not when it comes to young men," Mrs. Jolliffe had responded, completely unabashed. "Especially one the likes of Flora here, that's been kept cooped up at Gossinger, never getting to mix and have fun with people her own age."

At that point Flora had run out of the room wishing she were dead and Mr. Vivian Gossinger had never been born. She had never, *ever* thought anyone would guess her secret. Flinging herself down on her bed, she made up her mind that the next time he said good morning to her she would look as daft as she could; that way he couldn't possibly think Flora Hutchins had the brains to lie awake at night wondering what it would be like to step out into the soft green waking of very early morning and find him waiting for her by the weeping willow tree.

And I was standing under that tree, thought Flora, once again staring out the train window, *after the police left on the day of the funeral and Vivian came out into the garden to tell me I wasn't to worry about the future because he knew Sir Henry and her Ladyship would see I was all right. But I'm sure*—she pressed her nose against the pane of glass and closed her eyes—*that there was something else he wanted to say and didn't, because he kept circling the weeping willow as if it were a maypole hung with ribbons just to tangle him up into knots.* Perhaps he was having trouble finding the right words to tell her how sorry he felt about Grandpa's death, but Flora didn't think it was that.

Then, Sir Henry came out to join them. And it was at that moment Flora spotted the woman in front of the Dower House Nursery Garden across the road.

There had been no mistaking her. She was the gypsy-looking person in the mustard-and-black plaid cloak who had been at Grandpa's funeral. Who was she? And why the will-o'-the-wisp act? Those questions kept creeping back into Flora's mind, along with the realization of how little Grandpa had ever told her about his life and attendant relationships outside of Gossinger Hall. *I wish I'd asked him more—about my mother especially,* Flora thought, *but I always knew it made him unhappy to talk about her. As though there was . . . more wrong than the sadness that she died young.*

"Excuse me!" The voice came at Flora like a fist through a windowpane, shattering her thoughts like flying glass. The speaker was one of the men sitting across from her. The one by the window, not the one with the clerical collar. "Forgive me for intruding when it's clear you're miles away, Miss Hutchins," he said with a touch of primness. "But I didn't want us to reach King's Cross without reintroducing myself and telling you how exceedingly sorry I am about your grandfather's unhappy end."

Flora blinked. He was a youngish man with a head of beige woolly hair that looked unfortunately like a barrister's wig, and he had a long nose and a mouth that seemed to flap when he talked. He was wearing a Burberry raincoat. Where had she seen him before?

He helped her out. "My name is Ferncliffe. On the day of your grandfather's accident I brought a group of eleven-year-old boys from the New Church Preparatory School."

"I remember," said Flora.

"The boys were rather rowdy," Mr. Ferncliffe felt called upon to admit, "wound up like a bunch of alarm clocks all going off at once. It quite put me off teaching; but my mother thinks I ought to stick it out as a character-building exercise." He looked decidedly wistful, clearly hoping Flora would tell him that keeping himself cheerfully occupied as an early retiree was far more likely to make a man of him.

"I talked to you in the Great Hall, didn't I?" she asked. "About being worried that I couldn't find my grandfather; but I never dreamed, not for one single minute, that at the time he may already have been dead." Flora bit her lip.

The sad tilt of her pale face smote the science teacher with such force that the pen in his shirt pocket almost jumped out. He was beset by an almost overpowering urge to rescue her from a life of loneliness and despair.

Only looming thoughts of his mother demanding to know what had made him late for his tea prevented Mr. Ferncliffe from reaching across the laminated table for Flora's hand and imploring her to run off with him to somewhere unbearably romantic, such as the Isle of Skye, change their names to Jones, and hide out forevermore in a bed-and-breakfast. Mr. Ferncliffe, all five foot eleven of him, flamed with the intensity of his enthusiasm as he pictured the sweet, shy smile that would touch Flora's lips when she discovered fate had supplied her with a Young Lochinvar when she most desperately needed one. She would be so intensely grateful, so heart-wrenchingly humble, that he would have his work cut out for him trying to persuade her of his relief at having escaped the clutches of innumerable ravishing beauties.

Sadly, common sense returned full force. Possibly it would be best to tread the path of true love slowly. Sighing heavily, Mr. Ferncliffe adjusted the buckle of his raincoat in a heroic attempt at pulling himself together, and was able to address the object of his present heart's desire in a reasonably level voice.

"I expect you're wondering, Miss Hutchins, what brought me back to Lincolnshire?"

Flora hadn't been wondering anything of the sort. She had been thinking about those eleven-year-old boys and what a good thing it was that their school outing hadn't been spoilt. Luckily they had just departed in the coach when Grandpa was found in the garderobe. Then her mind had flashed to Mr. Ferncliffe vainly trying to control his youthful charges that afternoon and, unkind as it sounds, she couldn't help suspecting that at least one or two of the youngsters might have got a big buzz out of being at hand when a corpse was discovered in gloomy Gossinger Hall.

"I'm sorry," Flora looked full at Mr. Ferncliffe, "what was it you were saying about coming back to Lincolnshire? Did it have something to do with Grandpa's death?"

"You mean . . . yes, I suppose there would have to be an inquest. One of the boys—Boris Smith is his name—did come to me the other day wanting to know if the police would be around asking me and the lads from the day trip to give statements. Little ghoul! But if there is to be anything of that sort I don't know about it. The headmaster doesn't exactly make a habit of confiding in me."

Mr. Ferncliffe realized he sounded peevish, which was not the image he wished to promote. He proceeded to sink deeper in the mire by adding that the HM was inclined to treat all his teachers like servants. Fortunately Flora didn't seem to notice, and Mr. Ferncliffe finally got round to explaining that he had returned to the city of Lincoln because his mother (at least he didn't slip up and call her "Mummy") had been quite cross with him after his last visit.

"She was extremely upset that I didn't go up Lucy Tower."

"That's at the castle, isn't it?" Flora was trying very hard to sound interested and not wish that a suitcase would bounce off the luggage rack and come crashing down on Mr. Ferncliffe's woolly head so she could sit in silence until she reached King's Cross.

"My mother's name is Lucy," Mr. Ferncliffe said.

"Is it?"

"She is very attached to her name."

"It *is* pretty."

"So I suppose it's understandable," Mr. Ferncliffe conceded, "that she felt slighted that I didn't go up that blasted tower and think about her every step of the way. I tried to explain that the boys were out of control and I might have been tempted to forget about the wonderful view and push one or two of them off the top." He laughed rather shakily to prove he was only joking. "Mum—*Mother* wouldn't get off the subject for days. What did the trick was her reading about that bank robbery, the one that took place not far from Gossinger Hall." Mr. Ferncliffe rested his elbows on the table and steepled his fingers. "And I'll admit it was somewhat interesting that it turned out the man who did the holdup was technically only taking out his own money."

"Yes, that's what it said in the papers."

"Don't mistake me, Miss Hutchins, I don't have any particular sympathy for the chap, but I'm not sure it was right for his family to lock up his assets so he couldn't—legally, at any rate—get at them when he came out after spending fifteen, or whatever it was, years in prison." Repressing another of his wild urges, this time to confide in Flora that his mother kept a sharp eye and a tight fist on his own purse strings, Mr. Ferncliffe dropped his hands into his Burberry lap. "It would be different," he continued, "if the man had been put away for murdering young women in the backseats of cars."

"Did your mum see him as a sort of folk hero?" Flora asked.

"She didn't say." Mr. Ferncliffe shook his head. "She started talking about the Swineherd of Stow and how he left his life savings to Lincoln Cathedral. Mother said she couldn't believe I hadn't come home from Gossinger Hall with a pamphlet about this great philanthropist. Anyone would have thought *I'd* committed a crime. And one far worse than robbing a bank. So I decided to do my filial duty." Mr. Ferncliffe gave another of his unconvincing laughs. "Meaning I returned to climb Lucy Tower and see what I could find out at the cathedral about this swineherd, but unfortunately, yesterday being Sunday, there was no one in the information booth. . . ."

"Perhaps I may be of help to you, my son." The speaker was the gentleman seated next to Mr. Ferncliffe, who had been silent up until this point. "I'm returning to London after spending the weekend with my very dear friend, the dean of Lincoln Cathedral."

Here he cupped a hand to his clerical collar. "And it so happens that in the course of a delightful fireside chat we fell into a discussion of how saints appear so often in humble guise. The Swineherd of Stow is of course a splendid example of this."

"What a piece of luck," said Mr. Ferncliffe, ungratefully hoping that the man would say his piece and shut up. The train was now only about ten minutes from reaching King's Cross Station. That did not allow much time for Flora to realize she had fallen headlong in love with Leonard Ferncliffe and beg him not to leave her prey to the evils of London traffic.

"I regret I can provide you with only the sketchiest details," the clergyman's bland face expanded into a genial smile, "but I do not believe I am at risk of leading you into grave theological error. Indeed, I assert up front that there are those who claim the story is nothing but a pretty legend. You are free, my dear children, to decide," his kindly gaze included Flora, "without fear of heavenly recrimination, whether to believe that a certain swineherd of Stow left his life savings—a peck of silver pennies—to Lincoln Cathedral. He decided to do so it is said, as a result of his having been lost one winter night out on the marshes. The unfortunate fellow blew his horn, but no one heard, and he continued to wander in growing desperation until he heard the bells of Lincoln Cathedral, which led him to safety."

"It's such a nice story." Flora had heard it before, but never recounted with such benevolent charm. She found herself smiling, partly because she was remembering all those safe and lovely times when Grandpa told her stories about Lady Normina and the like, and also because the beaming face above the clerical collar was so clearly made-to-order for the job. It was impossible to imagine the man in any other walk of life than the one leading to and from the pulpit. She was vaguely aware that Mr. Ferncliffe was looking cross, but all thoughts were flung right and left at that instant by a voice booming out the words: "King's Cross Station!" over the loudspeaker. Within seconds the train was at a standstill and many of the passengers were on their feet, checking their watches and gathering up their luggage.

"Another stop on the journey of life." The clergyman picked up the briefcase that had been deposited at his feet and stepped into the aisle. "May I be of help lifting down your bags, my dear children?"

Mr. Ferncliffe, rising stiff as a soldier to his feet, replied that he could manage and produced his overnight bag from under the table. But Flora said she would be very grateful for a hand getting her two cases off the train, which led to the clergyman taking one and Mr. Ferncliffe the other and carrying them through the barrier for her.

"Are you sure you can manage the rest of the way?" The clergyman smiled kindly, as people with no time to dawdle brushed past them.

"I can help you down to the underground if that's where you're going." Mr. Ferncliffe asserted his right with a reckless disregard for his mother's feelings on the subject of his being late for tea.

"A splendid suggestion." The clergyman continued to beam as he sidestepped a woman with a black-and-tan beagle who lunged for his ankles as if suspecting he had drugs sewn into his turn-ups. "I will take it as a kindness, my dear young lady, if you will allow me to continue carrying my share of the load."

"You're ever so kind," Flora told both men, "and I'm really grateful, but honestly the cases aren't heavy and I've only got to get to Bethnal Green Station. From there I've been told it's only a little walk to where I'll be living." She noticed that the clergyman was looking rather sharply at Mr. Ferncliffe, as if sizing him up for the very first time. And for no reason that she could put a finger on, the world seemed suddenly as foreign as Mars, without a signpost in sight.

"Well then, my daughter," said the reverend gentleman, handing over her suitcase and watching the other man reluctantly do likewise, "we will leave you to go upon your way, trusting you will find as happy a sanctuary within the sound of God's heavenly bells as did the Swineherd of Stow."

"Honestly, I'll be fine." Flora had to raise her voice to be heard over the loudspeaker announcement that the train departing for York would be stopping at such-and-such stations on the way. "I'm going to be living rent-free in a nice little flat above a shop, so who could be luckier?"

Her words dealt a fatal blow to Mr. Ferncliffe's vision of Flora forlornly selling bunches of wilted flowers in Covent Garden and his fortuitous arrival in the midst of a downpour one gloomy winter afternoon, at which time he would buy up her entire stock before sweeping her off in a taxi to dinner at the Ritz, where she would melt at the touch of his hand and profess sweet bewilderment that a man of his urbanity and startling good looks would look beyond her plain face and meager circumstances to the woman within. Never mind; she proved herself to be of a shallow nature by saying good-bye to him without one longing glance. Whereupon Mr. Ferncliffe took himself off, determined to drown his sorrows in numerous cups of tea. Should he succumb to caffeine poisoning, so much the better.

The friendly clergyman, on the other hand, said good-bye with wholehearted goodwill and within seconds disappeared. As if, Flora thought rather wistfully while picking up her cases, he had been an angel sent to briefly lighten her load and had now been summoned back to the top office to be briefed on another assignment.

Flora stood for a moment looking toward the ticket

office on her right, fighting down the urge to scurry toward it and buy a ticket back home. Only—her feet started moving in the opposite direction—Gossinger wasn't anything like home anymore. It had become— her pace was quickening and she hardly felt the weight of her cases—more like a house of trick mirrors so that even what was once comfortingly familiar now looked queerly out of shape.

Sometimes it's better the devil you don't know, she thought, going down the escalator to the tube. *Like as not her Ladyship's sister could be a prize chrysanthemum, all eager to please and help me get settled in Wishbone Street. And if that name isn't a good sort of omen I don't know what is.*

Flora's mood of determined cheer lasted until she stood checking the metal chart on the wall to see what platform she needed. It was stupid to feel a prickle of unease and to suspect even for a second that someone was watching her. True, Flora had wondered if she were ever going to get rid of Mr. Ferncliffe; but it was certainly a stretch to suspect the schoolmaster of following her . . . even to make sure she got on the right train. And that nice clergyman couldn't have been more harmless. Turning away from the map, she decided that her problem was not being accustomed to crowds, particularly of the hurry-scurry sort. Talk about life in the fast lane! She was forthwith sucked onto the platform by the incoming rush of a train. And in her haste to get aboard without the doors closing on her, Flora didn't notice the woman with the dark and secret sort of face, wearing a black-and-yellow plaid cloak, start toward her before apparently changing her mind and entering the next carriage.

So when Flora got out at Bethnal Green she didn't look back over her shoulder. She was too busy relearning how to breathe after standing for what had seemed hours being crushed to death by people who seemed only able to maintain their balance by standing on her feet. And when she reached the top of the station steps and stepped out into the street, her sole thought was that if this grim and grimy place was London, she'd never feel at home.

However, walking past the narrow-fronted shops and catching snippets of conversation tossed about in strident cockney voices by the men and women engaged in closing up their market stalls, Flora had to admit this place was *alive*. And some might say that put it worlds apart from Nether Woodcock. Crossing at a traffic light she passed a woman wearing a sari. Stopping to remember how far she was meant to go before turning left on Wishbone Street, Flora saw two men in turbans coming toward her. They'd have stood out at Gossinger. *But here,* Flora turned the idea over in her head, *they aren't the foreigners. I'm the one who looks like I arrived in a cartload of cabbages.*

And here I am, Flora realized as she looked up at the number above the doorway. *This is Sixty-seven Wishbone Street.* Setting the suitcases down on the crumbling stoop, she tried valiantly to find something to like. She started with the shop windows, but there was something decidedly unfriendly about the iron bars at the windows. The sign above the scarred bottle green door read "Joe's Camera Shop."

Flora wondered enviously where Joe was now. She tried to convince herself that he had shown heart by leaving the curtains strung across the windows of the upstairs flat. But even from this distance the grayish material looked as though it would fall apart if dunked in lukewarm soapy water. When the key refused to turn in the lock, she wished with growing desperation that Lady Gossinger's sister Edna Smith would suddenly open the door and explain that she'd been in the back of the shop making a cup of tea to hearten the weary traveler.

But then the key turned suddenly and smoothly, as if it had been playing a little joke on Flora by pretending not to fit. Wedging the door open with her foot, she reached inside for a light switch. Failing to find one, she stumbled over the threshold, dragged in the cases, and continued the game of blindman's buff until her hand finally made contact. The room sprang into bleary light, provided by a naked bulb in the ceiling.

Flora sat down on one of the suitcases and began unbuttoning her coat with fumbling fingers. There was nothing to frighten her in the shop, because there was nothing there except a counter toward the back and two empty shelves mounted on the wall behind it. *But if I don't get up and take a look at the other rooms, I'll scare myself silly there's someone hiding behind one of those doors,* Flora told herself in a very firm voice. Exploring the kitchen immediately behind the shop wasn't much of an adventure. There was the sink and a dreadful old cooker in one corner and that was the extent of what could be reported to *Better Homes and Gardens,* apart from the staircase leading up to the flat.

And that's what's important, Flora staunchly reminded herself as she flicked on another light and ran up the steps. She found herself on a tiny landing that opened onto a sitting room, two tiny bedrooms, and a bathroom that would have given a field mouse claustrophobia. It was difficult, verging on impossible, to imagine Lady Gossinger ever living here, let alone making room for a sister and a couple of parents. It seemed to Flora that the rooms were empty of more than furniture. No one had left anything of their inner selves at Sixty-seven Wishbone Street. There was nothing to welcome a newcomer, and by the same token there was nothing to tell her she didn't belong.

"This," Flora said aloud, "is the exact opposite of Gossinger Hall, where everything happens in the middle of something else. I've come to a place that starts at the beginning every time a new person sticks the key in the door for the first time." She was standing at the sitting room window with the edge of one of the limp curtains clutched in her hand, but in her heart she was back at Gossinger. She could feel her grandfather's presence and hear him saying in his most loving voice: "Every ending is a new beginning, my Flora." Impulsively, she raced back down the stairs, knelt down in front of the larger of her suitcases, and was soon rummaging through the contents for the pair of scissors that she knew . . . well, was *almost* sure . . . she had packed. Yes, here they were!

Removing her hand mirror from its protective wrapping of two nightdresses, Flora stood it on the upper of the two shelves behind the shop counter and, the scissors poised in her hand, counted to three. Then, holding her breath, she unpinned her hair, shook it loose, lifted up a hank, and started to snip. She had the job half done when she was startled into dropping the scissors. The doorbell had rung.

"It'll be Lady Gossinger's sister come to see if I got here all safe and sound," she told the mirror before staring down at the handful of hair still in her hand. "What a fright I'll give her. A proper scarecrow, that's what she'll think I am." Flora carried the scissors with her to the door, just in case it was someone a lot more scary than Edna Smith come on the hop. After all, this was the city. And as it turned out she was wise to be prepared for the worst, because when she asked (while keeping the bolt on) who was there, the reply made her wish she could put her hair back on, if only to ward off the chill that made her sure she would have a stiff neck for a week.

"It's Vivian Gossinger."

So what if it is, Flora managed to remind herself as she released the stubborn bolt and opened the door. *This is my place even if I don't pay any rent and I didn't invite him, so he'll just have to take me as he finds me.* This spurt of defiance to the tenets of her upbringing stood her in good stead until Mr. Gossinger crossed the threshold and stood looking at her with wonder in his eyes.

"I've been cutting my hair," she whispered, handing him the scissors like a child caught stealing.

"I think it is most becoming," said Mr. Gossinger with obvious sincerity. "Were you planning to leave the long part or would you like me to even it up for you?"

"Yes, please," said Flora.

TEN

"Thank you for straightening me out, sir," said Flora in her best housemaid's voice.

"My pleasure," Mr. Vivian Gossinger assured her. "You look positively charming with your hair short, but I do hope you didn't feel obliged to cut it for the money."

"You mean to sell?" Flora nearly laughed but remembered in the nick of time that people of her sort were not in the habit of sharing a chuckle with their betters.

"Please don't think me impertinent, Flora, but I did wonder if you might be a bit short of the ready when it came to setting yourself up in this flat."

"That is kind of you, Mr. Gossinger," Flora stood in the center of the little shop with elbows at her sides as if holding a tea tray, "but Sir Henry advanced me some money on what I'll be getting from my grandfather's will. I'm not saying it's a lot." She realized she was gabbing on because she was nervous, mostly because she hadn't yet looked in the mirror to assess whether or not she looked like a chicken. "Grandpa tied up most of his savings for me to receive when I'm thirty. He may have been worried I'd meet up with the wrong sort of man, because I think that's what happened to my mother." Her voice petered out.

"I know Hutchins loved you very much," said Vivian.

"I'll manage fine. Especially when I get a job." Flora decided it was a good thing there wasn't a stick of furniture in the shop or flat above or she would have felt obliged to ask him to sit down, and then he would have felt equally obliged to stay awhile. "As for my hair," she touched the spiky ends, "it's not like it was my one beauty, as with Jo in *Little Women*."

"That's true." Vivian smiled. "You also have very pretty eyes."

Flora meant to reply that he oughtn't to say stuff like that. She wasn't a child anymore to be praised and handed toffees. Instead, she heard herself say: "Do you really think I have nice eyes?"

"Definitely." Vivian leaned closer so that his face was within inches of Flora's. "They're not an ordinary blue; they've got flecks of amber and bronze in them. Here, if you don't believe me, take a look for yourself." He went over to the counter at the back of the shop, picked up her hand mirror, and handed it to Flora.

"I'm afraid to look," she told him.

"Coward."

Flora found herself laughing, but she stopped and bit her lip when she peeked in the mirror. Her hair didn't look as if it had been to Vidal Sassoon. But she had to admit she did look different in a good sort of way. Her eyes seemed to have come alive and she found herself wondering if a touch of pencil and mascara wouldn't bring them out even more.

"Well?" asked Vivian.

"There's no point in having second thoughts, most of my hair is now in that wastepaper basket under the sink."

"You could have stepped straight from the pages of *Oliver Twist.*"

"Is that good?" Flora had to smile at him.

"You have to be the most enchanting urchin in all London." Vivian reclined against the shop counter, studying her intently.

"Not just Bethnal Green?" This was madness, but it was also magic. *It's this place,* Flora told herself, *and the feeling it gives that all sorts of wonderful things can happen because there's nothing here to get in the way. Only blank walls and empty floors. No rules set down in black and white.* Her heart turned over when Vivian cupped her face with his hand: For an exquisitely scary moment she was sure he was going to kiss her.

"I brought a picnic basket," he said, taking a good six steps backward, which as far as Flora was concerned amounted to a slap in the face.

"What did you say?" she asked, praying he wouldn't notice her embarrassment.

"I heard from Uncle Henry that you were moving in today and I thought I could help out by bringing over a meal. It's outside." Vivian was now crossing the room, talking over his shoulder. "Won't be two ticks."

Flora was tempted to bolt the door on him when he went out into the street, but reason prevailed. Perhaps he hadn't meant anything, or noticed that she'd gone silly on him. It wasn't like she'd puckered up her lips or thrown her arms around him, now, was it? And going on what the housekeeper before Mrs. Much had said, men could be awfully thick at times. In the minute taken by Vivian to return with a wicker hamper, Flora had herself back together.

"Really, this is kind of you, sir," she placed particular emphasis on the last word, "but you shouldn't have gone and put yourself out. Your family has already done plenty, letting me have the flat rent-free for a year."

"And so they ought." Vivian Gossinger set the hamper in the middle of the floor. "Your grandfather was an incomparable butler; Uncle Henry will never be able to replace him—or you, for that matter, Flora."

"That's nice to hear." Flora felt her guard slipping again and took refuge in saying sharply, "I hope that food didn't come from Fortnum and Mason."

"Not guilty on that score." Vivian flashed her his rare but oddly infectious grin. "I've had to cut a few corners lately on account of losing my job selling Macho Man beauty products for men. Everything in here," he tapped the basket with the toe of his shoe, "comes from good old Tesco's."

"I'm sure you still spent far too much," Flora protested.

"I didn't say I'm unemployed. They don't know about it at Gossinger, but for the last fortnight I've been working at a flea market only a few miles or so from here, and becoming quite the expert in cracked china."

"I'll never forget your kindness . . ."

"You sound," Vivian Gossinger brushed back a wayward lock of hair, "as if you're about to push me out the door."

"Well," Flora tried and failed to squelch a spurt of happiness, "I don't want to hold you up."

"Opening a tin of corned beef is no job for a woman. Besides, there are some things I'd really like to talk to you about, Flora. That afternoon in the garden after your grandfather's funeral wasn't the right time."

"You sound like it's something important."

"Nothing that can't wait until you've had something to eat." Mr. Gossinger knelt and spread a green-and-white check tablecloth on the floor before unpacking the picnic basket in earnest. In addition to the tin of corned beef, there were several packets of cheese, a loaf of sliced bread, a bunch of black grapes, and a carton of orange juice. "I'm afraid I forgot the mustard, but there is some butter in here somewhere." He again delved into the basket and triumphantly produced this item. "It's a man thing," he flashed his disarming grin, "being able to produce a well-balanced meal with only a couple of days' notice. I even remembered dessert. Look," he held up a packet of chocolate biscuits, "it says right here on the label: 'By Appointment To Her Majesty The Queen.'"

"You can't do better than that." Flora felt a pang at the memory of the letter she had written to the Queen about Grandpa's silver polish. "How about letting me lay the table? That's if you remembered the cutlery." Flora knelt down across the tablecloth from Vivian. There seemed no point in putting up any more fuss. Within half an hour he would be gone, and in all probability they would never meet again.

"I was determined to go whole hog." He handed her the knives and forks and sat back on his haunches.

"My word, sir," Flora could not repress a smile, "they're real stainless steel, made around 1960, by the looks of it."

"Are you sure?"

"Practically positive. Are you sure we ought to be using it?"

"I don't know," said Vivian, entering into the spirit of the thing, "I'm not sure whether any of the pieces are insured; do you think they should be?"

"My grandfather was the one who knew about old stuff." Flora set out the knives and forks. The change in her voice made it clear that at least for her the game had suddenly gone flat.

"You must have learned quite a bit from him, working alongside him as you did."

"Yes, being a maid in a house like Gossinger Hall gives a girl many opportunities to get to know a good piece of china or glass when she sees it."

"And silver," said Vivian Gossinger.

"That, too, but I'll never be a patch on Grandpa when it comes to knowing where and when a pair of marrow spoons was made and even the name of the smith." Flora spoke slowly and awkwardly because the horrible suspicion had entered her mind that a piece from the silver collection might have been put away in the wrong place. Had Sir Henry, or maybe her Ladyship, rung up Mr. Gossinger and asked him to go to Bethnal Green and ply her with kindness and corned beef sandwiches in hopes of eliciting a confession that she had taken it?

"I've been thinking," he said, laying a plate down between each set of knife and fork, "that you'd be an absolute whiz working in the flea market."

"Really?" Flora decided she had a wickedly suspicious mind. "I've always loved rummaging through the stalls. I think," she ran her fingers through the short hair so that it spiked up in truly elfin fashion, "I think it comes from always having so much fun playing dressing-up games in the trunk room at Gossinger. There was a lovely feather boa and hats and dresses such as ladies wore in the twenties. That was such a pretty fashion, don't you think?"

Looking at her glowing face, Vivian Gossinger regretfully decided that he could not tell her what he was thinking. What he did say was that he would be happy to introduce her to several owners of stalls in the flea market where he was employed if she thought she'd like to work there.

"Of course I would, but it wouldn't do."

"Why not?"

"Because," Flora—whose emotions had rarely had such a workout in so short a space of time—actually snapped out the words, "because I can't work alongside you, Mr. Gossinger! Sir Henry and her Ladyship would have fits. And I'd rather not think what my grandfather would have to say if he was alive."

"You think I couldn't handle the competition, because I've already lost one selling job."

"It's not that and you know it."

"Well, then, I promise I'm not going to be a nag if you'll agree to let me take you to the flea market tomorrow, just to see if there are any feather boas for sale."

"I'll have to think about it." Flora knew she was being weak, but the temptation was so strong . . . Vivian, sensing that the tide might be beginning to turn, proposed a glass of orange juice.

"I apologize for it not being a better vintage," he told her.

"I'm sure it's lovely." Flora took an experimental sip and nodded her head. *If he'd been entertaining a real lady he'd have brought wine with one of those unpronounceable names,* she decided. *And that's good. This way I know that when it comes right down to it, he hasn't forgotten we're from different worlds. So the best thing I can do is act natural so he doesn't think I've taken him wrong.* Flora promptly accepted her own advice and began buttering bread and cutting up corned beef. After which she and Vivian tucked in and made a very good meal, fortified by more orange juice.

"You know, it actually makes me feel a bit giddy," she said, which had the instant effect of turning Vivian Gossinger, who had been looking very cheerful, sober.

"I expect that's because you're worn out after packing up and leaving home." He swallowed the last of a grape and got to his feet. "Why don't I help you get those suitcases upstairs so you can begin to get settled?"

"Thanks." Flora scrambled up and wiped her hands together. See! It had all been over in a flash; he'd be out of here in next to no time and by tomorrow he would have forgotten all about her, his uncle's maidservant. "The stairs are through the kitchen." And she reached for one of the cases, but Vivian had got his hands on both of them and was heading past the shop counter and into the kitchen, where he stopped dead in his tracks.

"There's no table and not a single chair. I thought it would seem more like a real picnic to eat on the floor. I'd no idea it was a matter of necessity," he said.

"I'll get some furniture tomorrow."

"Furniture." Mr. Gossinger put down the suitcases. "Do you have a bed?"

"I'll get one of those, too."

"Well, I must say," he turned to face Flora, "I'm surprised at Uncle Henry and Aunt Mabel, letting you come to a place like this. They've got house accounts all over the place and it would have been easy as wink to have some pieces delivered."

"It wasn't their responsibility."

"You're wrong." Vivian looked angry. "They owed it to your grandfather to see you didn't walk into an empty place. And one would think after all that hoopla about Uncle—"

"About what?"

"Oh, you know," Vivian picked up the cases, "how Uncle Henry always went on about how Hutchins was the best butler that ever lived."

"That wasn't hoopla," Flora flashed back without a thought to respecting her betters. "Besides, Sir Henry and Lady Gossinger have their hands full right now, what with losing their entire staff at one go."

"I knew Mrs. Much was leaving."

"But you didn't know about Mr. Tipp?"

"What about him?" Vivian put down the cases for the second time and resettled his spectacles. "He's not dead, is he?"

"No, of course not!" Flora realized she sounded impatient and spoke more slowly. "It's just that he went off the same day as Mrs. Much to stay with a cousin in Dorset that was taken poorly all of a sudden and needed someone to help out."

"That's a weight off my mind," Vivian said somewhat ambiguously, and this time carried the cases up the stairs.

"I'm so sorry they're that heavy," Flora apologized. "It's because I brought half the bottles that were left of Grandpa's silver polish. It's silly, because I've got his recipe and could always make up some more; but there wasn't much else that was really his—except for his clothes—because of him never living in his own house."

"I don't think you're foolish about that." Mr. Gossinger, having put down the suitcases for the last time, was opening the sitting room door and taking a look inside. "Where I think you *are* foolish is in not taking my suggestion about working in the flea market seriously when you need so many things for this flat."

"I've got the money Grandpa left me."

"You said it wasn't all that much. Besides," sitting down on one of the upended cases, Vivian Gossinger looked reflective, "I have an additional brilliant idea. If you got on at one of the stalls that sells silver, you could make a little extra money selling your grandfather's polish."

"Yes, I suppose I could do that." Looking around the empty sitting room, Flora again had the feeling that she had stepped into a magical place, one that could become entirely her own creation. The threadbare curtains stirred at the windows that weren't sealed very well, but when Flora shivered it wasn't because of a draft.

"About those chocolate biscuits," she said.

"Did they make you feel queasy?" Vivian Gossinger got to his feet, overturning both suitcases in the process.

"No, it's just that I noticed they have the Queen's Warrant. I've read up about it, you see, and I know that's what it's called when a product has the words 'By Appointment' on the label. You're going to think what I'm going to say is silly. . . ."

"Try me."

"Okay, here goes." Flora took a deep breath. "I'd love more than anything in the world to get the Queen to give that warrant for Grandpa's silver polish. I used to lie awake nights when he was alive dreaming about it, but never saying a word because he'd have said it never could come true. And then a couple of weeks before he died, I wrote a letter to Her Majesty explaining that the product has been for sale for three years, which is one of the requirements, you know."

Vivian didn't say anything; he was thinking that he had come to Bethnal Green to ask Flora Hutchins if she really believed that her grandfather's death had been an accident, and now he could not do it, because only someone really vicious would kill the sparkle in her eyes.

"It's just a dream," Flora continued with a rush, "and no, I haven't heard back from the Queen. But I'm sure when a letter does come Sir Henry will forward it at once," she said, fetching up a smile. And at that moment someone buzzed the shop door. "My goodness, who on earth can that be?" She started to run down the stairs, but Vivian edged her against the wall and nipped down ahead of her.

"You're going to have to be careful, especially at night," he told her, feeling very much as if he had been put in charge of a bouncing puppy who would, with a guileless wag of the tail, welcome in miscreants of all sorts. "You don't know who could be out there."

"Getting ready to steal me blind?" Flora, being rather tired, stifled a laugh behind her hand as she crossed the empty shop to stand behind him.

"Or cosh you over the head," Vivian responded repressively, but forbore to paint an even nastier scenario.

"Cooee, it's only me!" a cheery voice called through the door. "Mabel's sister, Edna, from round the corner, with the bed I was supposed to bring over earlier."

"The what?" Flora said, whereas Vivian merely raised a bemused eyebrow and began somewhat reluctantly to undo the bolts. Both of them fully expected to find themselves face-to-face with a mattress and box spring swaying ominously in the wind and blocking the bearer from view. But what they actually saw when the door swung open was a woman who looked quite a bit like Lady Gossinger, with a roll of bottle green plastic under her arm and a boy of about ten or eleven at her side.

"It's the blow-up sort," Edna Smith explained as she stepped over the threshold. "And this here's my lad Boris, my grandson, that is. Say hello to the lady and gentleman and put a smile on your face, for God's sake."

The result of this instruction was to make young Boris look more sullen than ever, but he did attempt to make himself useful by kicking the door shut behind him.

"It's so nice of you to come round." Flora went to take the bed, if that was indeed what was tucked under her visitor's arm, while Vivian instinctively looked around for a chair, or something of the equivalent to offer Mrs. Smith by way of hospitality.

"So my aunt didn't forget and leave Flora to sleep on the floor her first night here. Thanks most awfully for filling in the breach," he said.

"You'll be young Viv . . . Mr. Gossinger."

"That's me. And may I say it's a great pleasure to

finally meet Aunt Mabel's only sister." If Vivian sounded distracted, it was because he couldn't shake the feeling he was actually looking at her Ladyship done up in fancy dress. The resemblance between the sisters was certainly very strong. They had the same build and puffy facial features. There was, however, a world of difference when it came to his Aunt Mabel's determined tweediness and this woman's mock-lizard-skin coat and tarnished-blond coiffure, arranged in loopy curls on top and a French twist at back. And their voices were as different as night from day, Vivian noted. This one made no bones about being a Londoner born and bred.

"It's a pain in the bum to blow up," Edna said, watching Flora cradle the bundle of green plastic. "One of my lodgers left it behind. If I remember right, he was the one what drove a lorry and had fallen out with his wife over her having a bit more than a cup of tea with the next-door neighbor. And Boris was on at me afterward to keep the bed in case one of the boys from his class should ever come over to spend the night. Not that he's holding his breath." This was said with a fond if somewhat worried look at her grandson. "A snobby lot they are at that school; enough to make you sick, but there it is. There's always some that thinks they're better than others."

Boris stared at the floor without comment, and both Flora and Vivian wondered if the boy was always this sullen or if it was just because he'd been dragged away from the TV, or possibly his homework—although somehow it was difficult to picture Boris being slavishly fond of algebra.

"Brings back a lot of memories, it does, standing here." Edna Smith was actually clacking around the shop room in high heels that looked dangerously unsuited to a woman of her heavyset build. "Whatever Mabel says different, Mum and Dad gave us the best childhood ever down here with all the secondhand stuff, mostly junk really, and upstairs, too—even though you couldn't swing a cat round in the flat without knocking everything off the mantelpiece."

"I'm sure your parents did a lovely job of bringing you up." Flora felt the warm glow that always came with meeting a kindred spirit.

"Ever such happy times I had here, helping Mum and Dad when they was too busy behind the counter." Edna dabbed at her eyes, streaking mascara onto her plump, rouged cheeks. "Most of the time they'd have me pretend to read a picture book, something easy because I was never what you'd call a brain. Anyway it didn't matter if it was *Puss-in-Boots* because really I was there to keep a lookout to see nobody was nicking anything. Made me feel ever so important, it did. And believe you me," this was said with a deep chuckle, "it wasn't the teddy-boy types with their sideburns and leather jackets you had to watch for, not on your life! Often as not it was the little old ladies stinking to high heaven of lavender water that'd be stuffing china ashtrays with 'A present from Blackpool' into their pockets." Edna Smith interrupted her memories to poke into the pockets of the lizard-skin coat. "Would you believe it, I meant to bring some tea bags so's you could at least have a nice hot cuppa, but what with one thing and another," her eyes shifted to her grandson, "I've come away without them. Never mind! It won't take a minute for Boris to nip home. We're in that block of council flats and he's got the key in his pocket."

"I'm not going." The boy came alive with a fierceness that startled Flora and Vivian, and they reassured him there was no need for him to fetch the tea bags because there was still plenty of orange juice left in the picnic basket so there was no question of anyone dying of thirst. Flora didn't mention that they didn't have a

kettle or any cups, in case Edna felt compelled to provide them.

"What's got into you, talking so rude, Boris!" She
looked more upset than seemed strictly necessary.

"I told you I didn't want to come and see her." The
boy directed a thumb in Flora's direction and promptly
got it slapped down by Grandma.

"It's dark out there, and raining too, by the sound of
it." Flora hoped this didn't sound too much like a criticism of Mrs. Smith, but there it was. For some reason,
the poor kid looked scared to death. The freckles stood
out on his pale face as if he had been stricken with the
measles.

"Extremely kind of you to offer, Mrs. Smith," said
Vivian, turning to Flora almost as if they were a couple.
"But we both understand Boris's reluctance to—"

"It's not because I'm afraid, if that's what you're
thinking!" The boy's raised voice quivered and he stuck
out his chin in the manner of a boxer welcoming his
opponent's punishing fist. "The dark doesn't scare me,
not one bit. It's just that I think it's stupid to go all the
way home for some bloody tea bags."

"There's no need to go using that word," scolded his
grandmother.

"I only said—"

"And I've told you never to say 'stupid,' it makes you
sound stuck-up. But I suppose that's what happens
when you send them to private schools." Edna now
addressed Flora and Vivian. "Of course, we don't pay
for him to go to there. Boris is on a sort of scholarship.
That's why I have to keep quiet about taking a lodger
now and then. Oh, the board of governors, they know I
do hairdressing, but if they was to get wind that I make
a bit of extra on the side they might stick it to me for at
least part of the school fees."

"I won't breathe a word," Flora promised.

"Anyway," Edna directed this to Vivian, "the gentleman I've got at present is a relative of sorts. Some kind of cousin getting on in years, with all the usual aches and pains, and it was no skin off my nose to offer him the back bedroom. I see he gets his meals regular. He's a nice man, is Mr. Phillips, wouldn't you say so, Boris?"

"Yes, Grandma." This was said with a noticeable lack of enthusiasm, but there was no telling if this was due to Boris's sour mood, rather than an active dislike of Edna Smith's male friend. "How about I blow up the bed, that's what we came for, isn't it?"

"That's really kind." Flora dared not look at Vivian Gossinger for fear she would catch him trying to repress a smile and that would set her off. And really it was unkind to think of laughing even on the inside, because the boy stood there looking as if what he wanted most in the world was a pair of boxing gloves and for someone to kindly volunteer to let him get in a good punch. "How about a chocolate biscuit," she offered, "before you start on the bed?"

"Thank you very much, miss," Boris suddenly looked almost cheerful, "but I can't possibly accept because Grandma here," he ducked his head in a mock bow in Edna's direction, "she's always gone and told me never to take sweets—and I suppose that means biscuits, too—from strangers."

"More for us, then," said Vivian with a smile for Flora as he slipped an arm around her shoulders.

"And I've had just about enough of your lip, Boris, my lad." Edna grabbed the blow-up bed from the smirking boy and used it to provide him a series of whacks on the bottom while herding him toward the back of the shop. "Now you'll take this upstairs to one of the bedrooms if you know what's good for you. Get it blown up and then sit your bum down on the floor until I'm good and ready to call you back down."

"Want me to make sure it's good and bouncy?" Boris stuck his head round the corner for an elaborate wink at Vivian before a series of thuds and thumps informed those left below that the boy was playing hopscotch on his way up the stairs.

"I'm too old for this game." Edna took off her high heels, tucked them under her arm, and hobbled across the room to rest her weary back against the shop counter. "Being a grandmother, is what I mean. But what was I to do but take him in when his mum— that's my daughter Lisa—did a bunk? And his dad was never in the picture from day one."

"Poor Boris." Flora eased out from the comfort of Vivian's arm and went to stand by the beleaguered older woman's side. "I was so lucky . . ." She was about to say this was because she'd had a grandfather who'd made up in the most loving and magical sort of way for her not having parents. But this would not have been exactly tactful, considering Edna had set aside the shoes as if even they were an insupportable burden for someone whose spirit had been broken by an eleven-year-old boy. Besides, Flora found herself wondering, with a lump in her throat, whether she hadn't been at times more of a pain than a blessing. Had Grandpa always told the truth, the whole truth, and nothing but the truth when he used to tell her she was the light of an old man's life? What about the time she'd lied about the man climbing through her bedroom window and muddling everything up, after she had just put the place to rights as instructed? Looking back, she counted herself extremely fortunate that hadn't been the end of Grandpa then and there. He might have had a heart attack. . . . The lump in her throat broke apart, exploding into particles of misery that flooded through her from head to toe. As it was, Grandpa must have spent many a sleepless night worrying that she would go from one wicked lie to the next until she ended up as some sort of confidence trickster.

"You look as though you could do with a stiff drink. Hold on a minute and I'll fix you right up." Vivian's voice wrapped itself around Flora like a warm woolly blanket, and it didn't matter a bit that he was talking to Edna. He was here, forming a bridge between the present and the past; and that was every bit as necessary as the glass he put in the other woman's hand.

"Orange juice," he was saying cheerfully. "Nothing like it for putting a smile on your lips and a song in your heart."

"You're a bit of a lad, aren't you?" The sparkle that appeared in Edna's eyes was of the determined sort, but still managed to offset the mascara in the hollows above her cheeks. "Not nearly so toffee-nosed as I thought you'd be, from Mabel's letters. Ever so hoity-toity is the way I've been picturing everyone at Gossinger Hall. Not just Sir Henry and that dotty old auntie of his, but even that butler bloke going in one door and out the other with the silver tea tray. Well, talk about silence landing with a thud!" Edna looked as though she wished the floor would open up and she'd reappear in China. "Trust me to say something tactless!"

"It's all right," said Flora. "I'd hate it if no one dared say Grandpa's name. It would make him seem more out of reach than ever."

"You poor little love, left all alone in the world. My heart goes out to you, dearie. And if there is anything at all I can do to make you feel less defenseless as you try to make your way, just remember old Edna is just a holler away. You'll have to come over for a proper tea, lots of nice bread and butter—none of that stuff with the crusts cut off. And that means you, too." She looked hopefully at Vivian. "That would tickle Mabel's funny bone, wouldn't it? You sitting in my council flat with a cup of char on your knee."

"I'd enjoy that no end, coming to see you, I mean, Mrs. Smith." Vivian's smile had a slightly thoughtful edge. "How about the day after tomorrow, if that suits?"

"Oh, yes, please!" It was quite ridiculous, but Flora, meeting his eyes, felt like Alice being invited down the rabbit hole into a land where wonders never ceased.

"I oughtn't to have made that crack about Mabel," Edna continued, sounding remorseful. "Say what you like, she did remember my birthday this year for the first time in God knows how long. Sent a present back, she did, with Boris that day." She tilted back her head and raised the glass of orange juice to her lips. "Oh, well! Bottoms up, as the actress said to the bishop."

"What day was that?" asked Vivian.

"There, I've done it again, haven't I? Gone running off at the mouth." Edna took another gulp perhaps in hope of steadying her nerves, and drained the glass. "I'd made up my mind, true as I'm standing here, that I wouldn't say a word about Boris being at Gossinger Hall the day your grandfather met with that horrible accident. And yes, it was that day Mabel sent him home with my birthday present." Her eyes sorrowfully met Flora's.

"You mean," Flora gently removed the glass before Edna could drop it, "you mean Boris was one of the boys on the school outing? I was glad, when I got round to thinking about it, that the coach had left or was just leaving when Grandpa was found. But of course they had to be questioned afterward. Oh, poor Boris! Do you think that's why he's been acting up?"

"It's a puzzle," Edna rubbed her eyes, "because I'd never have said Boris is what you'd call a sensitive child."

"Most eleven-year-olds are horrid little ghouls," Vivian offered encouragingly. "At that age I would have considered being in any way connected to Sudden Death a great adventure and would have wanted to crow about it to anyone who would listen." He reached for Flora's hand but let his arm fall to his side. Now he wished she hadn't cut her hair. She looked so cold without it—like an urchin child abandoned on a wintry street corner by a neglectful adult.

"But that's the funny thing," murmured Edna.

"What is?" asked Vivian.

"That Boris hasn't been his usual show-off self about being in the thick of things, so to speak. He won't say a word about that day, other than he saw his Aunt Mabel. And I only got that out of him because I found her birthday present to me in his coat pocket. Don't ask me what's eating him because I haven't no idea. But one thing I can tell you, I'd do anything in the world for that lad of mine . . . well, grandparents are like that, aren't I right, dearie?"

ELEVEN

Flora woke up the next morning to hear someone coming up the stairs. Still blurry from sleep, she thought it was her grandfather and that his death was all a terrible dream. But when she sat up in bed and rubbed her eyes, she saw that she was in the larger of the bedrooms in the flat and that it wasn't her grandfather but Vivian Gossinger who stood in the doorway with his hands full.

"Breakfast," he announced. "How do you like bagels? I picked some up from the shop a couple of doors down along with a cup of coffee for each of us."

"That was nice of you." Flora knew she sounded and looked stupid with the blanket she had found in the airing cupboard pulled up to her chin, and what was left of her hair sticking up on end. But to have smiled at him might have given him the idea that she was making the most of the situation. Strangely, she didn't focus on the upside-down nature of things that had Vivian serving her breakfast in bed.

"Just a small token of appreciation for letting me stay the night on the spare bedroom floor. I was extremely comfortable with the traveling rug I brought in from the car." Vivian set the tray on the floor and handed her a paper cup.

"You couldn't help your car not starting."

"That's kind of you to say," Vivian handed her a bagel, "but if Uncle Henry were here he'd point out I've always been the worst kind of slacker when it comes to anything mechanical, which would include remembering to fill up at the petrol pump. And as you can see I'm no better when it comes to putting a meal on the table, or I should say the floor? Look, I've forgotten to bring you a serviette." He crossed to the door. "Won't be a minute. There's bound to be one of the paper ones left in the picnic basket."

"I'll come down." Flora flung off the blanket as the door closed behind him. It wasn't just a matter of the incongruity of lying there like the Lady of Shalott afloat in her barge while Vivian raced around on her behalf that got her going. There was enough light creeping in through the gap in the tattered curtains to let her know that the day had been up and about its business way ahead of her. She hadn't taken off her watch last night and the hands pointed to nine o'clock. Opening the door, she called down: "I'll have a quick bath and get dressed, so if you want to go and get a tin of petrol, Mr. Gossinger . . ."

"Splendid!" His voice floated up to her. "No need to rush, because I may be a while. I'll go home to shower and shave."

"Be careful."

"Not to spill the petrol?"

"I meant crossing the street; there's so much traffic."

Flora felt a blush fire up her cheeks and she ducked back into the room and unpacked a towel from her suitcase. She must have imagined Vivian's laugh, because the sound of traffic was a permanent hum within the flat, sometimes interrupting its even flow with a louder rumble or explosion of tooting horns or the screeching of brakes. *I must stop this,* she thought while raiding her suitcase for something to wear. *I have to remember to remember that he's here as a representative of the Gossinger Family. Doing his duty as he sees it, because that's how men of breeding behave toward those who have served them.*

When she was standing in the bath, which was not much bigger than an egg carton, getting sprayed with lukewarm water from a makeshift showerhead, the feeling crept back—the one that explained why she hadn't been thrown into a tizzy when Vivian Gossinger had brought her breakfast in bed. She felt somehow as though the two of them had been shipwrecked together and after clinging to a piece of the wreckage, scarcely big enough for one let alone two, they had been cast up on a desert island where there was no one but them. Contact with the outside world was reduced to the occasional glimpse of a ship's silhouette skimming the blue horizon.

"You're deliberately escaping from reality," she scolded herself as she toweled herself dry and poked her hair. "I suppose lots of people would find that understandable, considering the shock of Grandpa's death. But I'm not going to let you make a complete fool of yourself. You'll go downstairs and thank Mr. Gossinger very nicely for stepping into the breach and then let him go back to his own life. And no wistful glances as he heads out the door, do you understand me?"

But when Flora entered the poky little kitchen at the back of the shop Vivian seemed so at home it was hard to imagine he lived anywhere else. He was sitting on a stool by the sink looking exactly like the model of Rodin's famous sculpture. "I found this outside the back door," he tapped the wooden seat, "the dustman's loss is our gain. I've been thinking," he added, "about Aunt Mabel's poor mother, having to cart every meal she cooked down here up to the flat. If you ask me, the woman had to die in order to give herself a rest."

"I expect they ate down here quite a lot," said Flora.

"What?" Vivian lifted his head. "Standing around the cooker with spoons in their hands?"

"It needn't have been as bad as all that. They could have squeezed in a table."

"Where?"

"Against that wall." Flora pointed to the space between the draining board and the staircase doorway. "There's enough room for a little drop-leaf table, and if they used folding chairs that wouldn't get in the way when not in use, I am sure it would have been possible to manage."

"Would it?"

Flora guessed what he was thinking and spoke more sharply than she intended. "There's no point in feeling guilty because you were born into a life where you had more than most. That's just the way it is and it's a waste of time to hit yourself over the head for it. Other people —my sort, you could say—get used to squeezing in together. Sometimes it makes for a special sort of closeness. I remember . . ." her voice went a bit wobbly, "that when I was little, I loved the bigness of Gossinger during the daytime, but it was always wonderful to be tucked in with Grandpa in our little rooms at night, with the curtains shut tight against the darkness and the clock ticking on the mantelpiece. That clock was like a member of our family, always chiming in without being spoken to . . . that's what Grandpa used to say."

Vivian sat still on the kitchen stool, wanting to speak but realizing Flora hadn't finished.

"Sometimes," she said, "on Sundays, we'd have tea together in our sitting room, Grandpa and me, Mr. Tipp and Mrs. Bellows—she was the housekeeper I liked best. She used to tell me stories about the Queen. She went to live in some place called Ilford . . ."

"I remember her."

"Yes, of course you would." Flora stood at the cooker, her concentration now on a chip in the enamel between the front burners. "Mrs. Bellows fixed up the cut in your head the night you drove into a lamppost coming to Gossinger."

"And you made me a cup of tea."

"Most of it went in the saucer, I was only about seven and I was so afraid you were going to die. Your face was white as the sink . . . is the way Mrs. Bellows put it. Anyway," Flora turned resolutely away from the cooker and looked at Vivian with a smile in her eyes, "back to Sunday afternoons. It was always a bit of a squeeze, the four of us, Mrs. Bellows, Mr. Tipp, Grandpa and me, getting around the tea table that wasn't much bigger than a lady's writing desk, but we managed to have some really jolly times. Sometimes Mr. Tipp even cracked a smile and Mrs. Bellows would say she'd mark that down on the calendar. Poor Mr. Tipp! I hope he won't have to be gone too long from Gossinger looking after his cousin who's poorly. He never went away before, not so as I can remember, and I'm afraid he'll be like a fish out of water."

Vivian wasn't at that moment particularly interested in Mr. Tipp. "What about that table?" he asked.

"The one in our sitting room?"

"That's right. Did you arrange to have it sent here?"

"It didn't belong to us," said Flora. "None of the furnishings did, not the clock or the corner cupboard or Grandpa's fireside chair. All that was there before he came. Leftovers from the butler before him perhaps, or it could be that some of the stuff was brought down from the trunk room; it always amazed me what was up there when I went exploring. Once, when Miss Doffit was with me, we found a pretty brooch made of different colored stones stuck down the side of an old brocade sofa. It wasn't valuable—just glass I expect— but it was fun to pretend it had belonged to Sir Rowland Gossinger's wife and that he had kept her a prisoner on bread and water in the trunk room because she wouldn't agree to give him a divorce so he could marry his true love."

"Were you sorry to leave it behind?" Vivian still had not budged from his stool.

"The brooch?" Flora brushed her hand across her face as if cobwebs from the trunk room still had her in their filmy hold. "I don't know what happened to it."

"I meant the table, the one in your sitting room."

"Leaving it behind was rather like saying good-bye to another old friend; but never mind, it still has the clock and Grandpa's chair for company." Flora smiled. "And maybe when Mr. Tipp comes home, Sir Henry will reward him for all his long years of service by making him butler. And there will be more Sunday teas and other happy times in that room. You're looking sorry for me, Mr. Gossinger, and that's because I've given you entirely the wrong impression. It's true all the major stuff— the furniture and so on—didn't belong to Grandpa. But when I got older and interested in flea markets, I'd bring home my astonishing finds. All sorts of things—a cushion with a cup and saucer embroidered on it, barley-sugar twist candlesticks for the mantelpiece, and once an early Victorian photograph frame so Grandpa could put my mother's picture on the tallboy in his bedroom. That way those rooms really got to be ours, even though we couldn't change the furniture or the wallpaper. And when I came away I brought most of those bits and pieces of memory with me in my bigger suitcase, along with those bottles of Grandpa's silver polish."

"I wonder you had any room for clothes," said Vivian.

"Well, you can see what I did bring got horribly crushed." Flora looked ruefully down at the damson-colored ankle-length dress which, along with the clunky shoes on her feet, had been another of her flea market finds. "I suppose I should have taken an iron to this, but I didn't want to keep you waiting when . . . when it was time to say good-bye and thank you for everything you've done, Mr. Gossinger, to see me settled into my new home."

"I'm sorry," Vivian stood up and nudged the stool under the sink, "but that wasn't the plan. I don't want to come off sounding abominably stuffy, Flora, but I think you may have had a little too much orange juice last night. Otherwise you would remember you promised to let me show you the flea market where I've been working these last few weeks."

"But . . ." Flora could have kicked herself for ranting on about her treasure hunts among the stalls, and at the same time she could not prevent a little spurt of pure happiness.

Vivian feigned disheartenment. "I expect you don't take my efforts to make something of myself seriously. You see me as just another member of the wastrel set, a chip off my forebear Sir Rowland's block, just playacting at making a living."

"That's not it!" replied Flora with surprising fierceness.

"Then you're worried about what your grandfather would say if he were here about your spending the day with me."

"Well . . ." There was that and the fact it was impossible not to wonder how many minutes, let alone seconds, there were in a day and how they could be stretched like a rainbow across the sky.

"And that's rubbish," Vivian told her, "because Hutchins was the most sensible of men and as such would have understood that I need to talk to you about matters that affect the reputation of the Gossinger Family."

"What do you mean?" Flora was startled into taking the two steps necessary to reach him. Without realizing what she did, she stretched out a hand to straighten his jacket collar. And by the time she got round to blushing it was too late because there was so much else to think about.

"That boy, Edna Smith's grandson Boris . . ." said Vivian.

"What about him?"

"It's clear, isn't it, that he's not been his usual self since that school trip to Gossinger."

"Meaning?"

"That," Vivian took hold of Flora's hand without either of them appearing to notice, "perhaps Boris saw or heard something that afternoon which has left him wondering about your grandfather's death and whether he might have done something to prevent it. We'll talk about all of this later out in the fresh air," Vivian said in a soothing voice while propelling her through the opening into the shop.

"No, I think we should discuss it now."

"Absolutely not. You look like you're about to faint."

"That's only because it's awfully stuffy in here." Flora wriggled away from him. "The windows won't have been opened since the last people left."

"No wonder I'm seeing spots in front of my eyes," Vivian was saying as they crossed the bare shop, then the jingle-jangle of the bell sounded and someone pushed the door open from the outside. "Stupid of me!" He grimaced. "I forgot to lock it when I came back in."

"Hello there! I bring greetings to our new neighbor!" The person standing at the threshold beaming at them was a middle-size man with the sort of tan that you don't get in England unless you were born with it courtesy of the genes that come from warmer climes. "I am Banda Singhh, very pleased to meet you, from down the road. Fish-and-chip shop, you know! Best in this neck of the woods. You must come and try some, on the house."

"That would be lovely." Flora hurried to shake Mr. Singhh's outstretched hand, suddenly feeling that the world was a lot less scary. "And it was so kind of you to come round."

"Yes, it was." Vivian took his turn pumping Mr. Singhh's hand while introducing himself and Flora, who had forgotten to do so.

"My wife, she would have come but she is cleaning out the chip baskets and shooshed me out the door. But I am to say you will like it here on Wishbone Street." Mr. Singhh's smile stretched even wider. "We came here straight from Pakistan and like it very much. Lots of very pleasant people, like one big happy family if you don't count Mr. Grundy who is not the sort to do more than pass the time of day. Poor fellow," Mr. Singhh now looked sad, "he has a bad back and a daughter who looks down her nose at him because he sells naughty underwear in his shop. A man has to earn his living, is what I tell him and now I must return to the grindstone before I find myself out of a job. My wife, Emel, she does not stand for too much slacking. You understand?"

"Absolutely," agreed Vivian while Flora nodded.

"But remember," Mr. Singhh was heading cheerfully out the door with a sideways wave of the hand, "do not hesitate to ask if there is anything Emel and I can do to be of assistance. Big or small, it is yours for the asking."

"What a nice man," said Flora as his footsteps retreated.

"With a prize of a wife by the sound of it," replied Vivian, picturing the woman up to her elbows in greasy water scrubbing out the chip pans.

"I think he got the impression we are both living here," Flora was saying when the door jangled open again and Mr. Singhh popped his head back inside.

"Sorry to make a nuisance of myself," his smile was still out in full force, "but Emel would hit me over the head with a bottle of our finest malt vinegar if I returned without asking what sort of shop you will be setting up to do our happy neighborhood proud."

"I'm not renting the shop." Flora couldn't help but sound apologetic. "Just the flat upstairs. The building belongs to Mr. Gossinger's aunt."

"She was formerly Mabel Bowser," Vivian informed Mr. Singhh, "who grew up here with her sister Edna—now a Mrs. Smith—when their parents had the premises."

"Yes, I know all about that!" The other gentleman looked as pleased as if he had been appointed Lord Mayor of London. "Emel, she is acquainted with this Mrs. Smith, a lady's hairdresser, quite good I believe. They worked together on the church bazaar last week. We don't go to the church—Methodist, I think it is—but we like to be friendly, you understand. All of us hoping to go to the same place, isn't that right? But not too soon, please!" Mr. Singhh put his hands together and looked so soulful Flora had to laugh.

"Think about reopening the shop," he told her, "and you, sir," inclining his head toward Vivian, "talk if you please to your aunt, tell her Wishbone Street does not look its best with one of its teeth blacked out. And now I will go away, before you get cross and tell me never to come back wasting your time."

"Wait a minute, please." Flora followed Mr. Singhh

out into the street. "I want you to know you could never be a nuisance, and there's something else . . ." she raised her voice as a bus rumbled past. "Would you happen to know what the shop was called when Mr. and Mrs. Bowser had it?"

"Ah, there's a question better suited I think to my son, who turned himself into an historian and went to work at the British Museum. A father must have his little boast, you understand?" Mr. Singhh nodded his head over his steepled fingers as a mother with a couple of toddlers in tow brushed past him on their way down the street.

"It was a secondhand shop in those days," prompted Flora.

"You forgive the slowness of my brain! It was before my time, you see. And businesses change hands as often as our friend Mrs. Smith gives haircuts." Mr. Singhh now pressed his fingers to his forehead and clicked his teeth together. "Ah, yes, it comes back to me, I think. It was called 'The Silver Teapot.' "

Flora was tempted to kiss him, but was afraid that might be against his religion—which, as it happened, was Church of England.

After watching him make his way down the street, she went back inside to find Vivian checking the bolts on the door.

"I expect you're wondering why I didn't ask Edna Smith about all that last night," she said. "But I didn't think about it at the time. It's true I will be having tea with her tomorrow, but suddenly it seemed important to know now. Because when you grow up in a house with a name, you get to think of places in a very personal sort of way. And it seemed—well, almost rude to keep thinking of my new home as a set of street numbers."

"But the shop has probably changed names several times since the Bowsers were here. What makes you think," Vivian stopped fiddling with the bolts to smile at her, "that it still wants to be called The Silver Teapot?"

"I don't know." Flora looked around at the empty walls as if seeing something written on them in a fairy hand. "Except that it seems strange in an enchanted sort of way that it should have had that name when your Aunt Mabel was here as a girl, and she should have afterward come to Gossinger where silver has played such an important role from the days of Sir Rowland right down to the present day." Turning to find Vivian looking at her in a very thoughtful manner, she added, "I mean that the Gossinger collection is still talked about as a talisman against evil days. And it works, you have to admit that. People pay money to view the house in good part because they want to see the silver, which is why . . ." her voice dwindled to a thread, "Grandpa was always so particular about its cleaning and why he made up his own polish. Oh, I am being ridiculous! Rattling on to you about your own . . . or what will be your own home one day."

"That sort of talk has an aging effect on me, and it's not even noon," Vivian said somewhat curtly. "Let's get out of here, before something or someone else happens to stop us. Fortune smiles." He closed the door firmly behind as they stepped onto the pavement. "It's warm enough that you don't need a coat at the moment and if the temperature drops you can borrow my jacket. No need to worry about wear and tear, it's paid for."

"What I am worried about," Flora stalled two feet behind him, "is that I didn't bring the key."

"It's right here." Vivian patted his pocket.

"And I left my handbag upstairs. . . ."

"Then you'll have to forget about powdering your nose."

"That's not the problem." Flora zigzagged around a group of people in order to catch up with Vivian. "I don't have any money for buses and I have no idea how far we are going."

"We are going to there and back to see how far it is," he said breezily, tucking her arm inside his as they passed a shopkeeper adjusting the awning above his entryway. "In other words, you and I, Flora Hutchins, are going to fritter away the day seeing the sights."

"But I thought we were going to your flea market."

"So we will, but we'll take the scenic route. Don't you want to see Westminster and Buckingham Palace?"

"I don't want you to get the sack."

"My boss is the understanding sort." Vivian smoothed down his hair, which kept getting blown about in the breeze. "Expects me when he sees me, that sort of attitude. Come on, he—or she—who hesitates is lost."

They were at a traffic light, which was green until they stepped off the curb; Flora felt a rush of exhilaration as they darted to the other side. Not only Vivian, but life itself was tugging at her, and she decided that this wasn't the moment to look back over her shoulder. She would allow herself the next few hours to not think about anything very much. Grandpa would think that wise. He wouldn't want me nursing my unhappiness every minute of the day, she thought, or feeling guilty for noticing that the sun is shining. And surely he would understand about Mr. Gossinger.

"You have to stop calling me that," Vivian said when they were sitting on the tube. "It makes me feel a hundred and five, besides which, it makes absolutely no sense after spending the night together."

"Would you please lower your voice." Flora spoke out of the corner of her mouth, very much aware that the woman on the other side of her was all ears. "Anyway, I couldn't possibly."

"Call me by my first name?" Now the man on the

other side of Vivian was listening under cover of his newspaper.

"Exactly."

"Why ever not?"

"Because—"

"Because you've got some silly idea that we come from different walks of life?"

"That wouldn't matter, at least not so much if Grandpa and I hadn't worked for your family." Flora got up and shook out the creases in her long skirt as the train got close to Oxford Circus. "And anyway, there's the other complication." She followed Vivian down the aisle.

"Which is?"

"That it would be like," Flora said as the doors opened and she skipped out onto the platform, "like calling Prince Charming Charlie."

"I didn't catch that." Vivian joined her after letting an elderly woman precede him off the train.

"Good! I mean, it doesn't matter." She really had to stop this giddy behavior before she made a complete idiot of herself. It was no excuse to claim that her world had been turned upside down and inside out. She had a lot to be thankful for: a place to live, the promise of friendly neighbors and even the hope of seeing dear Mrs. Bellows again, because looking at the stations listed on the chart inside the train she discovered that Ilford, where the old housekeeper now lived, was really very close.

"All right," Flora said as she and Vivian headed for the escalators, "I'll stop calling you Mr. Gossinger, if that's what you really want. But you have to promise—"

"Not to tell Aunt Mabel and Uncle Henry?"

"No, that you won't feel you have to keep me under your wing after today."

"You think you can take care of yourself, do you?"

Vivian glanced back over his shoulder at the press of people behind them as they rode the escalator up the exit. "Let me warn you," he now put his hands on her shoulders and spoke into her ear, "life has a way of getting complicated in London; not so long ago I was in the area of the palace, just minding my own business, and found myself in the thick of an antiroyalist rally. Thank God my picture didn't end up in the papers or Uncle Henry, avid monarchist that he is, would have ordered me never to darken his doors again."

"Yes, he and Grandpa shared that—their devotion to the Queen."

"Those two had quite a bit in common." Vivian resisted the urge to again turn his head, but the feeling that someone was watching them while being careful to keep out of sight wouldn't go away. He told himself that his imagination was playing havoc with his common sense, that he was probably reacting to nothing more than a prickling under his skin and the idea that there had been one person too many sitting behind a newspaper on the tube. Still, he had to restrain himself from gripping Flora's shoulders protectively. "Tell me, is seeing Buckingham Palace top on your list today after we take a walk down Oxford Street?"

"It was, but now I don't want this to end—riding the escalator, I mean. The only time I came to London before was when Grandpa brought me up to see Father Christmas at Selfridge's when I was five or maybe six. I remember I wore a royal blue dress with a hat to match and Grandpa had his umbrella. And the best part of that whole day," Flora looked at the people gliding past on the other side, "was riding the magic staircases— that's what I thought they were—and they seemed because I was so small to go up forever. And when we got to the top Grandpa let me go down again. Several times."

"Is that what you would like to do now?" Vivian asked as they stepped onto solid ground.

And he was rewarded not only by her bewitching smile but the realization that if someone were indeed following them, that person might begin to wonder if it were he, or she, who was the one losing touch with reality while going up and down the escalators at Oxford Circus.

TWELVE

"I'm afraid it's not Buckingham Palace," said Vivian when he and Flora were sitting in a crowded but scarcely up-market café on a side street, which had recommended itself by being the one where they had got off the bus after sight-seeing most of the afternoon.

"It's perfect," she assured him, picking up her knife and fork. "I love places where you can get sausage and mash and real onion gravy."

"But something's bothering you."

"You'll laugh," Flora speared a piece of sausage, "but I can't help feeling sorry for the Queen. I don't suppose she ever gets to eat real food in places like this that are packed full of life. And if you want to know, whilst I loved Westminster Abbey and the Houses of Parliament, I didn't like Buckingham Palace one bit. Of course I've seen it on television, but that's not the same as being there, is it? I thought it looked like a prison, with the guards there to make sure no one ever got out, rather than the other way round."

Vivian raised his teacup. "Here's hoping they've done a good job of fixing up the inside. It's amazing what a roll or two of carpeting will do for a place."

"I think we should offer a toast to Mrs. Much."

"That's right, she went to work there, didn't she? And for her sake let's hope she doesn't get the urge to wash the royal tapestries. Uncle Henry admitted to not being very pleased when he found out she'd given one of William Rufus out hunting in the New Forest a good rub-a-dub-dub." Vivian chuckled.

"Well," Flora swallowed a forkful of mashed potatoes, grilled onions, and gravy, "I don't suppose he was any more furious than Grandpa. Even Mr. Tipp's eyes got big when he heard what Mrs. Much had done. In a horrid sort of way, it was lucky for her that Grandpa wasn't around when it came time for her reference. Sir Henry always wrote them in accordance with Grandpa's assessment, you know." Laying down her knife and fork, Flora watched Vivian cut into his mushroom omelet. "Talking about that day when Grandpa died," she managed to keep her voice level, "we never finished discussing Boris and what it could be that has got him so disturbed. And there is something odd about that, considering you don't expect a child to get all worked up about the death of an elderly man he didn't even know. To be honest, I don't know that I could blame a group of schoolboys for thinking it rather a joke, in the best macabre tradition, that a butler was found stuffed down a medieval toilet. Think how many people, grown-ups many of them, get a spooky thrill out of visiting the Chamber of Horrors at Madame Tussaud's. So, given the circumstances, I think you could be right about Boris having seen or heard something at

Gossinger that has him thinking he might have done something to help Grandpa."

"And I think I may have been making a mountain out of a molehill," said Vivian, no longer feeling inclined to finish his omelet. "For all we know, Edna Smith could have been reaching into the old excuse bag in saying that Boris has been a different boy since that visit to Gossinger, because in true grandmotherly fashion she was embarrassed by his rudeness last night. Or, if there is something else bothering the boy, it could be something as simple as his having got into trouble with his teacher."

"Mr. Ferncliffe. It's easy for me to remember his name because I saw him again on the train coming up to King's Cross. Life is full of coincidences, isn't it?"

"Absolutely," agreed Vivian. "That's my point entirely, that whatever upset Boris, if anything did, had nothing to do with your grandfather's death, except that it may have happened to occur on the same day."

"You really believe that?" Flora shifted her chair as a waitress squeezed past with a loaded tray.

"No, I don't." Vivian shot her a troubled look. "I'm talking out the back of my head because I want to get off the subject and back to seeing you smile. You did put your unhappiness aside for a little while, didn't you?"

"Oh, yes!" Flora laid her hand on his without thinking for a second that doing so was again crossing that invisible line. "It's been a day I will always remember. The sort you wrap up in tissue paper and put away in a scented drawer, so you can take it out again afterward and find it still fresh and lovely. I can't thank you enough for Big Ben and St. Paul's, and perhaps most of all for agreeing to sit upstairs on the buses. Whenever I thought of Grandpa today it was in a happy sort of way, remembering how he managed to turn even ordinary outings to the fishmongers, or the shoe shop and such, into exploring expeditions."

"I'm glad." Vivian now covered her hand with his free one. "So how about we leave it that way with both of us having a good time?"

"Because now that I've started thinking about Boris I can't put *him* in a drawer," said Flora, shaking her head. "I haven't forgotten what it's like to be his age and have something awful on your conscience. Suppose he did know Grandpa was in dire straits and did nothing to help him? That could easily give him nightmares and make him behave badly because he's so angry with himself that he wants to be punished, even if it's for something else, such as being rude to his grandmother."

"Let's think about this." Vivian poured them each another cup of tea. "What if Boris slipped away from the rest of the group that afternoon? Perhaps he heard Hutchins, who had been suddenly taken ill, banging on the garderobe door in hope of summoning help."

"It wouldn't have happened that way." Flora placed her elbows on the table and cupped her chin in her hands, the better to concentrate.

"You don't think your grandfather was taken ill?"

"Of course I do. What else explains what happened, if he didn't turn giddy or faint and bend over that . . . hole and grip the sides of the seat in an attempt to steady himself? What I meant was that he would never have banged on the door, not even to let someone know he needed help. It would have been completely out of character."

"Flora—"

"I know it sounds like nonsense. I'm sure it's hard for you to understand how he was, how strongly he felt that one of the primary reasons for him being put on this earth was to serve the Gossinger Family. Grandpa's entire working life was devoted to making sure that life flowed as smoothly as possible for Sir Henry and her

Ladyship. I remember Mrs. Bellows once dropped the kettle, splashing him with boiling water, and he was much more worried about tea being late than he was about being scalded. I had to sneak the doctor into the house when Grandpa wasn't looking. So you see it would have gone against everything he believed in to create an uproar by banging on the garderobe door," Flora kept her head up, looking steadily into Vivian's eyes, "even if he thought he was dying."

"You knew him better than anyone."

"Not as well as my grandmother of course, or even my mother perhaps, but they've both been dead such a long time, so for years it was just the two of us. And one thing I don't want," Flora removed her elbows from the table and turned her cup round in its saucer, "is for you to think that Sir Henry didn't appreciate Grandpa or treat him like a person with feelings, because that just isn't true."

"I won't argue that one with you," said Vivian. "I know for a certainty that Uncle Henry had a very high regard for your grandfather that went beyond that of an employer for someone who had worked for him a long time."

"And her Ladyship was also," Flora tried hard to be fair, "sometimes very appreciative. She told me once that if I followed in Grandpa's footsteps I might make something of myself. And I think she was truly sorry when he died."

Vivian didn't know how to respond to that statement. For the last week or so, he had been torn between thinking himself a fool for even considering the possibility that Lady Gossinger might have had a hand in Hutchins's death, and the next minute believing himself an even bigger idiot for accepting even for a moment that Hutchins's death had been an accident. It was just too convenient that the man was removed from the scene before Uncle Henry could change his will. Surely he wasn't the only one having suspicions. Vivian reached for the bill that the waitress placed on the table in passing. Uncle Henry might be an old tortoise, but he wasn't a fool. And neither for that matter was Cousin Sophie. They had to know that the police would have looked at matters in an entirely different light had they been informed about that conversation in the tower sitting room, and that Aunt Mabel had been beside herself with rage at the prospect of Hutchins inheriting Gossinger Hall.

"You've gone quiet," commented Flora.

"Sorry. I was thinking."

"What about?"

"One thing and another."

Vivian wanted very much to tell her that he had come to Wishbone Street last night to fill her in on everything he knew for fact: that Sir Henry had planned to change his will and in so doing might have precipitated Hutchins's death. He wanted to explain that he had decided to keep his mouth shut because she had looked so tired and woebegone. But only overnight. He had still fully intended to talk things over with her in the morning and extract a promise that she would be on her guard, because now that her grandfather was dead Uncle Henry was talking about leaving the house to Flora. Making her the one standing between her Ladyship and her hopes of queening it at Gossinger Hall after Sir Henry died. But when morning had come Vivian had backpedaled once more. What good would it do to frighten Flora? Wouldn't it make more sense just to keep an eye on her until he could discover, among other things, if Boris Smith knew something that would confirm Aunt Mabel's guilt?

"Has the cat got your tongue?" Flora laughed, but her eyes were worried.

"I'm back to thinking about the boy." Vivian brought her face back into focus and felt his head clear.

He had made the right decision. There was a lot he could do without sending this young woman into a panic. No, he wasn't ready to go to the police; he didn't have any evidence, and it wasn't likely they would keep Aunt Mabel locked up on suspicion alone. He had another moment of acute doubt. Was he jumping to conclusions because he fancied himself some kind of first-class private eye? Was he damning out of hand a woman who had never been anything but kind to him? One who, when it came right down to it, had reacted to the blow dealt her by Uncle Henry very much as any wife might have been expected to upon being told her husband was leaving the family home to the butler.

"What about Boris?" said Flora.

For a few seconds Vivian looked blank. "That's right, I was back to him, wasn't I? Okay, we've decided he didn't hear Hutchins . . . your grandfather pounding on the garderobe door, but we're still left with the possibility that he did hear or see something."

"Such as?"

"He might have heard a groan."

"I suppose so. . . ."

"Or he could have peeked into the garderobe and seen your grandfather doubled over clutching at the seat."

"Then why didn't Boris go for help?"

Vivian wanted to end this. "Maybe he had no idea your grandfather was in serious trouble. If he did hear a groan he might have thought someone—one of his classmates perhaps—was playing ghost, and if he did see something he may have thought that . . ."

"That Grandpa had eaten a bad piece of fish for lunch," Flora pressed her hands together, "or something of the sort. Yes, I can see that at the time Boris might have been more embarrassed than anything else at barging in where he wasn't supposed to be in the first place. And that afterward he would feel afraid as well as awful. Particularly if there had been another boy, or boys, with him who might spill the beans."

"Yes, I can picture Boris shivering under the bed-clothes at night," agreed Vivian, "scared out of his wits that there'll be a knock at the door followed by the tramp of policemen's feet as they come to arrest him."

"Poor boy!" Flora finished the dregs of her tea. "How would it be if I got in touch with Mr. Ferncliffe to sound him out, just in case he knows something? Because if there is something worrying Boris it needs to be brought out into the open, for his sake. And I'll admit I need to know anything there is to be learned about how Grandpa died. You see, I always believed I would be with him at the end, holding his hand and saying it was my turn to tell him a good-night story."

"Don't cry." Vivian leaned toward her.

"I'm not." Flora dashed a hand across her eyes. "Perhaps you should go and pay the bill. Those three women waiting for a table are looking daggers at us."

"I'll do that." Vivian got out of his chair, and upon returning from the cash register saw Flora standing outside the glass door.

She smiled up at him. "A little fresh air is all it takes. A couple of deep breaths and I'm myself again."

"I don't know that this air meets government health requirement standards." Vivian placed a hand on her back and guided her past a movie theater and a pawn-shop to the corner, where fellow pedestrians stood in a huddle waiting for the signal to cross.

"You're wrong about that." Flora stuck out the tip of her tongue. "I can taste all sorts of vitamins and miner-als. Oh, I do think," she smiled impishly up at him, "that I'm going to like London a whole lot. I want to drink everything in, the history all mixed up with the right now. So where are we going from here? To your flea market, or will it be shut down?"

"Not if we hurry." Vivian glanced at his watch as

they crossed at the light. "It's only four-thirty and if we can catch the right bus—Speaking of which," he reached for her hand, "there's one pulling up right now. How are you at the hundred-yard dash?"

"Catch me if you can." Flora sprinted ahead of him, unencumbered by her long skirt, and joined the tail end of the queue seconds ahead of him. There was a moment's concern when they thought they might not be able to get on because the bus was already standing-room-only. But two women with bulging shopping bags immediately ahead of them suddenly decided to wait for the number 98 because it took a more direct route to where they were going. So Flora and Vivian were able to squeeze on board.

"This is fun," she said as the bus took off and they stood swaying in the aisle. "I'm finding my sea legs already."

"Well, don't get too comfortable, we're getting off at the next stop but one. I suggest we count to fifty and start making our way to the front. Don't worry about trampling people to death in the process, that's the way it works in the big city—kill or be killed." Vivian immediately regretted this quip because it brought back all the doubts he'd been having about his role in Hutchins's death. And this was compounded by the return of the feeling he'd had at Oxford Circus: that someone, some bland, anonymous figure, was watching them under cover of a newspaper or oversize shopping bag.

"Here," he said, grabbing Flora's hand and jostling her in front of the bus driver, "it's time."

"You make it sound as if we have to walk the plank!" She turned her laughing face up toward him. "All right, never say I'm a coward. I'll hold my nose and jump." She suited action to words, and a second later Vivian joined her on the pavement.

"Sorry, but we'll have to hurry if I'm to show up for work today." Vivian cut a corner sharply and crisscrossed a couple of streets and an alley between tall buildings so that they came out in the center of the flea market.

There were stalls under green tent roofs on either side of the road and, Vivian explained to Flora, some of the merchants did business inside the arcade. The air was thick with the cheerful buzz of voices as the vendors talked back and forth or informed their customers that selling at these rock-bottom prices would soon put them out of business.

"I love these places." Flora hovered in front of a stall specializing in toby jugs.

"What did you say?" Vivian was jostled aside by two women arguing over whether a piece was the genuine article or if the spider-web cracking in the glaze proved it was imitation.

"Early Woolworth's, that's what I say," insisted the one in the cherry wool hat. "I'll get it anyway, just because I like the colors. Anyway, my daughter-in-law, that's who I'm buying it for, won't know the difference."

"I said," Flora let Vivian lead her away by the hand, "that I'm glad you brought me. Can we come back another day when we've more time to browse?"

"You've forgotten that my idea was to find you a job here with my boss, if you like him enough to stand on your feet all day getting people to invest in cake stands and grape scissors."

"I haven't forgotten," said Flora as they passed by a stall with an eye-catching array of art deco hat pins and ivory-handled buttonhooks, presided over by a youngish woman in a plaid coat with masses of hair piled untidily on top of her head and a voice like a foghorn. "Oh, this one looks interesting!" She stopped, captivated by a blue enameled table, set out between flowered chamber pots and brass door knockers. "You never know what you will find crammed in among the junky stuff of this sort of setup."

"Actually," Vivian said, "this is where I work when I remember to show up."

"That's about it," rasped an unfriendly voice. Flora saw a huge man with a completely bald head and ruddy complexion ambling over from one of the other stalls to stand behind the chamber pots. She also thought she heard a small growl, but that could have been because the bald man definitely looked as though he was getting ready to bite someone. He jerked an enormous thumb in Vivian's direction. "I don't know why I keep the blighter on. Can't be for the good of my health because I get a pain in the you-know-where every time I see his stupid mug."

"I work hard when I'm here," Vivian answered cheerfully. "Come on, George, admit it—you love me like a brother."

"I'll say." The big man pulled a toffee from his shirt pocket, unwrapped it and shoved it into his mouth with the look of someone taking a tablet to stave off a heart attack. "My brother Bert isn't worth spit, got himself engaged to the woman I was seeing and had the nerve to ask if I'd loan him the money for the honeymoon. Not that she was any great loss!" George was talking out of the side of his face that wasn't bulging with toffee. "Bah! Who needs women? Nothing personal, you understand." He winked at Flora. "But give me a four-legged female any day."

"Was that a dog I heard a moment ago?" she asked, dragging her eyes away from the tempting rows of merchandise.

"Well, it sure as hell wasn't *me* making cooing noises to attract the customers." George bent down behind the counter, and when he reappeared he was holding a squirming bundle of rough-coated small dog with ears standing to attention. "This here is Nolly, son and heir of my little Samantha who's stayed home today."

"Oh, he's a darling!" Flora stretched out her arms impulsively. "Is he a Norfolk terrier?"

George glowered at Vivian. "You've got yourself a smart one. Which means you're not likely to hold on to her for long. Truth is, miss," he handed her the small dog, who had his paws out in anticipation, "his father was a mutt, but Samantha is a Norfolk, got the papers to prove it. She had three pups. Two bitches that I found homes for right off the bat, and Nolly here. I decided to keep him so he could be a comfort to his mum in her old age. But trouble is, they don't hit it off, not since he became a teenager."

"Oh, don't tell me he's a juvenile delinquent!" Flora nuzzled her face into the dog's fur.

"Can't trust him an inch." George shook his head. "Mouths off all the time, comes in at all hours, in with the wrong crowd, you name it."

"Wears a leather jacket and rides a motorcycle," Vivian added to the little fellow's list of sins. "The only thing you can say for him is that he shows up for work on time most days."

"I have to bring him along because he can't be left to his own devices." George folded his arms and scowled more fiercely than ever. "The last time I tried it he ate three cushions and a bar of soap. And with him not getting along with his mum, she's the one who's stuck home these days watching soap operas on the telly."

"What a tragic story," Flora said while getting her face frantically licked and looking at a particular piece of merchandise on the table.

"It could be worse." Vivian handed her a tissue. "At least George hasn't wheedled me into taking the little monster in lieu of wages."

"Oh, I'm sure Daddy would never part with you."

Flora used the tissue to dab at Nolly's eyes, which did appear to have moistened with tears.

"I might do just that," George now looked thoughtful, "if I could find him a good home. I think part of his trouble is that he's more of a woman's dog, likes to be petted and pampered, and as you might gather I'm not much for that sort of thing. No-frills-George, that's me."

Flora's eyes shone. "Do you mean it? You really would let him go to the right person?"

"My type of woman, an impulse buyer," said the big bald man with a man-to-man wink at Vivian.

"It's not an impulse, I've *always* wanted a dog! Sir Henry told Grandpa to get me one when I was little, but Mrs. Bellows was deathly afraid of them, so that was that. Oh, if you're not just pulling my leg, do please let me have him! I'll be so good to Nolly, and you can see him whenever you want."

"Sounds like my lucky day."

"Flora, think about this," protested Vivian, torn between amusement and concern. "George says Nolly can't be left alone without dire results. So what happens when you go out to work? I've been thinking," he addressed his boss, "that you might be able to use her here. No problem with references, I can supply glowing ones, and she does know quite a bit about antiques. Silver being her specialty."

"Is that so?" George scratched his chin.

"He's exaggerating; it's just that I grew up around it in Mr. Gossinger's uncle's house and have an interest. For example," Flora shifted Nolly into the crook of her right arm, "I've been looking at that teapot because it's the genuine thing, isn't it? Early Georgian, I mean? And, well, it has given me this shining inspiration."

"Which is?" Vivian raised an eyebrow.

"Remember," Flora turned toward him, her face full of sunlight even though clouds now obscured most of the sky, "Mr. Banda Singhh told us that the shop on Wishbone Street used to be called The Silver Teapot when Lady Gossinger and her sister Mrs. Smith lived there? Well, what I would like to do is stay at home, with Nolly for company, and start another secondhand business, under the same name. Doesn't that sound lovely?"

THIRTEEN

"I feel awful," said Flora as she and Vivian cut down the alley across from the flea market, with Nolly trotting cheerfully between them on his lead. "I never really expected George to make me a present of our friend here. But being a man, your boss probably decided that because I didn't have a handbag with me I must be totally impoverished."

"Or a recovering shop-aholic."

"That's unkind. I admit Nolly was a compulsion, but as a rule I am a very disciplined shopper."

"I'm sure that's true. After all, you didn't buy that teapot."

"Well, I couldn't afford it." Flora scooped up Nolly, who had started to yap at a poodle, making rude remarks about its haircut, forcing its owner to cut a wide berth. "Which was a shame, because it would have been a lovely talisman for the shop."

"Serves you right," said Vivian unsympathetically, "for telling George what it was worth; before that he hadn't a clue. And was asking how much?"

"Thirty pounds, but it would have been stealing to buy it for that, especially after he had given me Nolly," Flora said firmly.

"And one good turn deserves another, although I'm willing to bet George got the best of it."

"You're talking about my pride and joy." Flora set the little dog back on his feet and let him drag her toward a lamppost where he promptly asserted his territorial rights.

"No offense intended! I take your word he's a paragon!" Vivian nipped smartly aside as Nolly toddled toward him with the look of someone who had taken serious umbrage. "I'm sure he will mature into a pillar of his community, maybe take up politics and end up sitting in the House of Lords."

"Oh, I don't think he has those sorts of aspirations." Flora took a firmer hold on the lead. "After all, he comes from working people on one side of the family. And if he moved too far up in the world he'd have to worry about dogs with *proper* pedigrees looking down their noses at him."

"You have to stop that sort of thinking."

"Why?"

"Because it makes me long to hit you over the head with my rolled umbrella and bowler hat and I left both of them at home," said Vivian, as they made their way past shops where "Closed" signs were popping up all over the place, seconds before the lights went out and the iron grilles came rattling down. "Besides, I think you need to be directing all your thought processes to how you are going to stock your shop."

"The Silver Teapot, doesn't it have a lovely sound?"

A smile turned up the corners of Flora's mouth, adding a dimple to her left cheek, but immediately her eyes turned serious. "Oh, it's probably all wishful thinking. And cheeky to boot, because I haven't even spoken to Lady Gossinger about it."

"There hasn't been much time, given the fact that you only got the idea half an hour ago. Nobody but an ass would accuse you of dragging your feet in getting in touch with Aunt Mabel, although I do have to point out that we did pass a phone box on that last corner."

Nolly gave a little grunt to show what he thought of this pathetic jest, and hugged close to Flora's ankles to let her know he was hers, body and soul. "I was so fired up," she said, "that I didn't bother to think that Lady Gossinger might not at all like the idea of a complete novice as a tenant."

"You're far from that." Vivian got on the other side of Nolly and slipped an arm around Flora's shoulders. "Uncle Henry was always talking about the wonderful job you did with the gift shop at Gossinger."

"I was only helping Mrs. Warren."

"Now this is absolutely no time for false modesty. They didn't start making any money worth talking about until you got in on the act. In addition to the other stuff you brought in, think of all the silver polish you sold. Uncle Henry said it was impossible to keep on the shelf."

"That doesn't count because it just sold itself," said Flora. "People would come back again and again, filling up shopping bags with half a dozen bottles at a time if they had to travel a long distance. There's nothing like it on the market when it comes to removing tarnish without leaving any of that horrid white stuff. And of course visitors could see for themselves the superior shine it gives just from looking at the Gossinger silver collection."

"You see, you're a born salesperson! I'll take a standing order, whether or not there's a discount for buying in bulk." Vivian slackened his pace. Despite the clouds blanketing the sky, it was not chilly enough to make their walk unpleasant. "I have a couple of elderly female relatives whom I never know what to give for birthdays and Christmas, and I'm sure they would appreciate some relief from the usual bottles of lavender water and jars of bath salts. But let's get back to the matter of Aunt Mabel. Why don't you let me talk to her?"

"Because I refuse to hide behind your trousers." Flora stuck out her chin. "She might have trouble saying 'no' to you and that wouldn't be fair. I have to approach this in a businesslike manner and hope that she doesn't want too much rent."

"Then let's suppose that all works out," Vivian responded cheerfully, "how are you going to set up stocking The Silver Teapot? I know you said you have a little money from your grandfather, but will that be enough?"

"Have you ever been in a secondhand shop?"

"Of course!"

"We're not talking about classy antique places," Flora informed him crisply. "More on the lines of Oxfam, with the difference being that instead of the proceeds going to charity, I will be the lucky beneficiary in this case. What I'll do is talk to people like George and find out the names of suppliers of cheap but cheerful stuff—like oil lamps and china dogs. That will keep me going until I can get into what I really like."

"Such as silver?"

"That would be the ultimate." Flora bent to pat Nolly who was suddenly tugging on his lead in an attempt at going in the opposite direction. "Oh, dear, do you think he's homesick already? What's a mother to do?"

"Ask him if he'd like to stop for fish-and-chips."

"I don't think it's right to make empty promises."

"Flora, he's a dog. But if you must be so sensitive to his feelings I'm prepared to follow through, although you don't suppose he would prefer a curry?"

Nolly, having taken another sideways lunge, growled, and Vivian hastily said, "Fish-and-chips it will be."

"Oh, good!" Flora beamed at them both. "Because all this talk of high finance has me starving and I remember you didn't finish your omelet, Vivian. Do you want to go in there?" She pointed to a fish-and-chip shop three doors down. "Or would you rather wait until we get back to Bethnal Green and go to Mr. Singhh's place?"

"This is fine." Vivian disappeared inside the door, leaving Flora waiting on the pavement with Nolly. "What'll it be?" He stuck his head back out. "Haddock or cod?"

"Haddock, please."

"Why not? Considering you can write the meal off as a business expense. Vinegar on your chips?"

"Uhhmm!" Flora thought this one over.

"Don't tell me you have to ask Nolly or I'll start pulling out my hair."

"Vinegar, please."

Seconds later Vivian was back out on the pavement, handing over one of the two newspaper-wrapped bundles. "Is something wrong?" he asked as they walked, with Nolly doing a sideways trot, toward a bench screened by a tree overhanging a wall adjacent to the bus stop. "Come on, I can tell there's something wrong," he persisted as they sat down. "That's a frown masquerading as a smile on your face."

"It's not the food." Flora began unwrapping her package and inhaling the delicious hot oily smell of battered fish and chunky chips with crispy golden bits from previous fryings sticking to them. "This is going to be wonderful!" She broke off a piece of haddock, blew on it to cool it down, and handed it to Nolly who gobbled it down with the sort of show-off bad manners that would induce a man to tuck his serviette into his neck at an ultraposh restaurant. Then Nolly went back to looking over his shoulder and Flora followed his gaze, while saying to Vivian that he was going to think her stupid.

"About the shop?"

"No, not about that, although I know you would be justified. It's just that I don't think what's unsettling Nolly is that he wants to go scurrying back to the flea market and George. I know this sounds boastful, but I really do think he has taken to me in a big way."

"Who could blame him?" Vivian handed her a chip. "But I don't understand. What do you think is wrong with Nolly?"

"I think his protective instincts are up."

"Meaning?"

"He's got this silly idea," Flora offered Nolly another piece of fish, "that someone is following us. You don't have a jealous girlfriend, do you, Vivian? I'm sorry—I shouldn't have said that."

"Forget it." Vivian sounded decidedly curt, because now *his* protective instincts were aroused as he looked up and down the street. "Why would you take any notice of a dog? Especially one that looks as if he has fluff for brains."

"Because I had that same feeling, just before we got to the fish-and-chip shop. You know how sometimes you'll see a shadow out of the corner of your eye, and the moment you look round, it darts the other way. Nothing as solid as a real shape, but just enough to make you think someone is there. . . ."

Nolly gave a woof of agreement, but Vivian couldn't bring himself to sound as though he put much stock in Flora's feeling of unease. He hadn't sensed anything wrong, not since that morning at Oxford Circus, and he now made up his mind that he had been programmed by his concern for Flora's safety to imagine things. Why on earth would Aunt Mabel—even if she had murdered Hutchins—stalk Flora across London? No, it made no sense.

"You think I'm in an overwrought emotional state, prone to all sort of weird thinking. And I suppose you're right," Flora said and dug back into her fish-and-chips, making sure that Nolly got his fair share.

"I'm glad to see you haven't lost your appetite," Vivian said and they munched companionably for several minutes until a bus turned the corner. Getting hastily to his feet, he balled up their wrapping paper and tossed it into a conveniently placed bin before saying, "This is ours. It'll take us to within a few minutes' walk of Wishbone Street."

"I hope Nolly likes buses." Flora scooped up the dog and almost tripped over the trailing lead when climbing aboard the bus. "Shall we sit at the front so we can get off quickly if he gets sick?"

"I could ask the bus driver if they have any of those little bags that you get on planes in case of emergency." Vivian sat down beside her and lowered his voice. "But he didn't look like an animal lover to me." This lack was more than made up for by the woman with half a dozen shopping bags piled between her knees and her chin, who managed despite these restrictions to make cooing noises at Nolly. The dog promptly buried his face in Flora's skirts.

"We"—the plural just slipped out—"only got him today," Flora told the woman as she stroked him, "so it's understandable that he's a bit shy."

"They always are when you first get them," came the kindly reply. "I've had dogs all my married life and you'd think butter wouldn't melt in their mouths the first few days. But once they're sure you're going to

keep them, the honeymoon's over, and they'll start test-
ing your patience just like children. Do you have any
little ones at home?"

"No." Flora didn't dare meet Vivian's eyes.

"I was just picturing happy little faces and eyes getting all big with excitement when you walked in the
door with your surprise."

"We're not . . ." The bus swung wide around a
corner, in danger of mowing down several cars; Flora
had to make a grab for Nolly before he went flying off
her lap.

"We're not," Vivian completed the sentence for her,
"expecting our first child for a few months, and we can
hardly wait. So we thought we'd get the dog to break
ourselves in, isn't that right, dear?"

"A baby, how lovely!" exclaimed the woman,
readjusting her parcels.

"I was surprised, too," was all Flora could manage.

"No one ever told her where babies come from,"
Vivian said cheerily. This got a laugh from the woman
and a scowl from the supposed mother-to-be as Vivian
got to his feet. "Hold on to me, Flora." He extended a
hand to her. "We don't want you falling if the bus gives
a lurch before it comes to a stop."

"You really are the limit," she told him when they
were back on firm ground and Nolly was woofing to
get down. "Fancy telling a bunch of lies to that nice
woman; look, she's waving at us out the window."

"She wanted us to be a couple with dreams for the
future, so why disappoint her? I expect if there had
been more time she would have asked for our address
and sent us some hand-knitted bootees."

Flora tugged on the lead and marched ahead, nose in
the air. "Come on, Nolly. Now we'll never be able to
believe a word Mr. Gossinger says, and it is a terrible
thing when trust is broken between people."

"In other words, the pregnancy is off?"

"Definitely." It was impossible to repress a smile as Vivian fell in step beside her. They had just passed the block of council flats where Edna Smith and her grandson Boris lived when a man's voice spoke suddenly from behind them.

"Excuse me," the voice was as soft as a tap on the shoulder, "but would it offend if I had a word with you?"

"With me or the lady?" Vivian pounced around on the speaker, which was strictly speaking Nolly's job, but the wretched dog actually wagged his tail in greeting.

"Do I know you?" Flora looked into the man's face. A faint sense of recognition stirred, before slipping away. The gentleman—for he had yet to prove himself otherwise—wore a tweed cap and a sporting sort of jacket with a mustard tie. As for the rest of him, there wasn't much to say; he was in every way quite ordinary. *That's the only way I could describe him to the police,* she thought, gathering Nolly into her arms, *if he should suddenly pull out a knife or a gun and Vivian and I had to fight for our lives to get away.* She was wishing rather desperately that she was wearing one of her 1920's cloche hats so she could yank out a hat pin, preferably one of the rusty ones, should he try any funny stuff.

"Look here," Vivian stepped in front of her, fists clenched at the ready as he addressed the man, "have you been following us for most of the day?"

"Heaven forbid!" The response came in quite a jolly voice. "If you won't take offense—that is to say any more than you clearly have done already—I've had better things to do with my time. I've been putting in an honest day's work at the races. Made a bundle, by the way, and to celebrate my good fortune I'd like to invite Miss Hutchins to the pub—there's quite a decent one nearby—for a drink and a chat."

"Then we have met before?" asked Flora.

"On two occasions, as I am happy to remember."

The gentleman smiled broadly, showing teeth that certainly didn't look as though they belonged to the big bad wolf.

"I'm sorry . . . you'll have to remind me of where and when I made your acquaintance."

"Flora," Vivian took hold of her arm and tried to draw her on down the street, "he's feeding you the oldest line in the book."

"But he does know my name," Flora protested.

"Which of course means nothing," the man interjected smoothly before Vivian could do so. "I could have found out who you are, Miss Hutchins, from a neighbor or shopkeeper. Easiest thing in the world."

"Now he's trying to con you with apparent sincerity that he's on the level, but I'm not buying it."

"But this has to do with me," said Flora, "and I don't see any harm in going to the pub with him. There's usually safety in numbers, and I do admit I'm curious. . . ."

"He hasn't even told you his name." Vivian resented having to come off like a heavy-handed father.

"I know, and I understand why you're worried," Flora moved closer to him, "but you see I *do* have this feeling that I've met him before—"

"Then why can't he say who he is, right this minute?" Vivian glowered at the man. "Instead of making a mystery of it in order to lure you off to some pub? If in fact that's where he intends taking you."

"Because what I have to tell Miss Hutchins doesn't just involve ourselves, but a third party," the man said. "And she may find the situation calls for a drink."

"Is that so?" The ugly suspicion that had haunted Vivian ever since Hutchins's death now had him by the throat. Could this man be a plainclothes policeman? Come to probe Flora for information that would assist him in his inquiries? Vivian now cursed himself for not preparing her by voicing his own concerns. Instead, he'd played the knight in shining armor. Damn! He was worse than a fatuous fool, he was a heel! And Flora would hate him forever once she got past the horror of what she was about to learn about Aunt Mabel's reaction to Uncle Henry's will.

"You will come too, won't you?" She was looking at him with an appealing light in her smoky blue eyes as she hugged Nolly to her chin.

"What do *you* think?" he said, wishing he could kiss her right there on the street with people passing by and the copper—for that's what he surely was—taking notes.

"I'd really prefer to talk to Miss Hutchins alone," put in the other man. "Seeing that what I have to say to her is of a highly confidential nature."

"Well, that's too bad." Flora stood up as tall as was possible for her without wearing a hat. "Because if Mr. Vivian Gossinger doesn't come, neither do I. And that's final! There is nothing on earth you can't tell me in front of him, Mr. Question Mark."

"The lady always gets to choose." The man spread his hands in a gesture of capitulation and a few minutes later they were walking into the Blue Anchor, where the atmosphere was three parts slopped beer and two parts stubbed-out cigarettes. There was only room to inch sideways through the noisy throng and hope you didn't get jostled into the Ladies or Gents and get trapped inside until closing time. So there wasn't any opportunity to focus on the decor, but Flora didn't have the feeling of being transported back to the Boy and Fish where she had sometimes gone with her grandfather for a glass of cider on Sunday afternoons.

"Why don't the two of you find us a table," said the man, "and I'll get the drinks. What will it be?"

"A bitter lemon, please," said Flora, and Vivian said that he would have the same.

"Over there," Flora tugged at his arm, "those people

are just getting up. Nolly has been giving them the evil eye, which may have hastened their departure. Come on, before someone else grabs the space."

"I'm shuffling as fast as I can," Vivian told her. He narrowly missed getting hit in the eye by somebody brandishing a tankard while singing "Happy Birthday" in a loud, beery voice to an unseen entity. "Is it only me, or do you feel as though you're being compressed so you can go through the post?"

"I'm sitting down," Flora's voice floated toward him, "just two more steps to your right."

"Thank God, I was afraid I would never see you again." Vivian took his seat next to her under a broad window ledge filled with brass pots. "And I hope those plants aren't hogging more than their share of what little oxygen there is to go around."

"I think they're plastic."

"No, they're real ones grown to deceive the eye into thinking they are fakes."

"So people will forget to water them," Flora laughed, "and have to buy new ones?"

"Exactly," said Vivian, spilling out words in an attempt to stop himself from thinking about the ongoing nightmare of Hutchins's death. "The couple who run the market garden across from Gossinger were telling me, when I went across to buy Aunt Mabel a plant for her birthday, that it is getting harder to compete with the really good fakes."

"Have you ever minded about the Dower House and its grounds being leased?" Flora asked.

Whereupon Vivian was about to say his only regret was that it would have provided alternative accommodation for Lady Gossinger on her husband's death—which would have been getting onto a sticky subject. But he was stalled by the third in their party (not counting Nolly) approaching with a clutch of drinks in his hands.

"Here we are!" He set down the glasses and seated himself across from them. "To everyone's good health."

"And to the truth, please," said Flora. "Where *have* we met before?"

Vivian fully expected the man, now edging a finger around his foaming glass of bitter, to abruptly assume the manner of a professional policeman and explain that he had seen, perhaps spoken to, Flora at her grandfather's inquest. What he actually said was almost as upsetting.

"I'm the one you kindly gave a lift in your car, on the day of your grandfather's funeral," the man said. "Now don't leap out of your seats," he added, calmly sipping his beer. "I'm a reformed character."

"Since you robbed the bank at Maidenbury?" Flora gripped her glass of bitter lemon in both hands while Nolly sat very still on her lap, deciding—being occasionally a sensible dog—that this was not the moment to interrupt with the smallest woof.

"I know what you're thinking," said the man, as Vivian opened his mouth, "but believe me, that job doesn't count. I only took out my own money, all of which, if it will ease your minds, came from an honest source. A dear old auntie who left everything to me in the hope that I would behave myself if not short of the ready. Unfortunately, by way of some fancy footwork on the part of her lawyers, it was tied up while I was a guest of Her Majesty. And, yes, I will admit the fault, I don't have any patience with red tape."

"You're a crook!" Vivian closed the inch or two gap between him and Flora. In reward, he got a nip from Nolly.

"Recovering." The man produced a bland smile. "In fact I began to think seriously about entering the Church, but after trying it for a day I decided I could not take those tight collars and shiny black suits."

"It was you!" Flora exclaimed. "You were the priest

on the train to King's Cross! He was sitting next to Mr. Ferncliffe," she explained to Vivian, "Boris Smith's teacher, the one in charge of the school outing to Gossinger."

"A dull sort of fellow," the bank robber, alias man of God, said, "not at all your type, Miss Hutchins. I am sure your boyfriend here has nothing to worry about."

"You're the one who should be worried." Vivian leaned across the table. "The police are likely to be extremely interested when Flora and I pay them a visit and report our meeting with you."

The man shook his head. "Not a very Christian attitude. It makes me glad I decided against the Church. Here I am, breaking cover, because I wish to do Miss Hutchins a good turn. I appreciated her giving me a lift that day, and this is the thanks I get from you, sir."

"What sort of good turn?" Flora asked him.

"It has to do with a friend of mine."

"Go on," said Vivian, unable to put a lid on his curiosity.

"I'm talking about a fellow I got to know when we were both serving our country behind bars." He smiled blandly. "The way we looked at it, that was two more jobs, legal or otherwise, for the unemployed. My friend and I had been in the same line of business, con jobs, before going inside. Robbing the rich to help poor us is the way we'd looked at it. But after the first eighteen months or so we'd had enough of talking shop and neither of us was into woodwork; so naturally we shifted to personal stuff. And it was then that my friend —we'll call him Reggie, because that's his name—told me he was married to a great girl, but she died. Complications from asthma, I think it was. Anyway, Reggie'd get very down at times and blame himself for her death, because he was convinced that finding out what he'd been up to had put a strain on her heart."

"Why are you telling me this?" Flora asked him in a stifled voice.

"Because there was a child."

"And you are someone who likes to stir the pot," said Vivian, fighting down the urge to plant his fist in the other man's face.

"It was a little girl. After her mother's death she went to live with her maternal grandfather, who was butler at a place called Gossinger Hall, which I happened to know of because my old auntie, the one who died and left me the loot, lived not far from Maidenbury and liked to do her shopping and," again he smiled, "banking there."

"And you kept in touch with your friend?" Flora drew warmth from Nolly.

"He got out before I did, but he wrote and came to see me sometimes. I told you, Reggie was the right stuff, the sort to stick by his friends."

"But not the sort to stick by his daughter," Vivian said before he could stop himself.

"Or was it," Flora bit down on her lip, "that the grandfather of this girl insisted he stay away, because he thought that would be best for her?"

"No, that wasn't it. From what Reggie told me, the old man thought the girl was entitled to know the truth and to decide for herself whether or not she wanted contact with her father. He thought secrets were dangerous, but Reggie had made a promise to his wife, when she went back to her maiden name, that he would stay away from their daughter, so she would never have to know that he had been inside."

"Then why are you here?" Flora picked up her bitter lemon to demonstrate that her hands were quite steady.

"Because after you and I crossed paths I got hold of Reggie to tell him the grandfather was deceased and it might be time to forget some promise made under pressure and make up for lost time. He said he didn't think you'd want to know him, and I offered to come and . . ."

"Sound her out?" Vivian looked at Flora and got no response because she was staring into her drink as if it were a bottomless well.

"That was the idea," said the go-between. "Reggie wants you to feel free, Miss Hutchins, to see him or not as you see fit, but he also wants me to tell you that he thought about you always and sends his love."

"Are you going to tell us your name?" Flora needed time on safer ground.

"My friends call me Snuffy."

"I hope that's not," she managed to say severely, "because you've made your reputation snuffing out people."

"What a horrible thought!" He looked genuinely wounded. "I came by the name because I had an enthusiasm for snuff boxes in my youth. Still do for that matter, but I swear, I haven't added to my collection by unlawful means in a long time."

"Do you have any silver snuff boxes?" Flora discovered that if she channeled her thoughts straight ahead she could keep the shock of learning about her father in a separate part of her mind, to be taken out and mulled over when she stopped feeling as though she had taken a bullet between the eyes.

"As a matter of fact," Snuffy adjusted the knot in his mustard tie, "I have a couple of remarkably good Regency silver boxes, got them off a fence I used to know. An expert in all areas of the silver business. Worked in a museum at one time, I believe. But I've heard she's going straight these days, like myself and Reggie."

Vivian squeezed Flora's shoulder. "Perhaps he is, your father that is. I can't believe he's a heartless rascal, not with you for a daughter. It could be prison and your mother's death straightened him out. I've never been one to think a leopard can't change his spots."

But Flora got to her feet. "I think that I'd like to go home now. I appreciate the drink, Snuffy, and your kindness in finding me so we could have this talk . . ."

"About that," Vivian said to the other man while also getting to his feet, "how did you know where to catch up with her?"

"Nothing to it." Snuffy endeavored to look modest. "Miss Hutchins spoke on the train yesterday about coming to live in Bethnal Green in a flat above a vacant shop. So it was just a matter of putting my nose to the ground and sniffing out her tracks."

"So you did follow her!"

"Didn't have to, my dear fellow. A question here, another one there, is all this sort of thing takes."

Vivian didn't believe him, but chose not to stand and argue the point. It was clear Flora was desperate to get out of the pub, and so by the looks of him was Nolly, who indeed made a dash for the nearest lamppost the moment they were out the door.

Snuffy walked to the corner of Wishbone Street with them. "So," he said as they waited for the green light, "what would you like me to tell my friend Reggie, Miss Hutchins?"

"Ask him to come and see me tomorrow. In the daytime, that would be best, perhaps early afternoon, because I have to go out to tea at three. Unless," she bent down to restrain Nolly from pulling her into the road, "he would be at work at that time."

"I'm sure he can get round that if necessary." Snuffy tipped his tweed cap and was suddenly just another back mingling with those of other early-evening pedestrians heading toward the tube station.

"I don't want to talk," Flora told Vivian, "not yet." What she really wished was that he would go away. Because with him at her side it was impossible not to

wonder what he really thought about her being the
daughter of an ex-jailbird. It was one thing to believe
that she and Vivian could be friends of sorts despite
their different connections to Gossinger Hall, but this
altered everything. As they reached her door she wondered if Sir Henry and her Ladyship knew about her
background, and then was fiercely sure they didn't; she
had absolute trust in her grandfather that he would
never have shared her terrible secret with anyone else
whilst she was left in the dark.

"I'll have the door open in a jiffy." Vivian had produced the key and was inserting it in the lock.

"You don't have to come in." Flora was now able to
force her lips into a smile, although it made her face feel
as if it were about to crack. "Really, I'd rather you
didn't. You need to get back to your own life. And I'd
like to be alone until I can get used to the idea of not
being an orphan."

"Sorry, you're not getting rid of me that easily," Vivian told her. "Somehow—and you can put the arrogance down to my unfortunate background—I believe
we're in this together."

"You do have an undue sense of your own importance." Flora looked at him through suddenly wet
lashes.

"There's nothing undue about it," he said, switching
on the shop lights and pushing her gently through the
door. "You need me desperately."

"What do you mean?" She brushed a hand across
her eyes.

"You seem to have forgotten that Nolly does not live
by his looks alone. He has to eat. And it seems unlikely
to me that you brought any dog food along in one of
your cases."

"Oh, poor darling, what a wicked mother I am!"
Flora exclaimed. She dropped to her knees and cradled
the starving animal in her arms. "I don't deserve to be a

pet owner. Do you think there'll be a shop open?" she asked Vivian.

"You leave that to me. If there isn't, I may have to try to do some breaking and entering which at least would have the advantage of ensuring that you don't go accusing me of looking down my nose at your father."

"I never said anything like that," Flora said, stung.

"You don't have to." Vivian touched a finger to her cheek. "I can read your mind, my sweet."

What more was there to be said?

"Thank you," she murmured as Vivian headed for his car. "And don't run out of petrol, or forget to put the hand brake on when you park."

"He did that for me," said Flora, closing the door as his taillights disappeared down the street. "The dog food was just a lucky excuse so he could clear off for a bit and leave me to sort myself out. Isn't he the most special man in the whole world, Nolly? No, don't answer that! Tell me I have no business thinking about him in that sort of way, and that it isn't possible to fall in love with someone when you're a little girl and discover when you're all grown up that the man is even more wonderful than the handsome prince. That sort of thing is for fairy tales, and my life isn't turning out that way. How's that for self-pity?"

Nolly sat with his head tilted to one side, his ears adorable triangles and his heart in his eyes.

"I know what you are trying to say," said Flora. "It's that I should get you a bowl of water and some cheese crackers from that picnic basket on the counter. And that afterward I should think about what I'm going to say to my father, should he show up tomorrow. Oh, you think I should be guided by you, that if you try to take a nip out of his trouser leg I'm to take it he's not to be trusted. And if you snuffle all over him with enthusiastic kisses that will be the tip-off that he's truly sorry for everything that happened and all is forgiven. Am I right?"

Flora didn't have a bowl, but she did unearth a battered saucepan from the back of one of the kitchen cupboards, and while she filled it with water and set it down on the tile floor for Nolly to splash his face in, she thought about her mother, something she had trained herself not to do. Had she been terribly unhappy when she died, and was it fair for her mother to have extracted that promise from Reggie? *Oh, why didn't I ask Grandpa more about her when there was time? Poor Mummy!* Flora felt the tears lining her lashes. *How can I even think about blaming her for any of this? She just wanted to protect me, and what is kindest can't always be wise. Then again, maybe she was right.* Flora knew a moment of horror at the thought of her own father taking her away from Grandpa.

"Oh, you stupid girl!" she said out loud. "Instead of whimpering like a spoilt baby, you should be thanking your lucky stars for your wonderful, carefree childhood. No one ever had more in the way of love."

Flora went back into the empty shop, her mind a picture book of memories. *I didn't just have Grandpa,* she thought. *For a little while I had dear Mrs. Bellows to coddle me and tell me bedtime stories when he couldn't because Sir Henry had people for dinner. Those lovely stories about the Queen. Mrs. Bellows always made her seem so real—so that I understood, even though I was still a bit jealous when I was little, why Grandpa believed the sun rose and set on Her Majesty. And there was Sir Henry . . . He was never anything but kind, giving me toffees and encouraging me to make his home my castle. And I mustn't forget old Miss Doffit coming for visits and following me up to the trunk room, as eager as the child I was to dress up and pretend to be a duchess in crushed velvet cloaks and feather boas.*

"It was wrong of me," Flora stood and talked to

Nolly whose mustache was still dripping with water, "it was very wrong to blame Lady Gossinger because things changed after she came. After all, I couldn't expect to go romping through the house, sucking on toffees, my whole life long. If she never liked me much it was because I brought that on myself . . ."

She didn't get to finish cutting herself down to size because the shop door opened and Vivian walked in carrying a paper carrier bag. "What have you been doing?" he asked. "Deciding where you're going to put the shelves and what to put on them when you go into business?"

"No, I did a lot of soul-searching while you were gone. And I've decided that it's not the end of the world to find out I have a father who's been on the wrong side of the law. Maybe I'll like him, if he does show up, maybe not, but either way it won't matter all that much, because he didn't bring me up."

"And he can't change anything about who you are."

"Only to people on the outside, but there's nothing I can do about that, is there? So why waste time even thinking about it, when Nolly must be starving. I don't suppose you thought to buy a bowl? The old saucepan I found is rather disgusting."

"I thought of everything." Vivian was already unloading his purchases on the shop counter. "Three different tins of gourmet doggy chow, a tin opener, biscuits, a ball, some rawhide chews, and even a bottle of canine vitamins."

"You're marvelous. How much do I owe you?"

"Another night's lodging. The sad truth, Flora, is that I'm not happy in my digs. . . ."

"You're talking rubbish again. You've a bee in your bonnet that I shouldn't be alone. I expect you're thinking that my father might turn up here in the middle of the night."

"We only have Snuffy's word for it that you even

have a father." Vivian had been dwelling on this point during the better part of the drive back from his shopping expedition.

"But why would he make up such a story?"

"That's the question." Vivian got busy with the tin opener. "But I intend to be here tomorrow to help size up Reggie. Here, Nolly," he held out the bowl and the little dog gave the red ball a last look as if daring it to move while his back was turned before scampering toward his dinner.

"Wait a minute." Flora took the bowl out of Vivian's hands. "I think we should break some biscuits on top."

"Why? You want to make it into shepherd's pie?"

"No, silly, because I've seen people—the real doggy sort, you know, breeders and show types—do that on television shows where they explain how to raise champions."

"I'm not sure Nolly has that sort of future."

"No, I don't suppose he does." Flora laughed and put the bowl down. "But perhaps I can teach him to say grace."

"Some other time." Vivian took hold of her hand. "You haven't been upstairs yet, have you?"

"No, why do you ask?"

"Because, and don't drag your feet or I'll toss you over my shoulder and carry you up to the flat, I want you to tell me how you plan to decorate the place."

"I'm not sure I'll be doing much of that if I go ahead with the shop—which reminds me," Flora dodged around him and ran ahead up the stairs, "I should ring up her Ladyship tonight from the call box on the corner, before I chicken out. You don't think it's too late, do you? That's one thing I will have to splurge on, a clock for the . . ."

"What's the matter?" Vivian came up behind her as she stood transfixed in the sitting room doorway.

"I don't believe it!"

"Believe what?"

"The clock! The one Grandpa and I had in our sitting room at Gossinger, it's here on the mantelpiece, and . . ." she crossed the floor in a daze, "here's his fireside chair, the sofa, the bookcases and corner cupboard, and that's our drop-leaf table under the window! I don't understand . . . how did it all get here?"

"There's more as you will see when you check the bedrooms. I rang up Uncle Henry late last night after you were in bed and he found a couple of chaps to drive everything up here today. This morning while you were still asleep I had a spare key to the shop made and left it with Mrs. Smith, and she agreed to be here to let the men in at the appointed time. I know you, you're going to accuse me of being an awful busybody, Flora . . ."

"Oh, no, I'm not!" She turned to him, eyes blinded with tears. "You've given me a big piece of my life back and I don't know how I can ever thank you enough."

"You could agree," said Vivian, smiling at her, "to let me spend the night in the newly furnished spare bedroom."

FOURTEEN

"What's wrong, m'dear? You're looking frightfully glum!" Sir Henry Gossinger laid aside his sporting periodical in an attempt to give his wife her rightful share of his attention. "Was half asleep when the new housekeeper—still forget her name—came into the room and said you were wanted on the phone. Not bad news, I hope."

"I'm not sure what to call it." Lady Gossinger plumped down on a chair and stared into space.

"Ah, I've got it!" Her husband brightened. "Mrs. Frost, that's the woman's name. Mumbly sort of person, can never understand the half of what she's saying. But I imagine some people could say the same about me. Does her best, I suppose; trouble is, the place will never be the same without Hutchins. End of an era and all that." Sir Henry's face settled into unhappy lines. "Miss the chap more every day. Wonder how little Flora is getting along?"

"It was her on the telephone."

"What's that?" Sir Henry sat more upright in his chair. "Rang to say the furniture turned up all right, did she? Must say that was damned decent of Vivian to see to all that. Should have thought of it m'self."

"Just for once, Henry, would you stop talking to yourself and answering all your own questions?" Her Ladyship thumped a fist on her tweed-skirted knee.

"Sorry, m'dear. Unfeeling sort of chap you married, deserve better, you know." Sir Henry could not have been more contrite. It was plain from looking at her, at the shadows under her eyes and the new hollows in her cheeks that matched the tone of her voice, that Mabel wasn't herself. Hadn't been since Hutchins's death. "Should have realized you were feeling low," he said. "On top of everything else, Tipp had to take himself off. Couldn't help his cousin or whoever it was being taken ill, but damn inconsiderate not to have got in touch to let us know when he's likely to be back. I'll get you a glass of sherry, while you tell me everything little Flora had to say."

"I wish you would stop calling her that!" Lady Gossinger took refuge in anger because it seemed the safest emotion these days. "It makes you sound so fatuous."

"You're right, m'dear, she's a grown woman."

"And a wily one at that! It turns out she wasn't satisfied with getting the flat rent-free for a year. Now she wants to reopen the shop, selling secondhand goods. And believe it or not, she's somehow managed to get young Vivian into her pocket. He was right there when she was on the phone. I could hear him in the background before he took the receiver and explained to me what a wonderful idea this is."

"Isn't it?" Sir Henry stood at the drinks cabinet with the sherry decanter in his hands. "Seems to me Flora would do a bang-up job of running a place like that. Always thought she was wasted in our gift shop here. Hutchins worried about that, told me so. Wanted her to spread her wings. But she had it in her head it wasn't right to leave him."

"She's certainly making up for lost time!" Her Ladyship slumped back in her chair, which like most of the furniture was not designed for maximum comfort. "Oh, do give me that sherry, Henry, and don't pay any attention to my snarls. I don't mean to be such an ogre."

This was true; she was only making matters worse giving vent to her resentment of Flora. After all, Henry hadn't said anything recently about changing his will. He'd probably decided there was no rush, but she had not a doubt in the world that he still intended to leave Gossinger Hall to the girl. But that concern had to go on the back burner. What haunted her day and night— to the point that she couldn't eat or sleep—was the fear that what she had done would come to light. Henry might be a softie in many ways; he had never displayed the least suspicion that she might have stuffed Hutchins down the garderobe. But there were some things he would never forgive. And her attempt to undo a potentially fatal mistake had met with dismal failure. Her Ladyship gripped the arms of her chair and thought about hitting a certain person over the head with a heavy object.

"Here's your sherry, m'dear." Sir Henry placed the glass in her hand and hovered at her elbow. It occurred to him that she might have been wearing the same clothes for close on a fortnight, and her hair wasn't right, it stuck out in places where it shouldn't have and lay flat where it should have sat up. Sir Henry experienced an unusual urge to stoop and kiss his wife's cheek. Instead, he patted her shoulder before picking up his own glass of sherry and resuming his seat.

"This hits the spot." Lady Gossinger swallowed half

her sherry. "Nothing better than this, is there? The two
of us sitting talking things out. You're right, old bean,
as you almost always are. There's no sense leaving that
shop sitting empty, and it would be impossible to let it
with Florie living upstairs and having to use the kitchen
at the back to cook her meals. Much better to give her a
chance to make a go of things."

"My thinking exactly, m'dear. The girl needs something, a challenge if you like, to help get her over
Hutchins's death. Dreadful blow," Sir Henry shook his
head, "still can't get over his being right as rain one
minute and gone the next. Makes you think, doesn't
it?"

"Certainly does." Her Ladyship finished off her
sherry. "You've no idea, Henry, how I wish I hadn't
created a stink about your leaving Gossinger Hall to
your butler. Somehow what happened seems like retri-
bution."

Sir Henry could not quite view it that way, given the
fact it was Hutchins who had paid the penalty, but he
endeavored to make reassuring noises.

"And then I have to go taking it out on Flora." Lady
Gossinger got up and poured herself another sherry
without spilling more than a few drops. "Honestly, I
must be the most awful woman alive. Deserve to be put
in the stocks. But the truth is, Henry, I've always been
more than a little jealous of her."

"I say," Sir Henry looked startled, "you're not suggesting, old dear, that I ever had—don't quite know
how to put it—an eye for the girl?"

"No, of course not." Her Ladyship sat back down.
"What you had was a tendency to treat her like a
daughter. And that was a thorn in my flesh, seeing that
there was never any hope of us having children."

"Bound to be fond of her—she grew up here from
three years of age. Always about the place, as merry a
little thing as God ever made. Never could get anything

out of Hutchins about her father, but I assure you, Mabel, I never meant to hurt you by making too much of Flora."

His wife sighed. "I know you didn't. You're much too good to have realized I was harboring some unkind feelings. But enough of that. I told Flora I would talk to you about the shop, so why don't you go and give her a ring? Tell her we're both happy about her plans and we won't charge her anything until she gets on her feet."

"Are you sure that's what you want?"

"Positive. She'll enjoy hearing from you, and while you're on the phone I'll just close my eyes." Lady Gossinger suited action to words. "I've no idea why I've been feeling so exhausted lately, but there it is. I'm getting old, I suppose."

"Absolute bosh, m'dear, you're at your peak; wouldn't mind betting you'll live to be ninety!"

But as Sir Henry padded from the room he recalled thinking the same thing once about Hutchins. One never knew, did one?

Instead of being glad of the moment alone so she could chew on her thoughts, Lady Gossinger felt a twinge of panic when the door shut softly behind her husband. The walls seemed to close in to the point of suffocation and she felt an unreasonable urge to jump up and open the windows. *I wonder,* she thought, *if I'm losing my mind? Today when I was talking to Mrs. Frost I was convinced she'd been sent here as the new housekeeper to keep an eye on me, because the police don't really believe Hutchins died a natural death.* . . . Lady Gossinger was fighting down a fresh wave of paranoia when the door opened as quietly as it had just closed and Miss Sophie Doffit came into the room.

"It's only me, dear Mabel." She moved briskly across the Persian carpet for a woman of her advanced years. "I think we need to have a little talk. It's clear to me you can't go on this way, and I want to help you because I do appreciate your letting me stay on at Gossinger, long after another woman would have had my suitcases packed and put out on the doorstep."

"You're the last person I can talk to." Lady Gossinger buried her face in her hands. "You'd run immediately to Henry. I have to do what needs to be done all by myself."

"Not in your condition, Mabel," said Miss Doffit, plumping up a cushion and easing it behind her Ladyship's bowed head. "You have to trust me, dear, because you need me and there is nothing more that a woman of my age likes better than to be needed. You pour your heart out, and I'll pour us each a glass of sherry."

FIFTEEN

"The good thing about going out to tea at Mrs. Smith's this afternoon," Flora told Vivian, "is that I don't have to worry whether I'm dressed right or wrong for meeting my father for the first time. If he does turn up, I'll explain to him that I'm going out and he won't think I'm too eager or, on the other hand, not sufficiently enthusiastic. He'll understand that what I'm wearing has nothing to do with his visit."

"I think I have that clear," Vivian assured her. "The one who doesn't get it is Nolly; however, I have come to the conclusion that he is a very self-centered dog, who only really understands when you're talking about him."

"That's not true." Flora stood looking at herself in the mirror on the sitting room wall. It was one of the pieces delivered the previous day. And she loved it as she did the mantelpiece clock and the fireside chair, perhaps even more because as a little girl she had believed in the magic of mirrors after reading a book about one that had the ability to conjure up a beloved face from its store of reflections. Now Flora half-believed that if she turned her head at just the right moment, she would see her grandfather, a little shadowy perhaps, but there in the mirror, performing one of the tasks that had been part of his everyday routine in their sitting room at Gossinger. Making sure the door into the garden was locked at night, damping down the fire, or folding the serviettes just as he liked them. Memories of the best sort, the ordinary kind that settle deep in the heart, all there inside this shiny silver piece of glass.

As to her own reflection, Flora wasn't absolutely convinced that it couldn't be improved upon. She liked her hair short, although it did seem to need a little evening out. Perhaps she could arrange that with Edna Smith during tea. But the question remained: Would she look silly wearing a hat? She had asked Nolly's opinion and he had tilted his head to one side and pondered the matter as if it were of much more importance than either his red ball or a midday snack of biscuits.

Now Flora decided to pose the same query to Vivian. "Stay where you are," she instructed him, and disappeared into her bedroom to reappear wearing a black 1920's felt hat with a flower on one side twisted out of the same material. "What do you think about this? As you will observe, the black matches the braid at my neck and cuffs. I do love the combination of black and bottle green, don't you?"

"I can't say I have previously given the subject much thought." Vivian stood with his arms folded and a smile hovering around his mouth. "To be honest, I'm not sure about the hat. How about giving me a different angle to help me make up my mind?"

"Take a good look all the way round." Flora did a slow pirouette, her long skirts caught up in her hands to display black stockings and ankle boots. "Be honest now!"

"I'm afraid the hat has to go," Vivian told her. "It makes you look far too . . ."

"Silly?"

"Ravishing is the word I was looking for. But suit yourself. If you don't mind being stared at by men in the street while we walk to Mrs. Smith's, that's your business."

"You're just being kind," said Flora. "But I do love hats. They make me feel as if I should be speeding along honeysuckle-scented lanes in an old open roadster, sitting next to a young man wearing goggles and a cap, with a scarf streaming out behind him in the breeze."

"I have some goggles," said Vivian, "but they are the sort used for swimming."

"Listen to Nolly." Flora could not contain the happiness spreading through her like the promise of springtime. "That little bark is meant to tell us that he wants to be in the picture. Ladies who drove in those sorts of cars usually had small dogs sitting on their laps."

"I don't doubt you're right," said Vivian, crossing the room to the door, "except about the bark. I think Nolly hears someone outside the shop. And there goes the bell. Would you like me to disappear into one of the bedrooms when you let your father in?"

"That might turn things into a French farce, don't you think?" Flora smoothed her suddenly damp hands over her hips. "Imagine Reggie opening what he thought was the toilet door and finding you hiding in the bedroom. That's not how things are meant to go, when meeting your long-lost father. Besides," she followed Vivian out onto the landing, "you said you wanted to look him over and help me decide if he's on the up-and-up."

"I know I did," said Vivian as Nolly darted past them onto the stairs, barking at the top of his lungs, "but I began to think I was being an absolute clod, shoving myself in on what is likely to be a very emotional meeting. Of course, if you beg me to stay, I won't be forced to listen at the keyhole." He was torn between his desire to protect her and not wanting to dampen even one moment of her happiness.

"All right, I'll say it! I want you there. In fact, why don't you go down and let him in while I pace the floor and try to guess what he looks like? So far all I can come up with is a villainous mustache and a hand holding a bunch of flowers. Go on," Flora gave Vivian a little push, "before he decides I'm not home and goes away. I don't want to have to go through this heart-pounding business twice."

She went back into the sitting room and began rearranging the candlesticks that she had brought with her in one of the suitcases. The clock struck the half hour, making her jump but at the same time reminding her that she was surrounded by friendly things—the bronze vase filled with silk poppies that she had given to her grandfather one Christmas, the figurine of the Scottish bagpiper, the embroidered cushions on the familiar chair. They were all telling her that she was not adrift in uncharted seas; she was anchored firmly to her past.

As a result she was almost calm when voices reached her, accompanied by footsteps on the stairs and a woof or two from Nolly. Vivian ushered a tallish man into the room. He was holding a bunch of flowers and he did have a pencil-thin mustache, but the villainous aspect was lost when he smiled because he had a decided gap in his front teeth. He reminded Flora of someone. Yes, that was it! He looked rather like that actor, Terry-

Thomas, that Mrs. Bellows used to like so much. Flora wasn't tempted to cry "Daddy!" and run headlong into his arms, but she did decide that if he was still a bit of a bounder, it was the engaging sort. And she had a flash of why her mother might have fallen in love with this man.

"Hello," she said.

"I say! You have turned into a little corker!" The broad smile creased his cheeks and displayed the gap in his teeth in all its splendor. "Old Snuffy told me as much, but my word, I wasn't prepared! Would you mind if I sat down for a minute to collect myself? Don't get the wrong idea—I don't expect to dandle you on my knee after all this time, I'd just like to sit and look at you."

"Why don't I take the flowers?" suggested Vivian.

"Didn't bring them for you, old chap."

"A pity! Pansies are my favorites."

"Mine, too," said Flora, swiveling the chair around for her father to sit down in. "Grandpa told me, Reggie—is it all right if I call you that?"

"I'll say! And I know just what you have in mind, about the flowers. Grace—your mother—used to call pansies fairy faces." His expression turned mournful. "Lovely girl, don't know why she looked at me twice. Dash it all, seeing you does bring her back!"

"Then I do look like her?" Flora sat on the sofa, bunching her skirts about her knees, while Vivian wandered about the room in search of a vase and settled on a diminutive jug with an Italian scene painted on it. He left the room to fill it with water.

"Grace had fair hair, rather curly it was, and brown eyes. But I'm sure you've seen photos. Bound to have done. So it would be stretching it a bit, to call you the spitting image of her. But there is a marked similarity around the mouth and in the way you move. Don't suppose you remember her much?"

"I remember her hands touching my hair, and some-times I can hear her voice reading me a story. Other-wise it's just a feeling, I can see a room with light walls and pale yellow curtains and a picture of a gar-den . . ."

"Amazing!" Reggie's smile wavered on the edge of conflicting emotions. "That was our flat. Jolly little place. Only thing to strike a sour note was that dashed unpleasant landlady, always knocking on the door wanting the rent. I say, where's that little dog? Not trying to make a point, is he, that he's no time for a bad penny?"

"Nolly?" Flora called, and he came trotting up to her.

"I say! Jolly good show! You've got him well trained, I see."

"I'm afraid that's his only trick," Flora admitted.

"The way it should be." Reggie beamed encourage-ment. "Hang it all, I tell my clients, a dog's not a wind-up toy. Should be plain as a pikestaff the little beggars are entitled to their dignity, same as the rest of us. That's my current business: bringing peace of mind to the hearts and minds of those who don't have a voice in human terms."

"You're a dog psychiatrist?"

"Animal faith-healer."

"All sorts of animals?" Biting her lip as she pictured a gorilla throwing away his crutches when told to get up and walk, Flora gathered up Nolly, who hadn't gone racing over to sit at the feet of the master. "Do you mean lions and tigers?"

"What have I missed?" inquired Vivian, coming back into the room and setting the flower jug on the bookcase.

"Reggie's an animal faith-healer."

"Well, I suppose that makes as much sense as the other kind."

"I was just asking if he works with wild animals."

"Smashing idea! Love to try it sometime." Reggie did not sound one-hundred-percent enthusiastic. "But so far, my professional dealings have been with the domesticated species. I'm often the last resort when traditional methods, such as spaying and neutering," Nolly chose this moment to disappear under the sofa, "fail to break a dog or cat's habits. You'd be amazed at how many people are completely cowed by their pets. Fastest growing form of abuse in this country. Bally bad show, but there it is!"

Flora and Vivian could only listen entranced.

"I am currently working with a duchess who is afraid to put on her pearls because her Siamese cat lunges for her throat each time she wears them. Her Grace tried the obvious, buying the cat a jeweled collar, but no luck."

"But you've been able to help?" Flora refused to look at Vivian.

"Oh, I should say!" Reggie flashed his gap-toothed grin. "Not wishing to boast, you understand, I'm an absolute whiz at what I do. Meditation, that's the key— teach them that and you'll have the pussycats purring all day long. Better at it than dogs, but even dogs get it in the end. Dogs do better being regressed to their former lives."

"Not so many of them, perhaps," said Vivian.

"Some people think dogs are more suggestible," replied Reggie, and Flora found it impossible to tell if he took himself seriously, "but according to my findings they're more in touch with their feelings, and more liable to take risks on the path to true self-awareness."

A doggy yawn drifted up from Flora's feet.

"It all sounds most impressive," she made haste to say. "Don't you think so, Vivian?"

"Absolutely."

"Dash it all, I'm not aiming to become a household

name. Got properly cut down to size last summer."
Reggie looked instantly crestfallen. "A bit of a facer, all
right. A friend of mine, thundering good chap, gave me
a ticket to one of the garden parties at Buckingham
Palace. Seemed a chance in a million to have a natter
with the Queen about the corgis. From all you hear, she
could do with my sort of help bringing them into line.
But when I started to explain the virtues of faith-
healing and tried to give Her Majesty my card, two
men appeared out of nowhere and gave me a chair lift
out the gates. There was even a small bit about it the
next day in *The Times*. Luckily, I didn't lose many clients, even though they'd dug up the bit about me being
in prison, but it does dampen your faith in the Royal
Family."

"Oh, poor Reggie!" cried Flora, genuinely moved.
"What a horrid experience! But I don't think you
should blame Her Majesty. I'm sure she would have
loved to talk to you if those interfering security guards
hadn't hustled you away."

"Speaking of being in a hurry," Vivian looked at the
clock, "would you like me to ring up Edna Smith,
Flora, and tell her we're running behind and not to
expect us right away?"

"Oh, I say," Reggie got to his feet, "Snuffy did say
something about your going out to tea this afternoon,
and here I am rattling on and making you late."

"But you can't go yet," protested Flora. "I haven't
even offered you something to drink."

"You wouldn't happen to have a good malt whiskey
tucked away? No, I can see you don't. Well, another
time, perhaps. I've had a smashing time, my dear.
Wouldn't have missed it for the world and hope you'll
let me come again. Promise not to make a nuisance of
myself. But," he reached into his pocket again, "must
let you have my card. No, seem to have come without

one. Sorry to say, my phone is temporarily out of order, but that should be fixed in a jiffy."

"Well, don't go just for a minute," said Flora. "I've got my camera in the bedroom and I'd like Vivian to take a picture of you and me, Reggie, to record our reunion."

"Jolly good show, hope you'll let me have a copy."

Vivian snapped the father-and-daughter shot. And when that was done, Flora thought about giving Reggie a good-bye kiss on the cheek, but settled for shaking hands with him. When they parted at the shop door, she was both relieved and sorry.

"You look worried," commented Vivian as they strolled toward Edna Smith's council flat under gray skies webbed by clouds.

"I don't like leaving Nolly on his own, but I know I have to start sometime. And he wasn't invited to tea."

"That was a smart move, getting that photo."

"I'm going to show it to Mrs. Bellows when I see her, on the chance that my mother did bring my father to Gossinger. She may even have been at their wedding and be able to identify him and Reggie as the same person. And if Mrs. Bellows can't help, I'll talk to Sir Henry and show him the photo, too. I'm not so silly that I'll accept on blind faith someone who shows up out of thin air. But something inside me tells me Reggie is my father."

"I think you're right, Flora. If he were a fraud—and I have yet to figure out why he might be—I think he would have done his homework and padded his conversation with convincing details, ones that you'd identify. For instance, he might have asked if your grandfather still made his wonderful chocolate cake, or if you still had the patchwork teddy bear."

"Fancy you remembering Buttons!"

"I never saw you without him when you were little. For a while I thought you were Siamese twins."

"What did you think of him?"

"Buttons?"

"No, silly! Reggie."

"I rather liked him, but don't hold me to that. How about you?"

"The same." Flora stepped away from the curb as a bus rushed past. "I felt kind of sorry for him. It must get awfully tiresome having to live by your wits, but I don't suppose he's trained for anything but being a rogue."

"If you say 'Poor Daddy!' " Vivian took her arm, "I may be tempted to throw your charming hat under the next lorry."

"You wouldn't dare." Flora whirled away from him and started to run toward the corner. "I'd like to talk more about my mother to Reggie," she said when he caught up with her, "but I have the feeling he really didn't know her. And in answer to your unspoken question, sir, I do *not* feel as though I have survived an earthshaking experience. Now where is it that Edna Smith and Boris live? Did she say the third or the fourth floor?"

"Follow me," said Vivian. "Remember I was here yesterday to give her the spare key to the shop. That reminds me: I should ask her for that back."

"I think we should let her keep it, in case of emergency," answered Flora as they climbed the staircase hemmed in by stone walls on each side. "Oh, thank goodness, we're here."

"Yes, I was developing altitude sickness myself." Vivian buzzed the doorbell, and within seconds they were being ushered into a narrow hall with foil wallpaper in a geometric pattern that made the eyes cross. Music from a rock group crept out from under one of the doors, and a toasty aroma wafted its way from the kitchen at the far end.

"This is nice—I was looking out the window for

you!" Edna Smith, wearing a cotton frock with plums all over it, her hair piled up in galvanized loops and curls, led the way into the living room, which was decorated in black and gray with a lot of gold trim, and so many mirrors it was rather like being in a fun house. "Sit yourselves down—no standing on ceremony here. You'll find those chairs comfy. Set me back a bit, but you get what you pay for, I always say."

"This is a treat," said Flora, taking the black leather chair to the left of the small but fiercely hot electric fire. "We've been looking forward to this, haven't we, Vivian?"

"All day."

"Go on with you," Edna gave him a playful poke, "pull the other one, it's got bells on. Now do as you're told, sit your bum down across from your girlfriend."

"Oh, I have to tell you," Flora said quickly, as the heat from the fire worked its way up to her face, "I'm ever so grateful for your helping out yesterday with my furniture, letting the movers in and I'm sure showing them where to put everything."

"Well, you can't leave that sort of thing to men." Edna Smith placed a bowl of peanuts on each end of the black coffee table with the mirror top. "Arranging a room takes a woman's touch, and that reminds me— Boris is going to feel the back of my hand if he doesn't turn down his CD player. I let him stay home from school today even though I didn't believe he had the tummy-ache, not for all his moaning and groaning, but I told him he wasn't to make a lot of noise and bother Mr. Phillips, that's the lodger, the one I told you about. He's easy to please, but that doesn't mean the poor man will put up with having his eardrums ruptured." Edna's expression hinted at steel beneath the fleshy cheeks and heavy makeup. "I've decided I'm not going to put up with any more of Boris's sulks, so why don't you two sit back while I go and straighten him out before I bring in the tea? There's those peanuts for you to be getting on with. And maybe you'd like to have a look at the paper." She put that day's edition of the *Daily Mail* on the coffee table. "There's a bit in there, if you can find it, about the Queen coming to Bethnal Green to open the new wing of the children's hospital. I can't remember what date it says, but sometime soon."

"Boris isn't playing his music all that loud," said Flora when Edna left the room, closing the door behind her.

"It doesn't rattle my eardrums," replied Vivian, "but after meeting him the other night I can understand his grandmother's patience wearing thin."

"Or it could be the lodger is a miserable old crosspatch. Which is a bit of a shame, really, because I've been wondering if he isn't a relative, but really Edna's boyfriend come back into her life."

"You're such a romantic! My guess is the only flame the man wants lit is under his dinner. Don't you realize we men are all alike, taking the easy road wherever possible? I've been thinking, you're probably an excellent cook, Flora." Vivian picked up the newspaper.

"As a matter of fact, I am, but what does that have to do with the price of tea in China?" Flora hoped she wasn't blushing. "Why don't you look up that piece about the Queen coming to Bethnal Green?"

"You're thinking of that letter you wrote to Her Majesty about obtaining the Royal Warrant for your grandfather's silver polish. You're not worried that one of the corgis ate it, are you? Because I'm sure you will get a reply." Vivian flipped the pages and had just located the news item in question when Boris Smith came into the room, fresh-faced and stocky, with his sandy hair sticking up on end as if he had obeyed a grandmotherly instruction to put his head under the tap and towel it dry. His freckles and round cheeks gave him a somewhat engaging look, despite the scowl that looked to be the same one he had worn the last time they'd seen him.

"Hello, friends and neighbors," he said, plonking himself down on the settee, "Grandma told me to come and be nice to you. I'm supposed to say I'm sorry for being rude the other night."

"Are you?" asked Flora.

"Not really." Boris took a fistful of peanuts and tossed one into his mouth. "Sometimes it's just great to act rotten. It wasn't anything to do with you, really."

"Nothing to do with your visit to Gossinger?" Vivian laid the newspaper down.

"I wasn't talking to you." Boris crunched down on the peanuts and wiped his hands on his knees. "Look, I'm sorry," he met Flora's eyes, then looked away, "that the old geezer that was your grandfather snuffed it, but what's that to do with me?"

"Did you by any chance wander off on your own that day, away from the rest of your group?" said Vivian.

"Who's been telling you that?" Boris clung to his defiance by way of a shield. "Have you been up to the school to see Mr. Ferncliffe?"

"I happened to meet him on the train coming up to London," said Flora. *This boy does know something,* she thought, with a clutch deep inside. *Maybe he heard noises from inside the garderobe—sounds indicating someone was in trouble, but he didn't go in and check and now he's been sick with remorse.*

"Old Woolly Wig—that's what we call Mr. Ferncliffe—couldn't have told you anything. Because," Boris tried hard to sound nonchalant, "there's nothing to tell, except that I did sneak up to see my Great-Aunt Mabel, and why shouldn't I? I was hoping to get a fiver out of her, if you must know. But the old bat threw a fit when I went into that room in the tower so I cleared out fast. Gran says," he directed this to Vivian, "you're Sir

Henry's nephew." Boris breathed a little easier. It had been smart to say that, he decided, because it wouldn't do to let on that he had seen Mr. Gossinger and heard him talking to his uncle that day. That would only incur more questions, which could lead to disaster. At the thought of what could happen, Boris broke out in another of the sweats that had forced him to stick his head under the bathroom tap before coming into the room. Would they, he wondered, let him take his CD player to prison with him?

"Your grandmother said Aunt Mabel gave you a present to bring back." Vivian hadn't overlooked the sheen on the boy's face and the way he kept wiping his hands on his pants knees.

"Well, it wasn't for me, and, anyway, it was stupid. Gran gave it to the church bazaar."

"Here we are!" Nudging open the door, Edna appeared with a tray, which was swiftly taken out of her hands by the ever-courteous Vivian. "I toasted up some more crumpets because the ones I made before you came had gone hard as rocks. Having a nice chat, were you?" Her eyes switched to Boris, who was helping himself to more peanuts.

"We were talking about the Queen." Flora decided to shift the truth, partly because of something about Boris—the scowl that didn't go with the round cheeks and freckles tugged at her heart—and also because if she started to dwell on her grandfather's final day she might end up ruining the tea party. "When you said Her Majesty is coming to Bethnal Green it got me and Vivian talking about the letter I wrote her a few weeks ago. No, we're not best friends or anything like that," Flora said, laughing at the surprised look on Edna's face. "It was about my grandfather's silver polish." And she proceeded to explain about the Royal Warrant as Edna passed out the teacups.

"Well, what a lovely thing for a grandchild to do,"

said that lady, with a meaningful look at Boris. "And I'm sure you'll hear something encouraging before very long, dear. I've always thought the Queen has the kindest heart possible; it's her hair that makes her look so stern. I'd love to get my hands on it, soften it up a bit. Such a pretty girl she was!" Edna sat down on the settee next to Boris. "I remember how she looked coming off that plane when she came back from Africa after her father died, her eyes all misty and sad, and all of us knowing she'd never be young again. Only twenty-five years old, it doesn't bear thinking about. And I don't believe a word of it when people say she never played proper mum games like bubbles in the bath with her children and always put those dogs first."

Flora smiled. "You're like my grandfather. Mrs. Bellows, who was the housekeeper at Gossinger Hall when I was growing up, used to say that in Grandpa's eyes God came second only to Her Majesty. If you can believe it, I was quite jealous as a little girl of his devotion to the Queen. I remember kicking and screaming when she came on the television once and Grandpa interrupted the game of Ludo we were playing to watch her ride in an open carriage to the Opening of Parliament."

"Did you get sent to bed?" Boris let his scowl slip.

"I can't remember anything else except that I was obviously a horrible child."

"But the Queen doesn't know that." Vivian accepted a crumpet from the plate that Edna was handing round. "And unless one of us here blabs your past, it shouldn't ruin your chances concerning the Royal Warrant."

"I'm afraid," said Flora, shaking her head, "that my letter probably won't do the trick. What I really need to do is get a tin of the polish to the Queen. But short of smuggling myself into Buckingham Palace, I can't think of a way. And I really wouldn't want to end up like Reggie, being carried off in ignominy by security guards."

Now, why had she gone and said that? It meant explaining to Edna who Reggie was, which Flora didn't really mind doing, but she did begin to feel that she was becoming one of those awful people who hog the conversation to make themselves sound important.

"Ugh!" Boris said, showing more interest in his cup than in the abridged story about her long-lost father. "There are tea leaves floating like drowned flies in my cup!"

Vivian and Flora had each found themselves chewing on the occasional tough morsel, or sipping around them.

"Or are they flies?" Boris dipped in a finger and inspected it upon withdrawal.

"If you aren't the limit!" Edna got to her feet. "Showing me up in front of company! I should have sent you off with a clip on the ear ten minutes ago. And don't go playing any more of that loud music. Mr. Phillips wants you to take him a cup of tea, I forgot to tell you that when I came in. But it's no wonder my mind's like a sieve these days, with all your carrying-on."

"I hate that miserable old blighter!" Boris banged down his cup and kicked the coffee table leg for good measure.

"That's enough of that. Remember, he helps pay the rent here."

"Well, I wish he was dead!"

"And don't you go spitting in his tea."

"No, I'll put some poison in it instead."

"Who'd be a grandmother?" sighed Edna as the door banged shut on her grandson. "I tell you, I have to touch up my hair every day to keep the gray from coming back."

"Please don't feel bad," said Flora.

"It's hard not to get upset, and I am sorry about the tea. I ran out of bags, you see, and had to borrow some of the loose stuff from a neighbor. And hunt high and low as I did, I couldn't find my strainer. That's what I get, I suppose, for giving away the one I had to the church. But I was that upset at the time. A horrid dirty old thing it was, black as the inside of a chimney. Fancy, I thought, Mabel having the nerve to send *that* back with Boris. I suppose she thought I'd believe it was an antique and be so pleased I'd wet my knickers."

"What was it like?" The heat from the fire was really getting to Flora now, making her feel quite faint. "I mean, what shape was it?"

"Round," said Edna.

"Oh!" said Flora and felt the ground settle under her feet.

"I mean the inside of the strainer part and the cup underneath was round. The handles on either side made it a sort of oval. That was another thing," Edna was back to feeling put upon, "it was shaped like a bird and Mabel always knew I couldn't *abide* birds."

"Was it . . ." Flora knew without looking that Vivian had also tensed in his chair. ". . . Was it shaped like a swan?"

"Why, yes, I'd say that was it," replied Edna. "Is there something I need to know about that tea strainer?"

"Don't upset yourself," said Vivian. "If it's the one we think it is," he stood and reached for Flora's hand, "it's already been missing for two hundred years."

Sixteen

"I don't understand why Lady Gossinger would send that tea strainer to her sister. Unless she didn't know it was the one that had belonged to Queen Charlotte and created such an uproar when it disappeared." Flora and Vivian were walking back to Wishbone Street in a drizzling late afternoon rain.

"Of course she knew! She must have heard Uncle Henry describe it a hundred times." Vivian was clear in his own mind why her Ladyship had taken such a treacherous course of action. Mabel had been beside herself with rage about Uncle Henry's plans for Gossinger and had taken her petty revenge, one which had the added spice of being accomplished without her husband being any the wiser. "What an opportunity to laugh up her sleeve each time he brought up the subject of the purloined tea strainer!"

"But how did she come to have it?" Flora wrapped her arms around herself to make up for the folly of not having worn a jacket.

Vivian, without breaking pace, shrugged out of his and wrapped it around her shoulders. "Yes, that's the real question. The Family has searched Gossinger from top to bottom over the last two hundred years looking for that piece of silver. I know I did as a child."

"Me, too," said Flora. "And now that we know it really does still exist it's gone again, bought by somebody at the church bazaar who probably paid a pound for it and has no idea at all of its value. Or the fact that it rightfully belongs to the Royal Family."

"I am so angry," Vivian ground the words out through his teeth, "that I was about to walk us under a bus. One gets used to the heady roar of traffic and I wasn't looking both ways. Sorry about that."

"There has to be something we don't understand about what happened." Flora slipped her arms into the sleeves of his jacket and wrapped the fronts across her chest, missing the look he gave her. "Perhaps Lady Gossinger sent the tea strainer to Edna by mistake. Couldn't it be this way, that she had just found it and had it wrapped up waiting to surprise Sir Henry, and also had another package to send her sister of about the same size, and just got them mixed up?"

"You *do* believe in fairy tales, don't you?"

"I don't like to judge someone without knowing all the facts," Flora responded as they turned onto Wishbone Street. "And Edna did tell us that Lady Gossinger rang up to ask if Boris had given her the present and Edna told her she had sold it at the bazaar. Perhaps her Ladyship was about to ask for it back because she realized she'd made a terrible mistake."

"What we need to do is pray," said Vivian, "that whoever bought it didn't decide it was a piece of junk, as so often happens with bargains when you get them home, and pitch it in the dustbin."

"We have to think positively," Flora agreed, "but I suppose that's hard to do when you're getting drenched to the skin. Won't you take your jacket back?"

"We're almost at the shop."

"At least will you promise to let me help you find the tea strainer?"

"Of course. The legend is every bit as much part of your heritage as it is mine. More so, in fact."

"Because Grandpa loved the Gossinger silver collection?" Flora felt her love for the man walking beside her open up like a flower and it was difficult to keep her voice level. "It's really nice of you think that way, Vivian, but we both know it isn't so. What's wrong? You've got a funny look on your face."

"There's a woman standing outside the shop."

"What about it?" Flora had trouble seeing so far: The rain was coming down harder, so that the brim of her hat couldn't keep it off her face. "It's probably someone taking cover until this eases off a bit."

"Or waiting for us to get back." Vivian quickened his pace. "Yes, I was right! It is Cousin Sophie, with a suitcase at her feet."

"Miss Doffit? Whatever would she be doing here?"

"Another intriguing question," Vivian replied.

"Thank goodness you're back, both of you, although I was only expecting Flora," Miss Doffit exclaimed. "Luckily I've only been waiting here five minutes. But there's a dog inside that's been barking at me. And as you can see, the feathers on my lovely powder blue hat are sopping wet, which wouldn't matter so much, I suppose, if they came from the kind of birds that swim."

"Speaking of which," Vivian produced the key and stuck it in the lock, "I have a nasty suspicion I know what brings you here, Cousin Sophie. It has to do at least in part with a tea strainer in the shape of a swan. Although why my aunt didn't come herself, I can't begin to guess." He held the door open for the two women to get in out of the rain.

"Are you saying *you* have it? That Mabel has been worrying herself into a frenzy for no reason?" Miss Doffit had to shout to make herself heard over Nolly's frantic joy at being released from prison and reunited with Flora. Her old face crumpled in bewilderment, and if Vivian hadn't picked up her suitcase at just that moment she might have sat down on it.

"No, we don't have it," he reached inside to snap on the light, "but let's continue this conversation in the dry, shall we?"

"Vivian, you really shouldn't be so cross. You're making assumptions . . ." Flora brought up the rear with Nolly in her arms.

"Oh, it's all right, dear," Miss Doffit spoke softly now as they all stood in the middle of the shop, "there's no way to put the cat back in the bag once it's out, and I'm sure it's better this way. I haven't lived to be my age without accepting the fact that sometimes you're in the wrong because of trying to do right. The main thing here, Vivian, is for you to understand that poor Mabel is making herself ill over this business. She's terrified Henry will never forgive her if he finds out what she did, although why he would I don't know. Not if we all promise never to breathe a word."

"There's her sister," said Vivian grimly.

"But she doesn't know—"

"As of this afternoon she does."

"That was my fault." Flora's mouth quivered. "I let it out about the tea strainer being a long-lost treasure. But I really don't believe, even if her relationship with Lady Gossinger is rather cool, that Edna Smith would spill the beans to Sir Henry. Her life's complicated enough already. Anyway, if we can get the tea strainer back, surely that should be the end of it?"

"It would then be only the sister's word against Mabel's that she ever had the tea strainer and was so ungrateful as to give it to the church bazaar." Miss Doffit pulled off her hat and squeezed it out. "I remember my mother once giving a tiara to the Women's Institute for its summer fête. Which explains in part why we ended up with no money and I've spent my life, like a woman without a country, living in other people's houses."

"You're trying to break my heart," said Vivian.

"I suppose," Cousin Sophie smiled at him, increasing her wrinkles a hundredfold, "Mabel could say, if push came to shove, that she did give her sister a tea strainer, but it wasn't the Queen Charlotte one."

Flora put down Nolly the better to concentrate on Edna's defense. "I really think that this is unfair. Mrs. Smith strikes me as a decent person who is probably feeling every bit as bad as Lady Gossinger about all this. Even more so, perhaps, because she is very pro the Queen and understands that she—meaning Mrs. Smith —gave away something that belongs to Her Majesty. Poor woman, I don't suppose she'll get any sleep tonight."

"That's one of Flora's greatest charms," commended Vivian. "She has this boundless faith in human nature."

"I think she has lots of charming ways," retorted Cousin Sophie, "which doesn't mean to say I think Henry was right to—" Stopping just in time, she deftly changed course, "—to spoil her the way he did when she was little. But I was almost as bad, I imagine. We did have fun, didn't we, Flora, dressing up in the trunk room? One of the reasons I never married was because a duke never asked me, so it was great sport to pretend I was the Duchess of Devon, I think that was who I was. I seem to remember you aspired to being nothing more than a lady, in the titled sense of the word. And it's remembering those pleasant times that has me hoping, my dear, that you'll let me stay here with you for the next few days, even though I'll be glad to leave the treasure-hunting to you. That's something I really wasn't looking forward to, even though Mabel did give me money for taxis."

"I'll arrange for you to stay at an excellent hotel, Cousin Sophie," said Vivian.

"I'm not sure that would be a good idea." The old lady's face turned mulish. "What if I should fall in the night, with no one to hear me? And I do like a cup of tea when I want one. That's not unreasonable at my age, is it?"

"Of course you can stay here," Flora hastened to say. "The flat upstairs has two bedrooms, both of them furnished because Vivian was kind enough to ask Sir Henry to send all the pieces from the rooms my grandfather and I used at Gossinger."

"The bed in the smaller room is extremely hard," Vivian said. "Flora, I need to talk to you."

"We are talking."

"I mean alone. No offense, Cousin Sophie, but this is important as well as private."

"Of course, dear."

"Then why don't you let me take you upstairs so you can use the bathroom to dry off and change your clothes before going into the sitting room to warm up by the fire. It's one of those with the electric logs. I'll turn it on for you," Vivian told his cousin.

"And in the meantime, I'll take Nolly out," Flora said. "I won't go far, and I'll feed him when I get back."

When Vivian and Miss Doffit had gone upstairs, Flora found the dog's lead and attached it to his collar. She had a queer, unsettled feeling, but she told herself that one crumpet did not do much to fill the gap between lunch and dinner. And if that wasn't the reason, she decided as she and Nolly stepped out into the rain and headed for the closest lamppost, it had to be because it had been an unsettling day—meeting Reggie, to say nothing of the rest of the afternoon. But she hadn't imagined the strained look on Vivian's face when he said he needed to talk to her. And she didn't think he was worried about something as simple as her being let in for extra expense if Miss Doffit stayed with her. No, there was something more, and while her head told her it couldn't be anything ominous, her heart had different ideas.

She was back in the shop and had only just filled Nolly's food and water bowls when Vivian came downstairs.

"I wish we could go up to the flat," he told her, "but Cousin Sophie might overhear. And it's important that she doesn't. Why don't we sit on the floor as we did the night of the picnic? Flora, that night seems an eternity ago. So much has happened. You . . . happened."

"Do you want me to sit down because you don't think I can handle what you have to say standing up? Yes, that's it. You're scaring me, Vivian."

"Won't you?" He made a sweeping gesture toward the floor.

"No, I won't." Flora clenched her hands. "Please don't keep me in suspense."

"I should have told you that first night; I meant to—it was why I came, but I talked myself out of doing what I knew was right."

"Vivian, please don't look so sad." Her hand moved of its own accord and touched his cheek. "You're a friend, I never thought I could say even that much, but I have to." Somewhere outside herself she saw him take her hand in his and kiss its palm. "I trust you," she said, "and know that you did what you thought was best for me. Now tell me."

"It has to do with the day your grandfather died. . . ."

"Yes?" Her heart gave a couple of thumps and then went quiet.

"We were there in the tower sitting room—Uncle Henry, Aunt Mabel, Cousin Sophie, and I—waiting for tea."

"And I was late bringing it up."

"So you were." Vivian gave her hand a final squeeze. "It was after you left that Uncle Henry broke the news that he'd decided to change his will."

"But what could that have to do with . . . ?"

"Your grandfather's death? Everything, I believe, because what he had decided was to leave Gossinger Hall to Hutchins."

"I can't take this in!" Flora reached behind her as if gripping the back of an invisible chair. "Why would he do something like that?"

"The house is not entailed, so there were no legal constraints. His reasoning was quite sound, to my way of thinking, and hinges on the Gossinger silver collection." Vivian felt as though he were reciting from a rehearsed text. "The collection was brought to the house late one night in the latter part of the eighteenth century by the daughter of a local silversmith, who had grown up on the stories of the Swineherd of Stowe, the man who'd left his life savings to Lincoln Cathedral. This man, the girl's father, wished to make a similar bequest. So he asked her to take all the pieces that remained unsold in his workrooms, on the day of his death, to Gossinger. She was to request that young Sir Rowland take them with him when he next took his carriage into Lincoln and present them to the cathedral."

"So that's how it got there." Flora spoke through stiff lips.

"But things didn't work out the way the silversmith

intended. When the girl arrived, Sir Rowland was at the card table with a group of his drinking and wenching pals. He had been losing heavily all evening and in a last desperate bid to save himself from financial ruin, he staked Gossinger on the turn of a card. He lost. He must have thought he was saved by divine intervention when that girl showed up with baskets full of silver. He used the silver to stake another hand. And his luck turned. He not only got back Gossinger, but gained a small fortune as well. According to family records he gave *that* money, which may well have been more than the value of the silver at that time, to Lincoln Cathedral. But he refused to part with the pieces themselves, because he had all the superstitions of the gamester and believed that while the silver remained, Gossinger would be immune to all ill fortune. As for the girl, one legend says she and Sir Rowland became lovers. Another claims that, consumed with rage, she cursed him, and that her ghost walks Gossinger to this day."

"But why," Flora wanted to stay trapped in the web of the story but found herself inexorably tugged back into the present, "why did Sir Henry decide to leave Gossinger to my grandfather?"

"Because he knows Hutchins was a descendant of that silversmith's family."

Vivian rubbed his forehead. "Uncle Henry believes that Sir Rowland committed a great sin by going against a dying man's wishes and that in reparation, however belated, he should return the silver collection, along with Gossinger, which would have gone out of the family without it, to the rightful owner."

"My grandfather being the closest living descendant?"

"Yes. It's exactly the same thing as the tea strainer. Wherever it has been hiding all these years it must, if family honor is to be preserved, go back where it belongs. You do see what this all means, don't you, Flora?"

"Of course I do! I'm not completely stupid!" She picked up Nolly who had been sitting patiently, trying not to look as though he minded being left out of this momentous conversation. "You've just provided me with the motive for my grandfather's murder. Now are you going to tell me who murdered him?"

"You don't think . . . ?" Vivian blanched.

"That you—?" Flora's eyes stung. "How can you suggest I would think such a thing?"

"Because Gossinger would have come to me."

"But you don't like it!"

"That's true, but I might have equally disliked the idea of someone outside the family inheriting it. Let's be realistic: I could have sold it and lived rather nicely on the proceeds."

"We're wasting time," Flora said impatiently. "Do you think the killer was Miss Doffit?" The thought of the old lady now sitting placid as a cat by the fire being a cold-blooded murderess sent a chill through Flora. "Is that why you didn't want her to stay here?"

"No, I don't think she killed your grandfather. Although I don't like what I am thinking about her, because I've always been awfully fond of Cousin Sophie . . ."

"Then if it isn't her, and it obviously wasn't Sir Henry, then there's only one person left. And that's Lady Gossinger!"

"Aunt Mabel was beside herself when Uncle Henry broke the news about his will. He knew she would be, which is why he did it in front of Cousin Sophie and me. I suppose some might say that was cowardly of him, but his determination to follow his conscience makes him a hero in my eyes. And there's more, Flora. Now that your grandfather is gone, Uncle Henry is talking about leaving Gossinger to you instead. He may in fact already have done so."

Flora pressed her fingers to her lips in an attempt to steady her breathing before she could speak. "Please, don't you dare ask me if I realize what that means! All right, I'll say it for you. You're afraid that Lady Gossinger may make away with me next. That's why you've been staying here. I never did believe you ran your car out of petrol the other night. Everything's becoming clear, even to dim-witted me. I see now why you were so sure Boris Smith had seen or heard something that frightened him so much that he hasn't been himself since."

"I'm hoping to find out what that is," Vivian doubled his hands into fists, "because the problem is that I don't see how we can prove any of this without some evidence. It's all pure speculation, and to tell you the truth much of the time I believe I'm mad as a hatter. That *I'm* the one turning your grandfather's death into a murder story."

"You could have told the police about the will and let them reach their own conclusions. Didn't my grandfather deserve that much?" Flora spoke stiffly.

"And what if they couldn't come up with anything concrete? Aunt Mabel could have sat back and bided her time until, lo and behold, you met with an accident. I'll admit that there's a part of me that still can't believe she's a murderer. I always found her rather endearing, despite her faults. But no consideration of that sort would have stopped me from speaking out if I had thought it would settle matters up front."

"Do you think Sir Henry suspects her?" Flora put Nolly down. He was becoming unbearably heavy.

"No, I'm sure he doesn't. The man's completely guileless."

"So that takes us back to Miss Doffit."

"I think Cousin Sophie may have decided to throw

in her hand with Aunt Mabel as a means of ensuring she can never be tossed out from Gossinger on her ear. And that at the least she is here to find out if you have any suspicions. At worst . . . I'd really rather not think about that. But as I must, it seems to me that if Aunt Mabel is visibly at Gossinger, she might not be suspected if something untoward happened to you."

"Somehow I can't see Miss Doffit pushing me under a train."

"No, but she could be here to make arrangements with someone willing to do the job for the right price."

"Oh, this is beginning to sound ridiculous."

"I know," said Vivian.

"At least I now understand why you took me somewhat seriously when I told you Nolly sensed someone was following us. You aren't . . . you aren't thinking that Snuffy—and Reggie, too—could be mixed up in this?"

"The idea naturally occurred to me, but there reaches a point where it's impossible to know where paranoia starts or leaves off. I thought that if we could take it one step at a time—"

"But that's just what you didn't do! There was no 'we' about it. It was *my* grandfather that was murdered, not yours! And it's *my* life that you are now saying may be at risk!" Flora's eyes blazed with tears. "You had no business treating me like a child. If I act like one sometimes, that's up to me. No," she held up her hand, "don't touch me. The girl who said she trusted you isn't here anymore. Actually it's even worse than I let on! I allowed myself to fall in love with you! Can you believe that? Because *I* can't!"

"Flora, you must know—"

"I want you to leave, Vivian. I want you to pack up your Cousin Sophie and her suitcase and be out of here in three minutes, or I'll set Nolly on you both! And I'm not going to hate myself for this in the morning."

SEVENTEEN

When Flora woke up the next morning, her head throbbed and her eyes felt as though they had been rubbed in sand. For a moment she feared she had a hangover. She'd had one once when she was seventeen and went out dancing with some of her friends from school and returned home at what the current house-keeper had called a godforsaken hour. All Grandpa had said when he'd seen her was that he was glad she had taken a taxi home.

This was the same sick, muzzy feeling. The memories of last night floated mercifully out of reach. Until she sat up, upsetting the equilibrium so that they came back with such force that now her head really did feel as though it were about to explode. She had to stagger into the bathroom to get a glass of water, which she drank sitting on the edge of the bath.

Thank goodness for Nolly, thought Flora as the little dog came up and started nuzzling her feet. For his sake, I have to put myself on automatic, get myself dressed, and take him for a walk before breakfast. And it was surprising, she discovered, just how much can be accomplished using one-tenth of your brain. While out with Nolly she stopped at the grocer's shop four doors down, and chatted to the owners—a husband and wife who told her they originated from Middlesex. In addition to selling her the essentials for a few days, they lent her a kettle and saucepan. Nice people. On being handed a biscuit, Nolly certainly thought so.

She fed Nolly and boiled herself an egg, then put away the groceries and washed up the pieces of crockery and cutlery which had been sent up along with the furniture from Gossinger. And it was at that moment, with her hands sunk in soapy water, that a thought extricated itself from the fog inside her head.

"I don't believe it, Nolly!" Flora shook the water off her hands. "Maybe you'll say I'm a coward and don't want to face the truth, but I don't think it's that. I just do not believe that Lady Gossinger is enough of a monster to have murdered Grandpa! Yes, I can see her taking revenge on Sir Henry by giving away the tea strainer. That's in character. But the rest—no, and if you want to know why I'm so sure, Nolly, it's because Grandpa *liked* her. Oh, he never became as fond of her as he was of Sir Henry; that wasn't to be expected. But he would often get upset with me for not seeing her good points. And if he were here right now he'd tell me that it was entirely understandable for her Ladyship— or any wife, for that matter—to be beside herself on hearing that her home was being left to an outsider. If Sir Henry . . ." Flora reached across the draining board and snapped off a stalk of celery to nibble. "If Sir Henry," she repeated, "had told Grandpa what he planned, I know Grandpa would have been appalled at the idea that he might one day own Gossinger. It would have turned his world upside down and somehow diminished his life of service to the Family. You think I'm silly," Flora scooped up Nolly and laid her cheek against his, flattening his ears, "but I have to go by what Grandpa is telling me, even though you can't see him. Because Grandpa was the most sensible man in the world. And he's telling me that Lady Gossinger should not be blamed for what happened to him. Which leaves me *where,* Nolly?"

The little dog indicated that, much as he sympathized with her problems, he wanted to play with his red ball. So Flora put Nolly down and made herself start on the drying up. She put away the saucepan the grocer couple had lent her and stuffed the disgusting old one in one of the carrier bags, which she put under the sink to make do as a rubbish bin for the time being. And while doing all this, she was trying very hard not to think about Vivian. But it was impossible. Because one glance into the shop told her it was empty as it had never been before. He was wrong, she told herself; but the words lacked the conviction of last night. So she tried again. *All that time we were together, when I thought I knew exactly what was going on inside his head, I really didn't have a clue.* And then from the back of her brain another little voice piped up: *Is this what your anger with him is all about? Wounded vanity? Because it should be clearer to you now, you silly goose, why Vivian didn't know what to do for the best. If you can't believe Lady Gossinger murdered Grandpa, then think how it must have been for Vivian, harboring those awful suspicions! And at the same time wondering if he hadn't let his imagination run riot so that he was seeing bogeymen everywhere.*

Flora didn't get any further in trying to decide what to do about Vivian because at that moment the shop door jangled. She had forgotten to lock it on coming back in from her walk with Nolly, and she now saw Mrs. Much crossing the threshold.

"I don't suppose you expected to see me," Mrs. Much said, "but here I am, come to see how you're getting along."

"It's nice to see you," said Flora, coming toward her, "but how did you know where to find me?"

"That wasn't hard, dear." Mrs. Much held her handbag in both hands as she sized up the room. "I rang up Gossinger last night to ask if I'd left a book behind that was given to me by my past employer Mrs. Frome. And the new housekeeper put me on to Sir Henry, so naturally I asked about you and he gave me the address. Looks like you've got your work cut out for you, Flora. These walls will need stripping and painting." She moved in for a closer inspection. "Three coats if you ask me. And I'd be careful, if you choose white, to pick just the right shade. Nothing with a hint of gray, or the shadows from the window will make this wall in particular look dingy. Mrs. Frome, the lady I just mentioned, always preferred an off-white with a hint of blush. Oh, she was a gem to work for, God rest her soul."

"How about a cup of tea?" suggested Flora, to cut short praise of the late Mrs. Frome.

"No, thanks, dear, I just had one."

"Then why don't we go upstairs and you can tell me how you like your new job." *This is good,* thought Flora. *Perhaps by the time Mrs. Much goes, all those bits and pieces floating around in my mind will have assembled into some sort of sensible shape.*

"You've got things looking just the way you had them at Gossinger," Mrs. Much commented when they entered the flat and she had seated herself in the fireside chair. "Didn't you want to start all fresh, maybe buy yourself a nice Danish-modern suite?"

"No, I like being among old friends," Flora replied.

"There's certainly a lot of that at Buckingham Palace." Mrs. Much looked strongly disapproving. "All the furniture is as old as the hills and I've yet to see a fitted carpet. You wonder why one of Her Majesty's chums hasn't put a bug in her ear about talking to a decorator with some nice modern ideas."

Flora sat down across from her. "You don't sound too happy."

"Well, it's a job, isn't it?"

"Aren't things going smoothly?"

"Sometimes I suppose I expect too much by way of appreciation." Mrs. Much took out a hanky from her handbag and blew her nose. "You try to do your best and it's taken the wrong way. You'll remember the fuss that was made at Gossinger about me washing those filthy tapestries."

"Yes, I do."

"It was much the same as what happened the other day. You know how particular I am when it comes to toilets, Flora. Well, believe it or not, you should have heard the carrying on when it was found out that I'd put one of them sanitizing jobbies in one of the tanks. You know, the ones that make the water a nice royal blue. Oh, you'd have thought I'd committed murder, the way my supervisor carried on. It was only by saying 'yes sir, no sir, three bags full, sir,' to myself that I was able to keep my mouth shut and hang on to my job. If it wasn't that it doesn't do to keep jumping ship, I'd be looking for a new place tomorrow."

"Oh, I am sorry!"

"Well enough about old me; I'm here to see how you're coping with your grandfather's death. It'll take you a while to get over it, but then again I'm sure he wouldn't want you down in the dumps too long. So, how was things when you left Gossinger? What's going on with Mr. Tipp? I gave him my new address and was hoping he'd keep in touch, but so far not a dickeybird."

"He's gone to look after a cousin who's ill."

"Well, that's a turnup for the book." Mrs. Much put away her hanky. "I'm sure he told me he didn't have a soul in the world to call his own, but then again men are inclined to play on your sympathy when you're a single woman. And I wouldn't be surprised if he wasn't going a bit soft in the head. I remember a day, afternoon it was, when he did more talking than usual and looking back, I'm sure it was all a pack of nonsense."

"I do hope he's all right." Flora was really very glad when Nolly, who had not left his red ball to welcome Mrs. Much, came into the room and settled cozily down on the hearth rug.

"More important, dear, are *you* all right?"

"I'm settling in here and I have plans to open the shop downstairs. Lady Gossinger," it was a little difficult to say the name, "has said I can have it, which was very kind of her."

"And what is it you're going to sell?"

"Secondhand stuff at first, but eventually I would like to specialize in silver."

"Now you've gone and reminded me," said Mrs. Much. "I was hoping you might have some of your grandfather's polish with you. Because as you well know there's nothing to touch it on the supermarket shelves."

"Of course I can let you have some. I've quite a few bottles of it on the window ledge in my bedroom."

"Could you let me have two, dear?"

"I'll be right back with them."

"Thanks ever so." Mrs. Much reached into her handbag when Flora returned with a bottle of polish in each hand. "How much is it I owe you?"

"Nothing."

"Oh, I don't like to take them for free."

"You can pay me by telling people that nothing has ever cleaned silver like it and then send them here to buy some because I will be making up more from Grandpa's instructions and selling it in the shop."

"Well, that is good to know."

"And I've got even bigger plans than that." Flora sat back down and patted her skirt for Nolly to come and sit by her. "I'll let you in on a little secret, Mrs. Much: I wrote a letter to the Queen asking if she would consider granting Gossinger Silver Polish the Royal Warrant. So far I haven't heard anything, but I'm keeping my fingers crossed."

"Well, that does give me an idea."

"What do you mean?"

"That I'll take a bottle of the polish into work with me when I start my shift this afternoon."

"To Buckingham Palace?" Flora experienced a spurt of excitement. "But I wouldn't want you to get into trouble, not after that bother with the blue toilet water."

"Oh, it wouldn't be like that! I'll give one of these bottles to my cousin, the one that got me the job— Glynis is her name—and she works on some of the silver. Just leave it to me, Flora. And who knows—I could end up getting a rise!"

"If you're really sure . . ."

"Positive, and I'll be back in touch to let you know how things go. Well, dear, I'd better be off if I don't intend to ruin things by being late for work. Let me know if you hear from Mr. Tipp. Poor old soul. Perhaps it would do him good when he gets back to come up to London for the day and have me show him the sights." Mrs. Much continued to chatter as they went downstairs, wanting to know what Flora had seen so far of the big city and offering ample suggestions.

"John Lewis has a lovely soft furnishings department," she was saying when somebody banged on the shop door. Flora had a moment of panic mingled with hope, but of course Vivian would never thump on the door like that. And she opened it up to see Boris Smith looking up at her.

"Gran made me come." His eyes didn't quite meet hers. "She said if I was having another day off school I should come round and ask if there's anything you need doing." His freckles were spotlighted by the sunshine that slanted at a sharp angle off the rooftops. *I'm going to write to that teacher,* Flora thought, *because even if I don't believe Lady Gossinger had a hand in Grandpa's death, I have to find out if this boy knows something about what happened in the garderobe.*

"Hello, Boris," she told him. "This is a friend of mine. Her name's Mrs. Much."

"How nice." The response was made with blatant lack of enthusiasm.

"Mrs. Much has just promised to do something wonderful for me. She's going to take a bottle of my grandfather's silver polish into work this afternoon."

"And where's work?"

"Buckingham Palace."

"Is it really?" Boris perked up.

"Do I look like somebody that tells lies?" Mrs. Much gave Flora a peck on the cheek before walking away to catch her bus.

Boris watched her for a minute before turning back to Flora. "That's what my gran says, and she does, you know, tell lies."

"That's not nice of you to say."

"Even if it's true?"

"Then you need to talk to her." Flora suddenly wished she were a great deal older, with a much better understanding of children. "Do you want to come in?" she asked.

"No," Boris kicked one foot against the other, "I've got to go."

"We could talk."

"Thanks all the same." Boris was already moving

away, sliding his feet along the pavement. "I've just remembered there's something I have to do. Catch you later."

Flora was about to go back inside when she saw Mr. Banda Singhh talking to a delivery man outside his shop, and all at once, as if a torch light had flicked on inside her head, she remembered Mr. Singhh talking about his wife Emel and saying that she had worked with Edna Smith on the church bazaar. Dodging inside for the key and assuring Nolly that she wouldn't be a moment, Flora stepped back out into the street and hurried down to Mr. Singhh's place of business. The delivery van was no longer parked outside. When she pushed open the door of the fish-and-chip shop, she was met by the pungent smell of smoking hot oil. She found a woman with graying black hair drawn back low on her neck standing behind the counter.

"Good morning," the woman said. "First batch of chips all ready to come out of the basket, and we have some nice skate today."

"Sounds delicious!" Flora smiled at her. "But I really came in for a chat. Mr. Singhh was kind enough to come round the day before last, and—"

"So," the woman wiped her hands on her white overall before extending her right one across the counter, "you are the young lady from the empty shop! Banda, he was so pleased to meet you. Sadly, you have just missed him. He went down to the post office. I am his wife, Emel. Do tell me, if you please, how do you like Wishbone Street so far?"

"Very much," replied Flora. "Your husband helped convince me I will be happy here. Would you please tell him that I have decided to reopen the shop below my flat?"

"Certainly."

"He mentioned that you had worked with Edna Smith on the church bazaar."

"Banda," his wife's face lit in a smile that showed her beautiful, even teeth, "he is a man who pays attention to little things; there is not much that he does not remember."

"The reason I bring it up," Flora hoped she could keep the story short without making herself sound like the most awful busybody, "is that yesterday a friend of mine and I went to tea at Mrs. Smith's, and she mentioned giving a tea strainer to the bazaar, which it turns out—"

"Your friend, he was here not half an hour ago!" Seeing Flora's astonished face, Emel Singhh added quickly, "It must have been him because he, too, said he had been to Mrs. Smith's yesterday. And when he, just like you, asked about the tea strainer I was able to tell him that I was the one who sold it, to a woman I know quite well. She lives quite close by. That is what I told him. Look, that is him," Emel pointed to the window. "No, you have missed him. He is a fast walker. But go now and catch up with him."

Flora was out the door before Mrs. Singhh had finished speaking. Which way? She hated to lose a fraction of a second turning her head the wrong way. But there was no need to worry. She saw him immediately, no more than a few yards to her right and without thinking, she called out: "Vivian!"

He turned around at once. "I went looking for the tea strainer."

"And did you find it?"

"I was on my way to show you."

"And I was at the fish-and-chip shop."

"Great minds think alike." Vivian stood looking at her, the sun bringing out hints of gold in his brown hair.

"That makes for a great team," said Flora softly, seeing everything she needed to know in his eyes. "Let's go inside so you can show me the tea strainer. Do you really have it?"

"In my pocket," he assured her as he followed her into the shop. "Flora, we have to talk about last night. My thinking was that if I could bring you this," he pulled out the small paper-wrapped package, "you might find it in your heart to forgive me."

"There's nothing to forgive." Flora bent down to pat Nolly and throw him his ball. "I got myself sorted out this morning and I'm glad you didn't talk to the police about Lady Gossinger, because I don't believe she did anything more than possibly smash a few plates after Sir Henry told her about his plans to make that very silly change in his will."

"Flora, I'm happy you're no longer so upset, but—"

"I know what you're going to say, it's that I'm indulging in wishful thinking, but I don't believe that one minute. Vivian, I'm sorry for the things I said last night, including saying that I'd fallen in love with you. I only did that to make you feel more guilty, which was extremely immature of me. So you see," she gave him her most impish grin, "you don't need to be frightened at the prospect of being alone with me. Now, are you going to show me that tea strainer or do I have to snatch it out of your hands?"

"I want you to unwrap it."

"You have looked at it already?"

"What do you take me for?" Vivian gave a laugh that came from a warmth of happiness he didn't remember experiencing before. "I had to pay the woman who'd bought this big money, even though I told her it was of great *sentimental* value to my family."

"And you have no doubt it's the right one?"

"Take a look for yourself."

"My hands are shaking."

"All right, I have the paper off. Now take it."

"Oh!" Flora stared down at the tea strainer in her

hands. Someone, presumably the woman who had bought it at the bazaar, had made an attempt at polishing it, but there still wasn't much silver shining through the tarnish, which had turned it copper-colored in some places and a dull black in others. "What a beauty!"

"Both the design and the workmanship are truly exquisite, wouldn't you say?" Vivian bent over her as if admiring a newborn baby.

"It makes me want to cry." She brushed at her eyes.

"Just wait till we see it all shined up."

"But we could do that right now, I've some of Grandpa's polish upstairs."

"Then go and get it."

Flora handed him the tea strainer before racing up the stairs two at a time. She was back with a bottle in one hand and a handful of dusters flapping in the other before Vivian had finished rolling up his sleeves.

"What a good thing I thought to use these for packing up breakables," she said as he joined her in the kitchen. "Now bear in mind I don't possess Grandpa's magic touch when it comes to cleaning intricate detail, but with this product," she shook the bottle of polish vigorously, "only as severe a critic as he would notice the difference. The secret with polishing silver," she continued as she spread out a duster on the draining board, "is a firm but loving hand."

"I feel as though we should have a bottle of champagne on ice." Vivian stepped back so she would not feel he was breathing down her neck.

"It *is* rather like waiting for the Sleeping Beauty to awake after the prince's kiss." Flora dabbed some polish on her softest duster and got busy. "Look how it's coming up already! Stand back, because I want to see your eyes when I show you. Patience—this sort of thing can't be rushed. Oh, I can't tell you how many times I heard Grandpa say that! And how I wish he could be here for this moment!"

"So do I, Flora."

"I should be feeling sad, but I can't because I haven't felt so close to him since he died. It's as though he is right here in this room, watching me, saying, 'This is what I taught you, Flora.'"

"He taught you well," said Vivian as Flora turned and held out her hands: the tea strainer had become a brilliant silver swan resting on the clean duster. "I'm speechless."

"Do you think Her Majesty will be pleased?"

"Before we rush to ring up Buckingham Palace, I'd love to find out where it was made and the name of the silversmith. That way we could send it along with full credentials."

"That would be wonderful," said Flora. "Not that there's any doubt in our minds that it was the one Queen Charlotte brought to Gossinger, but it would be very nice to prove it. Oh, bother! Someone's at the door." She put the tea strainer gently back down on the draining board in the nest of dusters.

Vivian grimaced. "I hope it's not Cousin Sophie again. She spent the night at my place, and I was hoping she would stay put until I got back. But I did forget to tie her down."

"Well, she's bound to be pleased at the missing object's safe return."

But Flora opened the door to find not Cousin Sophie but her father, otherwise known as Reggie, standing outside.

"I say." He stepped nimbly inside and flashed his gap-toothed grin. "Hate to be a blithering nuisance but I was wondering if by some confounded chance I left my wallet here yesterday. Wouldn't you know, it had my last twenty pounds in it."

"You're fibbing, Reggie," said Flora, to which Nolly added agreement by thumping his tail.

"Smashing!" Reggie's smile stretched wider. "Admire a woman who sees right through me. Just thought I'd take a crack at it, a bit short of the ready, you see, but I'll be toddling along."

"Don't rush off," said Vivian. "You happen to have turned up at a rather opportune moment. I was just thinking," he said, looking at Flora, "about something our friend Snuffy said the other night."

"Oh, yes?" Reggie cocked an eyebrow.

"He mentioned a woman he knew—a former fence, who is an expert in silver. It stands to reason she would be, doesn't it? Because someone in that profession would need to know the precise value of the merchandise. And what I'm wondering is if in return for the loan of twenty pounds," Vivian pulled out his wallet, "you would be willing to ring up Snuffy and see if he can put us in touch with this woman."

"I say," Reggie looked from Vivian to Flora, "you're not getting yourselves mixed up in any funny business?"

"It's nothing like that," she told him. "We are just interested in getting an expert's opinion on a small piece of silver."

"Jolly good show! Lead me to the telephone. I'll give Snuffy a buzz and see if I can catch him."

"I only had it installed yesterday morning," said Flora as he picked up the receiver. Moments later he handed it to Vivian, who found himself speaking to a woman who answered to the name of Lucy and listened with apparent interest to the story of the tea strainer.

"She says she can see us now." He cupped a hand over the phone. "How does that suit you?"

"Perfectly," Flora told him, her face radiant.

"My friend Miss Hutchins is most eager to talk to you," Vivian told Louie. "She is descended from a Lincolnshire silversmith and is herself planning to open a silver shop."

"I had to make us sound important," he explained,

after hanging up. "Why don't you put on a hat and I'll walk Reggie downstairs." Flora knew the reason for this and said so five minutes later when they got into Vivian's car.

"You asked Reggie if he needed more than twenty pounds, didn't you?"

"It's that gap-toothed grin."

"I know, he's like a naughty schoolboy."

"And it was money well spent," said Vivian, putting the car in gear. "At least it will be if Lucy lives up to her reputation. Hold on to your hat, we're off and running!" And with that the car streaked out into traffic.

"Where does she live?"

"Earl's Court, shouldn't take us long."

"Not at this speed. Are we going under or over that lorry?"

"You do have the tea strainer?"

"No, I gave it to Nolly to play with!"

"All right, I won't ask again."

"Is that because we've arrived?"

"Give me another fifteen minutes."

Due to a shortcut not working out, it took a little longer than fifteen minutes to reach the block of flats where Louie lived. The outside didn't look much different from where Edna Smith lived. But a doorman in the entryway ushered them to the lift and accompanied them up three floors to the flat in question. Its door was opened by a maid in crisp navy and white who led them down a softly carpeted hall, hung with a mixture of traditional and modern art, into a large living room furnished in tranquil blues and greens.

Seated on facing sofas were two women. One was gray-haired and matronly. The other . . . Flora stood still and stared. The other was the witchy-looking woman whom she had glimpsed at her grandfather's funeral and later that afternoon walking across the road from Gossinger!

"I'm Lucy." The matronly woman extended a hand. "Excuse me if I don't get up, I suffer from gout and it's been giving me hell this past week."

"Good afternoon." Flora heard her own voice echoing Vivian's.

"And this is Evangeline, a friend of mine," said Lucy. "I hope that neither of you will mind that I rang her up after I talked to you, Mr. Gossinger, because I thought she would be quite interested in your tea strainer. Evangeline is also an expert in the field of silver. She is descended, as you are, which seems an interesting coincidence, from a Lincolnshire silversmith."

"You were at my grandfather's funeral." Flora took a half-step toward the black-haired woman with long purple fingernails, now rising to her feet with a swirl of her gypsy-style skirt.

"He was a cousin of mine, several times removed." Evangeline spoke in a throaty voice. "I hadn't seen him for years. That was my fault. I should have got in touch when your mother died, but I was embarrassed, I'm ashamed to say. Your grandfather once lent me quite a sizable sum of money to open a silver shop. It took some years to get off the ground, and by the time I could afford to pay him back—well, there aren't any excuses, I just never got round to it. And when I had the occasional moment of feeling guilty, I reminded myself he'd told me at the time that he didn't expect the money back."

"He had a great passion for silver," said Flora.

"It runs in the family," replied Evangeline. "I did want to talk to you at the funeral, but you slipped away before I got the chance. And afterward I took a walk out to Gossinger and saw you in the garden, but you were talking to this gentleman here," she indicated Vivian, "so I decided not to intrude. It began to seem that we weren't destined to speak the other day. I spotted you at Kings Cross underground getting into another carriage. But now here we are."

"This is all very interesting," said Louie, "but am I going to be allowed a look at this tea strainer?"

"Flora has it." Vivian nudged her gently forward. "We're interested in knowing approximately when it was made."

"I don't go in for approximations." Louie pulled on a pair of cotton gloves and picked up an eye loupe from the coffee table. "If I can't give you the month I can certainly give you the year. Hand it over now, I'm not going to run out the door with it! Ah, yes!" she exclaimed. "You are correct, Mr. Gossinger, it is a little marvel. I think you should take a look, Evangeline."

"If I may?"

"Of course," replied Vivian.

"There's no doubt," Evangeline's voice grew even more husky, "this is the tea strainer purchased by Queen Charlotte on her way to Gossinger Hall from our mutual ancestor, Flora. His name, if you don't already know, was Thomas White. One day, if you wish, I will show you his record book. It provides a detailed description of this tea strainer. He made only one."

"I have to sit down," murmured Flora. "This is almost too much to take in. . . ."

"Oh, I can tell you a lot more, almost all of which I uncovered after I last saw your grandfather. I'm quite sure, Mr. Gossinger, that what he didn't know was that Thomas White's daughter wasn't Sir Rowland Gossinger's mistress as has been suggested. Neither did she put a curse on him. She became his first wife. A secret marriage, but one that produced a son, and according to my genealogical research, that would mean that my cousin—Flora's grandfather—was the living heir to the title your uncle inherited. Oh, one other interesting fact," Evangeline placed the tea strainer back in Flora's unsteady hands. "The name of that girl who brought the silver to Gossinger Hall and won the heart of Sir Rowland . . . it was Vivian."

It was at that moment of stunned silence that a male voice was heard calling, "Mother, I'm home!" And Louie leaned back on her sofa with closed eyes as Mr. Ferncliffe, man of science and teacher of eleven-year-old boys, walked into the room.

EIGHTEEN

"I wonder if Mr. Ferncliffe knows that his mother was once part of the underworld?" said Flora.

"That's the third time you've asked me that since we got back here." Vivian leaned back in his chair and watched her get up to close the sitting room curtains which had so recently hung at Gossinger.

"Sorry."

"Don't be. I know what you're doing. You're reaching into the bag for things to say so that I won't keep thinking about what your cousin Evangeline told us about the family tree. It does put a different complexion on Uncle Henry's motives, doesn't it?"

"For deciding to change his will?" Flora sat back down across from him.

"Or saying he was going to, which isn't the same thing. I don't like what I'm thinking, Flora, because

Uncle Henry has been a second father to me. But what if he did know—and if Evangeline could dredge up the information, so could he—that it was your grandfather to whom the title and everything else truly belonged? For all we know, Evangeline, or someone else, could have been in touch with Uncle Henry and threatened to expose the true state of affairs. That would certainly strike many people as a rather compelling motive for my uncle to get rid of the sole obstacle to his wealth and position. And how clever it would have been to point suspicion away from himself by announcing that out of the goodness of his heart he was going to leave Gossinger Hall to his devoted butler!" Vivian dragged himself out of his chair and began pacing, or rather walking around Nolly, who was lying in his path. "I hate myself for suspecting him, Flora, but it's beginning to seem rather sinister to me that Uncle Henry wanted me and Cousin Sophie there when he put Aunt Mabel in the picture."

"Did you get much sleep last night?"

"Not a lot."

"I didn't think so, because you are talking a lot of rubbish," said Flora. "Of course Sir Henry had to tell you what he intended. You're his heir. Grandpa was devoted to Sir Henry, and his devotion was based on his belief that he was a truly good man. And one thing I can tell you is that my grandfather was not a fool."

"I have to be the world's worst brute," said Vivian, "putting you through another evening on this painful subject."

"It isn't upsetting me, not tonight. And that's because I've felt so strongly today that Grandpa isn't really gone; he'll always be here when I need him most. Warm and real and very much my guardian angel, just as he was in life." She turned her head as the phone rang. "I wonder who that can be?"

Nolly showed his annoyance at the noisy interruption by attacking the cord, and Flora had to step over him to pick up the receiver. He continued to yap for the few minutes that she spoke to the caller.

"That was Mrs. Much," she told Vivian, hanging up.

"Anything important?"

"Odd, to say the least. I forgot to tell you that she came round this morning and said she would take a bottle of Grandpa's silver polish with her to Buckingham Palace when she went to work this afternoon."

"In hope that Her Majesty would be dazzled by the new brilliance of her silver and ask if a new polish was being used?" suggested Vivian. "Which would in turn jog her memory regarding a recent application for the Royal Warrant?"

"That was the general idea. But as it turned out, Mrs. Much sprained her ankle getting off the bus and didn't go in to work today. The odd part is that someone telephoned Buckingham Palace to say that a member of the staff would be bringing in a bottle supposedly filled with silver polish, but really containing an explosive. The result was the biggest rumpus ever, with bomb squad people pouring through the palace. Mrs. Much got wind of it through her cousin who also works there." Flora pressed a hand to her mouth and sat down on the arm of the settee. "Oh, my goodness, I am dense! *Boris!*"

"What about him?" Vivian went over to her.

"He was here as Mrs. Much was leaving, and I told him about the polish."

"Why, the wicked little devil!"

"This shows he really is disturbed, doesn't it?"

"I'll say!"

"Poor Edna, I'll have to tell her." Flora felt thoroughly miserable.

"You don't have any choice." Vivian pulled her to her feet and put an arm round her. "Cheer up, maybe this is what it takes to get that boy some help. And speaking of taking action, I've decided to look in on Uncle Henry and Aunt Mabel tomorrow to see if I can't get a better perspective on things." Vivian was now back to pacing around Nolly again. "The trouble is, it's the old story of never practice your profession on your relatives."

"I don't understand," said Flora.

"It's something else I never got round to telling you."

"What is?" Flora was thoroughly confused.

"That I *do* have what comes close to a full-time job. I work for a private detection agency owned and operated by a couple of my relatives. I think I may have mentioned them to you in passing. They are elderly women—"

"The ones you send lavender water to at Christmas?"

"That's them. They're sisters. And the agency is named Flowers Detection because their names are Hyacinth and Primrose. As of the last month or so they have been working on a case in Switzerland. Or I hope that's where they are. It's hard to keep in touch with them when they go undercover, which is why I haven't been able to discuss our situation with them. And that's a major pity, because they would have had the answers while I was still asking the questions," he added glumly.

"So your job with George at the flea market was just a front?"

"A woman had taken to flogging her mother's knickknacks. Nothing of any great monetary value, but the rest of the family was mad as hell so I was hired to catch her in action. That's the sort of job I handle mostly," said Vivian, "the stuff that doesn't have the police begging to get first crack at the action. My stint at Macho Man, the toiletries-for-men people, was a little more interesting. There I was brought in by the chairman of the board's ex-wife to find out if he was lying about the extent of his income."

"Do you like it?" Flora asked. "Being a private eye?"

"Yes, I do. Fortunately I'm not dependent on what I earn, because at the moment I'm not worth all that much. Hyacinth and Primrose have yet to be tempted to cut me loose on a big case."

"Well, I think you're going to amaze them one day soon with your brilliance," Flora said firmly.

"So you're not upset that I didn't tell you about this before?" Vivian wanted very much to take her face in his hands.

"No, of course not," replied Flora. "We've only begun to know each other, and I wouldn't like to think you spilled out your heart to just any girl after that short a time."

"But there's a difference. Not every girl lets me spend the night on our first date."

"I'm obviously a very shallow person."

"I think you're entirely wonderful."

"You're only saying that," Flora was having trouble breathing, "because you want me to be shallow one more time."

"I'm getting to like having my own room here."

"Oh, all right!" Flora tossed a pillow at him in an attempt at putting the mood back where it belonged. "Let's go out for fish-and-chips. Nolly is tired of eating out of a tin."

NINETEEN

When Flora looked out of the sitting room window the following morning to watch Vivian drive off, she saw the flags hanging off buildings up and down Wishbone Street, and wondered what was going on until she remembered Edna Smith saying that the Queen was coming to open the new wing of the children's hospital. Which Flora had taken to mean in a week or two. And she hadn't assumed that Her Majesty would pass down Wishbone Street. But those flags certainly indicated that was a possibility, if not an assured thing.

Flora thought about Edna while she was making her bed (Vivian had left his tidy) and after plumping up the cushions in the sitting room decided not to put it off any longer and telephoned her to talk about Boris. It took several rings for Edna to answer, and when she spoke it was with quite a bit of huffing and puffing, because she had been halfway down the first flight of steps from her flat, on her way to the hairdressing shop, when she heard the phone and turned back.

"I thought it was someone from Boris's school," Edna said, "wanting to know why he hasn't been in class the last few days. I know I shouldn't give in to him letting him stay home, but I'll tell you, Flora, I'm afraid if I come down heavy that boy will just run off. His mother was a great one for that game. Well, that's why I'm raising him, isn't it, while she's God knows where. Sometimes I think I'm at the end of my tether."

This is not going to be easy, thought Flora. *And there's Miss Doffit worrying that Edna might decide to blackmail her sister over the business of the tea strainer. As if she'd have the energy, poor woman.*

"I hate to do this to you, Edna, really I do," she said, "but it's about Boris that I'm ringing up. There was an incident yesterday that I think it's important for you to know about." And she went on to explain about Mrs. Much and the silver polish.

"Oh, my heavens! The boy's going to end up in prison, I don't see any other end to it. And just a few weeks ago I'd have sworn on a stack of Bibles there was no more harm in him than the usual boy's mischief."

"It's not as though he caused any physical harm. . . ." Flora suddenly wondered if she had made too much out of a boyish prank.

"But to phone up Buckingham Palace and put the wind up the poor Queen, I don't think I'll ever be able to look her in the face on the telly, let alone go out and watch her drive past at noon today. Oh, and I was so looking forward to it, I'd bought a new coat and shoes, but there's no use upsetting myself about that. I'll go and yank Mr. Boris out of his bed this minute and try to get that boy to talk to me. See if I can't reach him somehow."

Flora hung up the phone and wandered listlessly

about the flat for several minutes until she got herself
motivated again and sat down to make a list of things
she needed to do. The first thing she wrote down was
"sewing machine." She had liked to sew ever since Mrs.
Bellows had taught her to stitch, and it would be fun to
make a cloth to cover a display table for the shop. Her
pencil began to move rapidly. Find a carpenter, talk to
George from the flea market about suppliers, buy a cash
register—preferably one of the lovely old brass ones.

The list went on to a second page, and after that it
was time to write a letter to Mrs. Bellows asking when
Flora could go and see her in Ilford. By the time Flora
looked at the clock it was close to eleven. When she
glanced out the window she could see people lining
the street waiting to catch a glimpse of the Queen. If
she didn't take Nolly out now, it would be an impossible crush.

As it turned out, Nolly appeared to be quite taken by
the crowd, perhaps because it brought back memories
of his life at the flea market with George, and Flora had
trouble persuading him to stop showing off and come
back inside the shop.

"You'd have been charging for your autograph
next," she scolded, taking off his lead. "I think we'll
watch for the Queen from the sitting room window.
That way you can't embarrass me by— Oh, well, never
mind, there goes the phone. I do hope it's Vivian, he did
promise to ring, didn't he?"

It was Vivian, and her heart did another of those
queer flip-flops.

"Let me guess," he said, "you and Nolly just got
back from a walk."

"That's true, but it isn't really such a clever guess,
seeing there's really not a lot to do here at the moment.
What about you?"

"After being with Uncle Henry again I've decided
that my suspicions of last night mark me as a ranting,

raving lunatic. As for Aunt Mabel, she looks awful. Uncle Henry says she's been sick quite a bit lately, especially in the mornings. If she weren't the age she is, I'd be predicting a visit from the stork. And, Flora . . ."

"Yes?"

"Something else has happened here. A body was found yesterday buried under the compost heap of the Dower House Nursery Garden."

"A person's body?" Flora sank down on the arm of the settee. "I mean . . . not a dog or a cat?"

"It was a man."

"Vivian?"

"Yes?"

"I am wondering," Flora had trouble squeezing the words out, "if it could be Mr. Tipp? When Mrs. Much was here yesterday she mentioned he'd told her he didn't have any living relations. So how could he be staying with his ill cousin?"

"Mrs. Much could have misunderstood."

"Yes, she said that could have been it; it's just that I'm suddenly thinking that I wasn't always kind to Mr. Tipp. I'm fond of him, but sometimes as a child I used to call him Felt-Tip behind his back because his first name was Philip and I thought Philip Tipp was such a silly sounding name."

"Flora, I'm sure he's all right."

"Yes . . . of course, he must be."

"I'll be back before you know it."

"Please don't speed."

"Promise."

"Good-bye," and Flora pressed the disconnect button because she didn't want to let go of the receiver immediately. When she finally put it down and stood, she saw she had sat on her hat. She made herself go downstairs and steam it out with the kettle, and had almost completed this exercise when the doorbell rang. As she went to the door she thought that she seemed to have been doing that a lot lately, starting something and getting interrupted in the middle. Who would it be this time: Edna? Boris? Reggie? She hoped it would be nice Mr. or Mrs. Singhh! Nothing *complicated* about either of them.

It was Miss Doffit. "I was worried about Vivian," she said without preamble, stepping spryly inside, looking as though she were going to a garden party in soft shades of mauve and blue and topped by one of her smartest feathery hats. "I'm terribly worried because he didn't come home last night."

"But he phoned," said Flora, "I was right there when he spoke to you."

"Oh, that explains it!" Miss Doffit's face plumped up in a smile. "That's why his voice sounded funny; I thought it was because his kidnappers had a gun at his back."

"You didn't really!"

"I'm just teasing, dear. Being an old lady, I love to see young love in bloom. I suppose you've thought that Henry and Mabel will be a little surprised at first. Henry, of course, will take it well. He's always been so fond of you. Just as I have. But Mabel's bound to kick up a stink. And of course there will be talk among the local people and among those in Vivian's set. There are always those who don't like to see a girl like yourself do well. But that's what I'll be there for, to help smooth the way, and it will make my last few years on earth among the happiest of my life, because I do so love to be needed."

"Miss Doffit," said Flora, locking the door, "you're thinking we're back in the trunk room at Gossinger playing make-believe. This is real life, not a fairy tale. Vivian and I are *friends*. That's all there is to it. I know it seems odd his being here so much, but there are reasons—ones that I'd rather not go into right now— that have *nothing* to do with romance."

Miss Doffit's face fell. "Oh, my dear girl, I do hope you haven't been feeling so depressed over your grandfather's death that you've been contemplating something foolish?"

"Not for a moment."

"What a relief. Because I'm so looking forward to being in the thick of things. You will let me help pick your trousseau, dear? Mine is still in my bottom drawer. I found it just a little while ago when I looked through some things I had in storage. It's amazing, some of the things that turn up at such times." Miss Doffit looked thoughtful. "My parents threw away money like bath water, and yet they were the most confirmed hoarders of stuff that most people would have got rid of years ago. But I'm obviously no better, because I've continued to pay out money since their deaths on storage fees. And I'm going to let you into a little secret, Flora."

"What is it?" Flora was only half listening. She kept thinking about the body of a man found across the road from Gossinger. She couldn't shake the creepy feeling that had taken hold of her the moment she'd hung up the phone and was cut off from Vivian's voice.

". . . It's about the tea strainer."

"What is?"

"The secret I'm about to tell you."

"Oh. I'm listening."

"It will explain why I was so relieved when Vivian rang last night and said you had got it back. Because, you see, I was the one who found it the first time and gave it to Mabel. I knew she would be thrilled to be the one to place it in Henry's hands and see him really smile at her. She was going to surprise him with it on his birthday. That was my idea. So romantic, don't you think? Henry isn't the demonstrative sort. I'm sure he's extremely fond of Mabel, but like most men he needs to be reminded once in a while that his wife is a desirable woman. But—not wishing to be unkind—poor dear Mabel doesn't have the figure for nylon nighties or that sort of thing. However, I couldn't help but think that if Henry saw her standing there with that tea strainer in her hands, even wearing one of her shapeless woollies and tweed skirts, he was bound to find her irresistible. I pictured them," Miss Doffit's eyes turned dreamy, "gazing hand in hand at the tea strainer, while love blossomed anew. Given all that, how could Mabel not realize how much she needed me in her life? Meaning I would never again have to worry about putting the occasional foot wrong and one day being shown the door."

"But where was the tea strainer all those years?" Flora asked. Curiosity pushed aside the dark uneasy feeling that had settled on her like the mist on the day of her grandfather's funeral.

"All I can tell you, dear, is where I *found* it. Which was in a lacquered box at the bottom of an old tea chest, which was in storage along with the rest of my parents' things. My guess is that one of my forebears was present the day Queen Charlotte came to tea, and took it. I'd like to think it was a child who did it, for a prank, although I do have to admit that I don't come from unblemished stock. A brother of mine had to leave the Bank of England because he took an unauthorized increase in salary."

"Miss Doffit, if Vivian were here, he would call you a marvel!" And Flora could not resist giving the old lady a hug.

"Thank you, dear. And now, don't you think we should be getting upstairs? You were going to invite me to look out the window and watch the Queen ride past? Or did you plan to stand outside? I'm afraid I'm not much good in crowds anymore, but I don't want to spoil your pleasure."

"I was going to watch from upstairs," Flora assured her, "because given the crowd, the view will be better."

"Oh, good. You know, I have never stopped being thrilled at getting a glimpse of Her Majesty. I think it's because with so many people saying how strongly I resemble her mother, I feel particularly close to our dear Queen." Miss Doffit certainly sounded giddy with excitement as she followed Flora across the floor.

Flora led the way upstairs into the sitting room, where Nolly came toddling over to her, insisting on a pat on the back for behaving himself while she was gone.

"He's not much of a watchdog, is he?" said Miss Doffit, who had stationed herself at the window and was taking something out of her blue leather handbag. "At least not when you're here. He did bark when I was standing outside the shop the other night, but I suppose he feels safe when his mummy is home."

Why did Flora instantly feel that she had never felt less safe in her entire life? Was it because Nolly gave a little whimper just as she bent to lift him up? She remembered he had made a similar sound the day Reggie had rung the bell. But he hadn't made a sound when Mrs. Much had shown up. Flora had put that down to his having by then really settled into his new home, and being much more interested in his red ball or in taking a nap than in who came in or out. But was it that women didn't arouse his protective instincts? Now he was sniffing his way to the door, which Flora had closed behind her on entering the sitting room, and his whimper turned into a growl. And it wasn't the sporting kind he used to let the red ball or his other toys know who was boss. This was the real thing. He was telling her that someone—a decidedly unwelcome someone—was outside, creeping ever so softly up the stairs. Not that Flora really needed to be told, because she heard the tiniest creak, no more than a whisper really, of a stair board under foot, followed by a pause, which seemed to freeze in time, so that Flora seemed to see Miss Doffit larger than life . . . standing by the window with a pair of glasses in her right hand, and the blue and mauve plumes of her hat fluttering in the breeze.

"It has to be Vivian," Flora said, through lips that couldn't quite get themselves around the words; but of course she knew it wasn't Vivian because even if he had flown he couldn't possibly be back here this soon. "Oh, my goodness, why am I standing here like a rock?" She charged at the door, but it was too late: before she could turn the key in the lock, she found herself shoved aside by the door being pushed inward, and someone stepped into the room.

It was Mr. Tipp, looking more skeletal than she remembered. But he most definitely was not dead. In fact, for all his stooped posture, wispy hair, and sunken cheeks, Mr. Tipp held the gun he was pointing at Flora in a gloved hand that looked to be rock steady.

"Why, whatever is *he* doing here?" Miss Doffit asked in a voice that was also amazingly level.

"I wasn't counting on your being here, madam." Mr. Tipp had the grace to flinch when looking at one of his betters. "I'm sorry as how it should have turned out this way."

"Well, let's not worry about *your* feelings," the game old lady responded crisply. "Think about mine and poor Flora's and put that silly thing away."

"Ever so sorry, but I can't do that, madam."

"Then I'm just going to have to stick my head out the window and scream bloody murder."

"If you do—pardon the impudence—I'll have to shoot you in the back of the head. Now I'm not saying that would be as much fun as talking to Mrs. Much about the possibility Hutchins was murdered, and laughing up my sleeve. But it wouldn't keep me awake nights if I had to put a bullet through you, Miss Doffit. It's not like you has the Gossinger name. And with me that's all what counts."

"I think he means business, Flora." The old lady spoke without a quaver. "I have to tell you, dear, that Henry never liked him."

"Neither did Grandpa."

"I knew that," said Mr. Tipp, "and that's why it gave me no end of pleasure to bump him off. Not as I wouldn't have done it whatever my personal feelings, because, you see—I suppose you could say I was like Hutchins in one way at least: I had to think about the good of the Family. My own people has been at Gossinger for hundreds of years. I'm part of the place in a way Hutchins and you, Flora, never could be. And then to hear Sir Henry was going to leave the dear old place to him—I couldn't never let it happen."

"Always listening at keyholes," said Miss Doffit. "That's what Sir Henry always said."

"It didn't matter to me none what Sir Henry thought about me. He was entitled. He's master of Gossinger." Mr. Tipp moved the gun an inch closer to Flora. "I have to say that I don't know as I'd have gone about getting rid of Hutchins, if I hadn't seen that schoolboy coming out of the tower sitting room."

"Boris?" Flora wished she dared move to pick up Nolly, who was shivering at her feet.

"That's him. He'd gone in to talk to her Ladyship on account of her being his grandma's sister. She'd told him to get out, and he was livid as only little kiddies get. He said someone should stuff the old bat down the garderobe. And something about the way he spoke gave me the notion he'd been up to something. As well he had. Him and another boy—Edward somebody. When I dragged him off to the garderobe by his ear, I found the whelps had locked Hutchins in the garderobe."

"He . . . Boris . . . he didn't see what you did to Grandpa?"

"He cleared off. Then I went and did what had to be done to save Gossinger for the rightful heir, which is Mr. Vivian."

"Did you make Grandpa write that note, the one saying God save the Queen?" Flora wasn't just talking to play for time and pray for a miracle; she needed to know as much as this demented man would tell her about her grandfather's last moment.

"No, I wrote that." Mr. Tipp's lips crept upward into a thin smile. "I was never fond of you at the best of times, Flora, always making free of the house when you was little. Playing dress-up with Doffit here, in the trunk room, like you was Sir Henry's own family. So I thought as how it would be getting in a nice little jab to put down those words and make you think Hutchins's last thoughts was of Her Majesty, not his precious granddaughter."

"I should have realized."

"But there was another note, one what Hutchins did write and put under the door, saying two boys had locked him in and he needed to be let out. That was typical of him, and I have to say I admired that part of him, the one that wouldn't let him make a big commotion if there was any other choice. And with Mrs. Much and you, Flora, along with myself, going past the garderobe as often as we did, it was likely he'd have been let out quick. If it makes you feel any better," Mr. Tipp's face seemed to soften in a way that somehow made it even more unpleasant, "Hutchins wasn't what you'd call fighting fit when I opened the garderobe door. The stuffiness had obviously got to him, and he wasn't none too steady on his feet. As I reached out to him he passed out, made my job easy as a wink. And the rest wasn't no harder."

"What do you mean?" Flora and Miss Doffit asked the question one on top of the other.

"Persuading that boy, Boris Smith, that him and his pal was the cause of Hutchins's death. I kept the note, the one where Hutchins wrote he'd been locked in, and used it after I found out Sir Henry still hadn't come to his senses and was thinking he'd will Gossinger to you, Flora. Now, even *you* can see as how I couldn't let that happen, so I sought out Boris, nothing to that, what with him being related to Lady Gossinger. And I moved in with him and his gran so I could be ready at any given moment to turn the screws, so as to get him to help me with the rest of my plan."

"And what was that?" Flora extended a hand in the hope that Nolly would jump up and let her pet him, but was deterred from any further attempt at movement when Mr. Tipp moved the gun a shade closer.

"At first I thought I could get away without having to go through all the work of getting you boxed up and put alongside Hutchins." Mr. Tipp shook his head, possibly at his own naïveté. "My idea was for Boris Smith to ferret out something what would make you look bad in Sir Henry's eyes and cause him to change his mind. It wasn't like I was worried about making people suspicious about two deaths in a row, because it was clear to me they'd think it was Lady Gossinger who was at the back of them. And I wasn't all that bothered about that, because she wasn't Family, in the real sense. And like lots of folks I always thought Sir Henry should have looked higher for a mate."

"This is all very interesting," said Miss Doffit. "At my age one doesn't expect this much excitement in a year, let alone one day."

"I wasn't really clear how I was going to proceed," Mr. Tipp informed her, "not until Flora here and Mr. Vivian Gossinger came to tea with Mrs. Smith the other day. I got Boris to fill me in afterward about everything what was said—all about how you wrote to the Queen, Flora, asking about whatever that stamp of approval thing is for Hutchins's silver polish and how you hadn't got an answer. The bit about you being jealous of Hutchins's fondness for Her Majesty when you was little. And then to top it all off, when I sent Boris down here yesterday to see what more he could find out about you, he came back and told me about Mrs. Much taking a bottle of the polish to the palace. Yes, I think that did put the cap on my arrangements, when I phoned up and said there was explosives in that bottle," he concluded smugly.

"Mrs. Much didn't go in to work yesterday."

"No matter, it's all the same in the end. Because when you go to shoot the Queen, there's already all this built-up evidence—a good thing I watch thrillers on the telly. They'll even think you got this gun from your jailbird father or one of his crooked friends."

"Shoot the Queen?" gasped Flora, suddenly ice cold, but rigidly determined. "You can't make me do that. You'll have to shoot *me* first."

"Me, too," Miss Doffit said firmly.

"Oh, I think I can make you." Mr. Tipp's smile now gave off a terrible kind of radiance. "I've always been painfully thin, but I'm still a remarkably tough old bird." And with this he grabbed Flora's arm and began yanking her toward the window, all the while keeping Miss Doffit in the eye of his gun. "There's no need to put up such a fuss, Flora. I'll be behind the curtain holding your arm and helping you squeeze the trigger. But yours will be the only fingerprints on it. Then afterward I'll be forced to shoot Miss Doffit. And when the police rush in . . ."

"They'll find your gloves in your pockets and figure it out."

"No, they won't, because I'll put them in that chest of drawers and anyone as finds them will think they're

yours. It's lucky, isn't it, not that it really matters, that I
have very small hands, no bigger than yours now I look
at them."

"You can't do this." Flora strove to speak calmly.
"How can you believe the Gossinger Family to be more
important than the Queen—she's this country's anchor!
Britain could fall apart without her!"

"What I'd like to know," said Miss Doffit, as excla-
mations from the street below suggested the imminent
arrival of the royal car and Mr. Tipp elbowed her aside,
"in fact, I'm extremely curious to know how you got in
here, when the shop door was locked."

"I took the spare key that Mr. Vivian Gossinger left
with Mrs. Smith."

"That's right, so you bloody well did!" cried out a
voice from behind them. "As if it wasn't enough that
you frightened my poor Boris until he couldn't think
straight— Oh, I managed to get the lot out of him just
now, and now it's your turn to be shaking in your
shoes. This is a grandmother you're dealing with, Mr.
bloody Phillips! And to think I agreed to lie and say
you was a relative, because you said otherwise the
neighbors might think there was hanky-panky going
on! Fat chance, you little bugger!" Edna stood in the
center of the room and appeared to Flora's distorted
gaze to swell until she was the height and breadth of a
teeth-gnashing grizzly bear.

"You get over here," screeched Mr. Tipp, waving the
gun wildly because it was clear even to his crazed mind
that the moment could easily be lost. It would take only
a second for the Queen's car to pass safely under the
sitting room window.

"You bet I will!" Edna Smith was already lunging
toward him, cracking what looked like a whip against
her side. Mr. Tipp, with a flashing glance below, knew
that if he were to shoot now, it would make everything
meaningless. The royal car would stop short of the dan-

ger point. The gun wavered in his hand and then went off. The bullet hit the ceiling as Edna Smith, hairdresser to the core, wrapped the cord of the curling iron she had removed from her overall pocket around his throat.

"That's the ticket," she rasped triumphantly when in the space of seconds she had him on the floor. Flora moved in to complete the process by smashing him over the head with one of the candlesticks from the mantel. "Never know what will come in handy, do you?" Edna sprang like a schoolgirl to her feet.

Meanwhile, not to be outdone, Miss Doffit leaned out the window to shout for help. Seconds later, a pair of regal legs emerged from the royal car, and the voice of Her Majesty rang out, brooking no argument from bodyguards or anyone else. "Don't anyone attempt to stop me. I'm going in! They've got Mummy in there! They've taken the Queen Mother hostage!"

EPILOGUE

"Her Majesty was wonderful," Flora said to Vivian that evening, as he hovered over her as she lay at his insistence on the settee. "She kept everyone calm, including her security people."

"The hand that rocks the Empire."

"That's the feeling she creates. That she's not only the Queen, but Mother to all her subjects. She asked just the right questions, and would you believe it, Vivian, that she listened with great interest when I explained the part Grandpa's silver polish played in all this! She asked me for one of the bottles on the window ledge and said that Gossinger's Polish sounded absolutely right for one of her seals of approval, so long as it really did live up to my enthusiasm."

"That seems highly encouraging," agreed Vivian. "It sounds to me as though you may find yourself mixing in such high circles in the future that you won't have time for me anymore. And I really can't say I blame you, because I wasn't much help in all this."

"That's not true," Flora exclaimed. "You got in touch with Edna Smith to warn her about Mr. Tipp, and you asked her to pass the message along to me immediately. It was my fault you couldn't reach me directly because I hadn't replaced the receiver properly."

Vivian rubbed a hand across his brow. "When I was talking to you on the phone you were so worried that the body that had been discovered was Tipp's. I found out just before I left Gossinger that the remains were those of an elderly homeless man. Then I remembered your telling me that Mr. Tipp's Christian name was Philip. Which brought to mind two things: that Mrs. Smith's lodger was supposedly named Phillips, and that Uncle Henry had never liked the man and only kept him on out of a sense of obligation. Neither did your grandfather think much of Tipp. And as you said yesterday, one man's judgment of another must sometimes be taken into serious account. But," Vivian smiled at her, "let's not talk any more about this. Unless you want to?"

"No, I think I need to let it all settle for a bit. And you must still be reeling from the news that Lady Gossinger is indeed going to have a baby."

"Imagine how Uncle Henry is feeling! He was barely coherent when he rang just now to say the doctor had been out this afternoon to see Aunt Mabel and said she is nearly three months pregnant. You know what this means, Flora, there's a fifty chance that I won't get stuck with either Gossinger or the title."

"You really don't mind?"

"If what Evangeline told us is accurate, we Gossingers have been living under false pretenses for two hundred years. Anyway, I'd much rather be a self-made man." Vivian's grin assured her he meant every word. "Now tell me what you have planned for tomorrow."

"Yes!" Flora sat up and cupped her chin in her hands. "It is rather glorious to know there *is* going to be another day. Evangeline rang up just before you got here. She wants to repay me that money Grandpa lent her, with interest. I was surprised at how much it was. Enough for me to buy some silver, including that teapot your friend George has for sale, and start the shop the way I'd really like it. Instead of having to sell second-hand odds and ends. And Evangeline has offered to help further the education my grandfather started."

"Speaking of your newfound relation . . ." Vivian reached for Flora's hand. "You do realize that, from all she told us, you and I are also related."

"*Very* distantly."

"And what a very good thing that is," he said, sitting beside her on the settee and raising her fingers to his lips. "I wouldn't at all have liked to find out we were first cousins."

"No, that wouldn't have done at all," said Flora, turning a face to his that was lit, not by the glow of the fire, but by the discovery that the world was as bright and shining as the Gossinger silver after she had helped her grandfather polish it, in those magic days when she was a little girl and knew they would all live forever.

About the Author

DOROTHY CANNELL is the author of six mysteries featuring Ellie Haskell, including *The Thin Woman, The Widows Club,* which was nominated for an Agatha Award as Best Novel of the Year, *Mum's the Word, Femmes Fatal, How to Murder Your Mother-in-Law,* and *How to Murder the Man of Your Dreams.* She is also the author of *Down the Garden Path.* She was born in Nottingham, England, and currently resides in Peoria, Illinois.

BANTAM MYSTERY COLLECTION

____57204-0 **KILLER PANCAKE** Davidson • • • • • • • • • • • • • • • • $5.99

____56860-4 **THE GRASS WIDOW** Peitso • • • • • • • • • • • • • • • $5.50

____57235-0 **MURDER AT MONTICELLO** Brown • • • • • • • • • • • $6.50

____57300-4 **STUD RITES** Conant • • • • • • • • • • • • • • • • • • • $5.99

____29684-1 **FEMMES FATAL** Cannell • • • • • • • • • • • • • • • • $5.50

____56448-X **AND ONE TO DIE ON** Haddam • • • • • • • • • • • • $5.99

____57192-3 **BREAKHEART HILL** Cook • • • • • • • • • • • • • • • • $5.99

____56020-4 **THE LESSON OF HER DEATH** Deaver • • • • • • • • $5.99

____56239-8 **REST IN PIECES** Brown • • • • • • • • • • • • • • • • $5.99

____56976-7 **THESE BONES WERE MADE FOR DANCIN'** Meyers • • $5.50

____57456-6 **MONSTROUS REGIMENT OF WOMEN** King • • • • • $5.99

____57458-2 **WITH CHILD** King • • • • • • • • • • • • • • • • • • • $5.99

____57251-2 **PLAYING FOR THE ASHES** George • • • • • • • • • • • $6.99

____57173-7 **UNDER THE BEETLE'S CELLAR** Walker • • • • • • • • $5.99

____56793-4 **THE LAST HOUSEWIFE** Katz • • • • • • • • • • • • • $5.99

____57205-9 **THE MUSIC OF WHAT HAPPENS** Straley • • • • • • • $5.99

____57477-9 **DEATH AT SANDRINGHAM HOUSE** Benison • • • • • $5.50

____56969-4 **THE KILLING OF MONDAY BROWN** Prowell • • • • • $5.99

____57191-5 **HANGING TIME** Glass • • • • • • • • • • • • • • • • • $5.99

____57590-2 **FATAL DIAGNOSIS** Kittredge • • • • • • • • • • • • • • $5.50

Ask for these books at your local bookstore or use this page to order.

Please send me the books I have checked above. I am enclosing $____ (add $2.50 to cover postage and handling). Send check or money order, no cash or C.O.D.'s, please.

Name _____

Address _____

City/State/Zip _____

Send order to: Bantam Books, Dept. MC, 2451 S. Wolf Rd., Des Plaines, IL 60018
Allow four to six weeks for delivery.
Prices and availability subject to change without notice. MC 2/98